ADULTS

Emma Jane Unsworth is an award-winning novelist and screen-writer. Her novel, *Animals*, has been adapted into a film, for which Unsworth wrote the screenplay. The film premiered at Sundance Film Festival 2019. She also writes for television and various magazines.

www.emmajaneunsworth.com
@emjaneunsworth
/emjaneunsworth

ADULTS

EMMA JANE UNSWORTH

b

THE BOROUGH PRESS

The Borough Press
An imprint of HarperCollins*Publishers* Ltd
1 London Bridge Street
London SE1 9GF

www.harpercollins.co.uk

First published by HarperCollins*Publishers* 2020
20 21 22 LSC 10 9 8 7 6 5 4

A catalogue record for this book is available from the British Library

HB ISBN: 9780008334598
TPB ISBN: 9780008334604

This novel is entirely a work of fiction.
The names, characters and incidents portrayed in it,
while at times based on historical events and figures, are
the work of the author's imagination.

Set in Perpetua by Palimpsest Book Production Ltd, Falkirk, Stirlingshire

Printed and bound in the United States of America by LSC Communications

For more information visit: www.harpercollins.co.uk/green

To my mum, Lorraine.
Sail on, silvergirl

PROLOGUE

SOHO SQUARE

I sit and wait for her, my feet swinging under the bench. She'll come soon, and she'll know where.

Adrenaline. I squeeze my own arms. Tap my toes. God, I hate waiting. Is that what I've been doing all these years? Waiting, for her? Maybe all those therapists were right. Maybe therapy isn't just a bad stand-up show you don't have the balls to take on the road.

I look around, at the other people chatting and posing and repositioning themselves, whiling away this cold Friday. It's a few weeks before Christmas and the city is all lit up. People are smiling too much, drinking too much, wanting too much, wearing too much tinsel. Nothing points to the ephemeral nature of life quite like tinsel.

I look towards the north gate of the square and it's then that I see her. Dishevelled, pulling on her coat. She scans the benches, spots me and freezes. I wave. She tilts her head to one side and bats her eyes, as though appealing to some ancient understanding between us; as though this has all been a scripted episode, some kind of

1

brilliant shared joke. I stare at her emotionlessly. I am not playing. She stares back. It's checkmate with the old queen.

She starts to walk over. I almost don't recognise her with her clothes on. Which is a strange thing to say about your mother.

A FEW MONTHS EARLIER

HELLO, WORLD!

It is 10.05 a.m. and I am queuing at the breakfast counter of my co-working space in east London. The weather outside is autumnal but muggy and I have over-layered. I am damp at my armpits and wondering whether to nip out and buy a fresh T-shirt at lunch. I made dhal for dinner last night from a budget vegetarian cookbook I picked up in a charity shop, and let me tell you, it was astonishing. I am creating a social media post about a croissant that I am pretty sure will define me as a human.

I stare at my phone. I am happy enough with the photo. I have applied the Clarendon filter to accentuate the photo's ridges and depths, making the light bits lighter and the darker bits darker. I added a white frame for art. The picture looks – as much as pastry can – transcendental. However, the text is proving troublesome. I've tweaked it so many times that I can't work out whether it makes sense any more. This often happens. I ponder the words so long, thinking how they might be received, wondering if they could be better, that they lose all their original momentum. I get stage fright. The rest of the world has fallen away around this small square of existence. It's like that bit in *Alien 3* where Ripley says to the alien:

You've been in my life so long, I can't remember anything else. I used to think it was about motherhood. Now I know it's about social media.

I stare at the screen.

PASTRIES, WOO! #PASTRIES

Is this the absolute best depiction of my present experience? I cross out the WOO, and the comma.

PASTRIES! #PASTRIES

I stare at it again. I try and recall the original inspiration; to be guided by that. It's the least I can do. I interrogate myself. That's what the mid-thirties should be about, after all: constant self-interrogation. Acquiring the courage to change what you can, and the therapist to accept what you can't. What is it I really *want to say* about pastries? How do pastries truly *make me feel*? Why is it impor-tant *right now* that I share this?

I delete the exclamation mark and stare at the remaining two words. They are the same word. The only difference is that one is hashtagged. Do they mean the same, or something different? Is there added value in the repetition? Is it worth leaving one un-hashtagged, so that the original sentiment exists, unfettered by digital accoutre-ments? It's so important to get all this right. I want people to know instantly, at a glance, that this post is about pastries in their purest form. This is Platonic Pastry.

I delete the hashtag so that the post simply says:

PASTRIES.

Full stop or no full stop? A full stop always looks decisive and commanding, but it can also look more cool and casual if you just

4

leave the sentence hanging there, like, Oh I'm so busy in my dazzling life I don't even have time to punctuate. The squalid truth is I over-punctuate when I'm stressed/excited. I can go four exclamation marks on a good/bad day. Exclamation marks are the people-pleaser's punctuation of choice. It makes us seem eager and pliable. Excited to talk to you! You!!!! I always notice other people's punctuation. When someone sends me a message with no exclamation marks or kisses, I respect them. I also think: are they depressed? Did I do something to offend them?

Sometimes, I see people using whole rows of emojis, and I just want to hold them.

PASTRIES

Perfect.
Yes, I think that probably says it all.
Hm.
Is it enough, though, really?
Oh god. I just. Don't. Know.
'Can I help you?'
I look up in fright. It is my turn at the counter.
'Uh . . .'
I look at the croissants on the rough stone plinth. I see now that there is a problem. I'm pretty sure – and I am very observant – that one of them is from yesterday. It looks stiffer than the rest, the way it's hunched at the front, like it's all uptight. It is a decidedly different texture and colour to the rest. I don't know whether this suggests age, or some kind of bacterial contamination, or what. How did I miss this? I know that I am definitely going to get that croissant if I ask for a croissant.

I am paralysed. I do not know what to do. I do not feel able to ask for a specific croissant, although I certainly feel I deserve one. I do a quick calculation. There are eight croissants there and the defective one is on my side rather than the server's, so really it's unlikely I'll get lumped with it. I exhale. I decide to go for it. I need this experience, to fulfil my . . . planned experience.

I speak. 'One croissant, please.'

The server nods, but then for some reason known only to herself, goes to take the CROISSANT OF CALAMITY from the front. I shout: 'Oh, hey! Excuse me! Could I please not have that croissant?'

I say it with fear and also with absolute rectitude.

The server's tongs twitch. She says, slowly: 'They're . . . all the same.'

I say: 'Could I just have one from the back please? Thank you!'

Everyone is looking at me.

She speaks slower still, as though I am an idiot. 'But . . . they are all the same.'

'That one is a slightly different hue, I believe,' I say, quieter.

She peers at the croissants. The person behind me in the queue comes forward for a look, too. The barista abandons the Gaggia and comes over. The cashier. They all look, and then they all stare at me.

'It was a preference really,' I whisper. 'Please, just put any croissant in a bag.'

She puts the croissant in a paper bag. It hits the bottom with a ding. I press my card on the reader and will it to bleep. Bleep for Chrissakes, bleep fucking fuckbud fucker.

It bleeps. I pelt.

I run into the Ladies, sling the croissant in the bin and have a short cry. It's fine, though. People cry in WerkHaus all the time. They have these little soundproofed booths near reception for private calls, but mostly people just use them for crying in.

When I'm done crying I take a piss. As I wipe, I check for blood, as always.

I look at my phone.

PASTRIES

The sentiment remains the same, even if the truth has turned out differently. And it's the sentiment that counts.

PASTRIES

In a way, it's perfect. Factual. But I'm still not 100 per cent. I recall something Suzy Brambles once said in her 'Incontrovertible Gram Tips'. She said: 'Go with your first draft.'
I change the words back to:

PASTRIES, WOO! #PASTRIES

Right. I feel almost ready to go on this. As a final check, I text Kelly. Kelly is my oldest friend and most trusted social media editor.

Pls will you check one thing for me before I post

No no I said no more of this

Please

No, you're driving me mad with this daily bombardment

It's not every day!

Mate, it's most days

Please I'm having the worst day already!!!! I was just served a defective pastry

No

I beg of you

I am not endorsing this behaviour

What behaviour???

This lunacy. I don't think it's healthy. Or authentic

Authentic???

You said that we 'grew up together' in a post the other day. We were 22 when we met

It made a better story! Anyway we almost did, in that we both grew up in the North!

WTF

Charlie Chaplin once lost a Charlie Chaplin lookalike competition

DOUBLE WTF

Well we inevitably put a filter on ourselves, don't we? Even as honest people moving through society

Stop intellectualising your problem. Life is not a lookalike competition

Just sent you the post, pls review and feed back

FFS

She'll read it. I know she will. She doesn't do much while she's waiting for her receptionist shift to start – other than watching blackhead-removal videos, which I think somehow give her a sense of universal equilibrium being restored.

She replies after a few seconds:

It's fine. Really don't know what you were concerned about

Thank you x

I bestow a kiss! I hope she really feels that 'thank you'. My politeness-verging-on-grace. Then after a few seconds I send:

I hope you took time to really consider it and didn't just
rush off an answer?

She doesn't reply.

She does that sometimes, Kelly. Shuts down. She did a much bigger version when I was getting together with my ex, Art – back in those heady days of hard wooing – and I asked her to check the things I was sending him. Sometimes you just need a second opinion, you know? What are friends for?

Kelly's from the North, too. She's Yorkshire. The white rose to my red. She's an angel in my lifetime but she has started to publicly undermine me and to be honest it's starting to grate. Example: last week I posted a photo of a leaf-covered bench in the park with the words:

Autumn, you've always been my favourite

and she commented:
Do you think liking autumn makes you a more complex person?
A few days later I posted a charming vista of a field and she wrote,
Mate, there's nothing in this picture
It's not the kind of thing you expect from a beloved friend. BUT – if you had to ask me who knew me best, who *loved* me best, who *I* loved best – well, I do know what the answer would be. Kelly thrills me, it's as simple as that. She thrills me. We might have drifted apart a bit of late, but we have the kind of friendship that can weather emotional distance. It's very easy-come, easy-go. Like an open marriage.

Kelly has a son, Sonny. I've known them twelve years, although technically I met Sonny first. He's fourteen now. Kelly got pregnant with her university ex, whom she told me she swiftly outgrew. He now has a baby with another woman and is a proper truck-blocking activist. He and Kelly once stayed up a tree for six weeks, while she was pregnant, and I think it was during that time she realised the relationship was really over. It's going to be a make-or-break holiday when you're crapping in a carrier bag and arguing about who has more snacks left because there's no electronic entertainment. Kelly still has a star tattoo on her wrist from when she used to be an anarchist. (She never turned down a cheeseboard, though. I think you often find that with anarchists – they still like the small comforts.)

The last time I saw Sonny, a couple of months ago, I told him to stop looking at girls with long fake nails on Instagram because they were emulating porn stars. He said I was nail-shaming them. He told me his friend pressed the wrong button on a vending machine in America and got the morning-after pill instead of a drink, so what did I have to teach him? People are depressed about the totalitarian state we're heading towards – a world where our internet use will be restricted to viewing the shiny, ham-like faces of our unelected leaders – but at least it will save the kids from porn. Every cloud.

I've told Kelly that we have to respect social media more than the younger generations because we're not digital natives. We were raised in print. This shift has been a major cultural and psychological upheaval in our lifetimes. We didn't get email until we were at university. The internet can throw some curveballs. I once ordered a bureau off eBay and when it arrived it was a miniature one, for a doll's house. I thought it was a bargain at £1.99. Plus, we weren't brought up natural broadcasters. We've had to catch up, and too quickly. I remember that move towards daily (hourly; constant) documentation. Years ago a friend drove me mad on a hike, stopping to take photos all the time for her Facebook. I was very frustrated, as I wanted to keep walking. It was like being in a constantly stalling car. Now, I'd be the one scrambling to the nearest cliff face for a signal.

Speaking of which.

It's time to bite the bullet. I add a last-minute impulse hashtag. Really going now!

#shameabouttheservice

I post the picture. The waiting begins. It's like that conundrum of the tree falling in the empty forest. Does it make a sound if there's no one there? If you put something on social media and no one likes it, do you even exist? I have calculated that with my number of followers I can measure a successful post on the basis of approximately ten likes per minute. Still, there's no formula for it – I've tried everything. One time I even arranged a day trip to Heptonstall to photograph Sylvia Plath's grave (literary, tragic, it ticked so many boxes!) and so many people lit their little hearts for it that it was worth the £100 train fare. I used to do things for their own sake, but now grammability is a defining factor.

We're almost at a minute and no—

Yes! There's one! And two! And three and four! Thank you. Now we've broken the seal, it all gets sexy. Someone comments, 'Yumstrels.' I dabble with the notion of liking the comment. It's a commitment, liking comments, because once you start you really have to follow it through and like all of them. Really it's best not to start, plus it looks less obsessive, less like you're monitoring things. I just left this here and walked away! What, you think I have nothing better to do with my day than refresh this inanity?

I'm waiting for any likes, but really I'm waiting for the women I currently admire online. It's been moving this way for a few years and recently it calcified. I want the women to want me more. I wait for a name that means something. I wait for a sign. There are certain people whose attention I am keen to attract. Margot Ripkin. Buzzface Cruise. Wintering Marianne. Suzy Brambles. Suzy Brambles more than the rest, perhaps, because she just started following me back (two days ago! I've been following her for years), so it feels as though we are now connected. As we should be. Entwined, you might say.

Suzy Brambles. Oh, Suzy Brambles, with your hostile bob and black Citroën DS and kickboxing lessons and almond eyes and lips like you've been sucking on a frozen Zeppelin. What's not to like? And I like. I like and like and like. The first post that ensnared me was a charred corncob on a beach barbecue, with the caption: *The adventure is already inside you*. I was pretty lost on the adventure front at the time, so that corncob spoke to me on many levels. This morning, Suzy Brambles has been kicking up leaves in Dulwich. She is such a playful thing! I have watched the video five times already. Suzy Brambles only posts in black and white. This is because she has real integrity. I watch the video of her in the park again. Each time I watch it, I find something new to admire in her choice of composition, angle and filter.

I look at the time. It is almost 11 a.m. How did that—

ART SAID

'That thing is the first thing you look at in the morning and the last thing you look at at night.'

We were in bed. It was a week or so before we broke up. I was looking at my phone while we were having sex. I see now how that might have been interpreted as rude – some might even say offensive. He put his hands on my shoulders and said: 'Stop.'

I stopped.

He said: 'Jenny, somehow I just don't feel like I have your full attention.'

'You do!'

'I don't. Even when you're here it's like you're not here. It's like half your head is somewhere else.'

It was. Half my head was in Copenhagen, where Suzy Brambles was having a splendid time. The earthenware in one particular eaterie was 'lickable'.

Art said: 'I feel as though this constant interfacing has become a wall between us.'

I almost said: *But does sex require one's full attention?* Eating doesn't, after all – and that is arguably as important as sex.

I looked back at my phone. I smiled at Suzy smiling.

Art pulled himself out from under my legs, sat on the side of the bed and whipped off the condom. He rubbed his face. 'Okay,' he said. 'We have a problem.'

I finished my comment, a simple, single red heart emoji – the classic choice; just . . . *enough* – clicked the phone to sleep and looked at him. Art said: 'You are on that thing when we eat, you are on it when we watch TV, you are on it when we go for a walk, and now you are on it *when we are having sex.*'

'It was a slow bit!'

'It was sex, Jenny. Not a film.'

I looked at him and tried a cute: 'Sometimes it's as good as the movies, though.'

'Mmmmmmmm.'

It was a long sound, that mmmm. Like a door buzzer, or a hornet trapped in a jar. I watched the sunlight on the wall flicker. Summer was almost over. *First thing in the morning and last thing at night.* There was a time – even in my life – when that slot would have been reserved for a lover.

Art said: 'Are you in love with someone on the internet?'

'No!' I said. Which was almost not a lie.

He said: 'I've noticed a direct correlation between you growing more distant from me and closer to your phone.'

He said: 'It's like I can't get to you when you're there. Your eyes are all wide and you're plugged in like a happy little robot.'

He said: 'Except you're not happy.'

'How do you know I'm not happy?'

'Because you're never satisfied.'

I took his penis in my hand. 'Maybe that's just me.'

I WALK

back into the main office. It's all creative types in here – advertising and media, mostly. There's a lot of lino. A lot of dachshunds. Lots of plants that are real-imitating-plastic. You see men with visible pocket watches high-fiving over MacBook Airs and you worry about what this means for evolution.

I work for an online magazine, *The Foof*, and it is as awful as it sounds. My editor, Mia, is fucking terrifying – stupidly; admirably? – socially fearless. I think this is her seventh or eighth start-up. Art called her a 'delectable oaf' (not to her face). I'm anxious to please her because I'm an approval junkie and have a teacher–pupil dynamic with people in positions of authority. You should see me getting a smear test – it's like I'm trying to *sell them* my super-clean vagina. I thought I'd offended Mia on Friday when I told her UV uplighters for teeth were imbecilic, unaware that she was wearing one (I thought she was slurring on her anti-depressants) – but then she liked one of my pictures on Sunday and I breathed a sigh of relief because I knew everything was okay. Saturday was fraught – I spent a lot of it questioning my whole life and worth. Even though I don't respect Mia, I fear her and professionally that's ultimately a good thing because it means I want to impress her, so I give my work my all. I'm only really effective around people I want to impress. Otherwise, my energy deadens. I'd churn out dross if I actually felt comfortable around my boss. Vague social terror: that's my motivation.

15

The Foof has a permanent office here, in the loosest sense. There's a sign – *FOOF TOWERS* – in fluffy pink letters across the back wall. The sign could be taken down at any given moment. So could the wall.

I make my way across the main space to my desk. I don't come in every day so I share with Gemma, who writes the horoscopes and product reviews and is so cheerful I want to punch her. (Sorry, I don't want you thinking that just because I work in the media I'm a fucking idiot.)

I sit down and start to compose an email, which is what I do after any unsatisfactory social interaction.

DRAFTS

Subject: That Croissant

Dear Breakfast Maven, Queen of the Granola,
You know and I know that croissant was prehistoric. It was yesterday's batch, that's why you were trying to palm it off on me. I deserve a fresh croissant, do I not, for my £3.50? In America, that kind of hesitation within the service industry would be unthinkable. JUST GIVE ME THE CROISSANT I WANT NEXT TIME, FOR THE LOVE OF COMMON DECENCY.

Kind regards,
Jenny McLaine
The Foof (columnist)

THEY SAY

it is crucial to incorporate mindfulness into your daily routine. I like to get on it every few hours, just to be sure. After I've written the email, I take a deep breath and count to ten in Hindi. I even have an app to remind me to take time out regularly. It shouts *TAKE A BREAK, BABY!* in an Austin Powers voice (I chose the voice from six options). It's a little obnoxious, but it's good to know something cares.

I check le status of mon croissant. Thirty-five likes. Dear sweet Christ alive. You've got to be kidding. The thirties are disastrous numbers, they really are.

As I'm studying the post, I realise that I have automatically tagged WerkHaus and, while I am displeased with the morning's events, I do not want anyone losing their job on my account. I've seen *An Inspector Calls* – several times – with my mother. I know how much people in the service industry can take things to heart. My life is a perfect war zone of potential consequences.

I go into Edit Post and de-tag the location. Too late! Someone from WerkHaus – Joel from The Little Green Bento Den – has commented:

Was it the hench one with the underbite? She's a right Orc

Fucking Joel. I consider what to do. I don't want Suzy Brambles or any other notables thinking I am endorsing this bile. I also don't want to get into an argument with Joel that could last several hours and get my blood up. I've sacrificed entire emotional half-days before now to online altercations. And I've got a column to write. Digital is not at odds with the flesh, as some might argue; this all has a very physical effect on me.

I type back at Joel:

Putting the miso in misogynist as ever, I see

There. That, I think, is smart and final. No coming back from that. Now we can all relax.

I stare at my comment.

Oh god. No it's not smart at all. It's over-handled and ham-fisted, like all my comments. Do you even get miso in a bento box? Fuck my life.

I delete the comment and Joel's comment and just as I'm regretting deleting Joel's comment (it looks cowardly, to delete without comment, and he's the kind of fucker who'll notice and comment again) – I put my head in my hands.

'MORNING, WOKERS!'

I look up. Mia is standing over me. She's wearing a blindingly white dress with a giant turtleneck obscuring the bottom half of her face. She looks like a Victorian who just got back from space. Mia's Boston terrier, Simone, is by her feet. Simone once shat my initials perfectly on the office floor. You can call me paranoid, but there was no denying it was a definite 'J' and an 'M'. Another victory for meaning. My point is: you know someone judges you when their dog judges you. *No language skills, but what a critic!* Etc.

'How's my fave ginger whinger?' says Mia, in a voice that cuts right through my face and straight into my being. She is holding a turmeric-coloured drink and a twisted copy of *Vogue*.

'I really hate it when you call me that.'

'Don't be a hater, bébé. Buzz on the chans is there's a new personal drone that doubles as a clutch bag. When you're out you just fling it in the air and it captures your night from above from all angles.'

I really think I could shoot Mia, possibly in the face, if her opinion of me wasn't so important to me.

'I don't need an aerial reminder of how appalling my night was,' says Vivienne, the features editor. Vivienne is six foot and wiry, with thick veins ribbing her arm muscles. She looks like the kind of woman who's spent a lot of time smoking on Spanish beaches. I am certain she has killed. I don't think I've once seen her smile and she isn't on any social media – which only adds to her menace, and her valour. Vivienne and Mia are friends from fashion college. Anyone can see Mia's always been the one with money and ambition and Vivienne is the cerebral sponger. Vivienne doesn't give zero fucks; she gives minus fucks. Every time I am near her I want to whisper: *Teach me how to eat an artichoke, Vivienne.*

'Are you completely sectionable, Viv?' says Mia. 'That's the teenage-girl angle. Pictures from above make everyone look like a teenage girl. If you partook in popular culture I wouldn't have to tell you this.'

'I do not partake,' says Vivienne. 'I am a puppetmaster.'

'Well, I've ordered a sample clutch drone,' says Mia, 'which I shall be trying out, in the name of investigative journalism.'

Vivienne says: 'Speaking of which, I'm going to patronise that new Israeli near Kings Cross at lunch. I may not be back for a few days.'

'Jenny!' says Mia, as though she has just remembered my name. 'How was your weekend?'

'Busy! A few drinks, a private view, you know.'

'Yes, I saw your picture.'

'Oh, did you? Great, thanks,' I gush.

'Are you not going to ask me what I got up to?'

'What did you get up to?'

She scrutinises my face. 'I went . . . for a meal . . . which I know you know, because you liked other pictures around the same time mine went up, so why didn't you like mine?'

Vivienne adjusts her neck. She knows the score. She *keeps* the score.

'I must have . . . missed it? You know how sometimes it randomly reorders things.'

'Hmm.'

The truth is, I like every fifth or sixth thing Mia posts – not always because I like them, but to sort of say hi and remind her of my existence. I don't want to look rabid. I thought I was managing my affection well. Evidently not.

'And how is Art?' Mia asks.

'He's fine! Busy.'

She clasps her hands. This again.

Suffice to say that Art has a lot of hangers-on. A lot of women of a certain age. I know that's unfeminist to say, but it's a phenomenon that brings out the worst in me. At exhibitions, launches, shows . . . He's the sexy, shaven-headed photographer. The hot thug. I can see it in their eyes: he's a welcome, regular escape from their non-pussy-licking husbands.

'Can he make drinks on Friday?'

'I'm not sure.'

'Not even one?'

'One drink?'

'Yes.'

'I'll ask.'

'Do that.'

'I will.'

'Appreciated.'

'So,' Mia continues. 'What's the column this week?'

'Co-habitation with women versus co-habitation with men. A nostalgia piece, in part, about my uni days.'

'Juicy anecdotes, searing insight, rounded off with everywoman wisdom?'

'Check, check, check!'

She hesitates.

'Just, keep it on the hi-fi, rather than the low-fi.'

'Spice it up,' says Vivienne. 'S'boring. You're like someone in a Sunday supplement moaning about their shoes.'

Mia says: 'Now, now. But yes, Jenny, it's true. We're all bored stiff with your vulnerability. Save it for your therapist. We need bold voices, not weak cries for help. We want ferocity. Strength. A roar from the lady jungle, not a whimper. This is the frontline of feminism. We have work to do. Remember the name of your column: INTENSE MODERN WOMAN.'

'I mean, it's an oxymoron though, isn't it, having a *column* in a feminist magazine.'

Mia stares at me. 'Do you mean a column as in an erection? Are we still doing phallus chat? COME ON. Brand too strong for some punk-ass bear to stop this wave. Make it gain traction.'

I swallow. 'I understand, Mia.'

I do not.

She starts to walk away and turns back to say: 'The headline of this conversation is: don't hold back. Explode everything about what living with other women is really like. Put a grenade up the arse of that female utopia.'

'Got it.'

Simone follows Mia, giving me a hefty side-eye.

Vivienne walks to the kitchenette zone and starts wrenching at the coffee machine. 'Why are you chewing your fingers?' she asks me. 'Anxiety?'

'No, it's because I think I'm fucking delicious.'

I check my likes once more (forty-two, I should really kill myself) and start to write.

I stop typing every two minutes or so and let my thumb and thoughts zip round in a fast, looping flight. This, this, this, this. Back to work for a few sentences. Back round again. This, this, this. My head teems.

This is how I think:

I am doing what I should be doing: writing. Oh that's quite good. I can do a good sentence when I put my mind to it – no wait, it's terrible, why am I so terrible? Am I so terrible because of that time I kissed my male friend even though I was in a relationship because I have no way of separating platonic heterosexual friendship from groundwork for a sexual encounter? Oh, there's something about politics! I should know more about politics. I will like it so that people think I know about politics. Or am I so terrible because I once tweeted a line of my own poetry after I'd been up all night and someone replied: *Pull your head out your ass once in a while*, and it was the brother of someone I once dated. No I am terrible because someone once commented on a column – apropos of nothing – *YOU HAVE NO INTEGRITY*. I am obsessed with whoever wrote that. How dare they be so right about me. It was the top comment, too, so it lives forever as the first thing you see beneath the piece – I can't believe it can't be removed on legal grounds. Ugh, this woman with the self-care haikus is awful. Her podcast is no. 2 in the charts. I should do a podcast. But what would my podcast be about? Maybe politics. Maybe politics for people who know nothing about politics. Like me. I am A WOMAN OF THE PEOPLE. I just need to find the time. I don't know how people find the time to do podcasts. I can't even find the time to finish this senten—

My phone pings with a message. I pounce on it.

It's one of my lodgers. Sid.

Hey have you seen the half avocado that was in the fridge?
x

She sends me daily micro-aggressions like this.

I reply:

> Yes I ate it for breakfast, thought it would be okay as you ate half my sourdough last week x
>
> That wasn't me, that was Jonah, as you know I am gluten free x
>
> He was staying in your room for the night tho x
>
> He is his own person, why am I accountable for his actions? x
>
> Fine, I'll buy you another avocado. A whole one x
>
> Not much good to me right now is it? Not to worry! Thank you, I do appreciate you replacing it x

I keep telling myself this lodger situation is only for a while, but I don't know how I'll ever afford to live in that house on my own. I just probably need to work harder, somehow. I should be a slashy. Journalist/podcaster/politician. How hard can it be to be a politician anyway? They're all floundering and resigning these days. I can flounder and resign! Especially for cash. I'll give it some thought when I get some time. I have three lodgers at the moment: Sid, Frances and Moon. They're all in their early twenties, which makes me feel great. Usually, when I get in, they're colonising the lounge. The other day when I got in they'd been at an all-day festival at Victoria Park. Swathed across the sofa, bleached and feathered, they looked like a gang of crooked fairies. The evil fairies that kill babies. Those kind of fairies.

Mia comes over. She has a print-out of my column in her hand.

'Well it's not going to start the revolution,' she says. 'But it might light a few torches in some under-educated backwaters. Now, do you have any candid photos of these days?'

'I'm sure I can root something out,' I say.

'Excellent. Keep it halal.'

I look at my nearest desk-neighbour, confused. My desk-neighbour whispers: 'She's trying to make it a thing. Like kosher.'

I nod at Mia. She gives me an empty fist bump and walks away.

I pull out my laptop and start to go through my scanned old photos, but I end up looking at photos of me and Art. I stall over a photo of my mother and Art in a bar. They have their arms around each other. I recall how my mother burst in that night – in stilettos – and shouted (she always shouts, to be fair – no no: she *projects*): 'Get me a seat, would you? MY BALLS ARE KILLING ME.' Everyone in the bar looked – which was what she wanted, of course. Art thought she was the most. Showboats, both of 'em.

'Your wit's hers,' Art said, more than once.

However, one likes to think the apple fell a little further from the wit tree, rolled a good way across the field of wit, coming to rest at the foot of Wit Mountain.

Anyway – she was so nice to him that night. Too nice. She'd never been nice to anyone I'd introduced her to before. But she was all over Art from the get-go. When he went to the Gents, I said: 'You seem . . . very eager to please him. Not like you.'

After all, she'd said it countless times: *Darling, who needs a man when you have a detached house, a personal trainer and a Teasmade?*

'What do you mean, it's not like me?' She did innocent eyes.

I did cynical ones. 'You've always been rude to my boyfriends.'

'I like his energy. It complements yours. And mine.'

I sat back. 'Are you making a play for him? Because if you are, this situation is veering horribly close to cliché.'

'Pahaha! Making a play – what a notion.'

'Because you actually described yourself earlier as a "gymslip mum". You actually used those words.'

'It's as simple as this: I think he's good for you.'

'I'm good as I am. I don't need anyone to make me better.'

'I know that. But I also know—'

'What?'

'How it gets, sometimes.'

In my head I thought she might mean 'lonely', but I didn't want to push it, and anyway Art was coming back. And how could she be lonely, this woman who professed to be constantly harangued and harassed by the voices of spirits, which invaded her thoughts like rampant toddlers, or so she said. I once asked her: *How do you switch off?* She winked and raised her gin glass to me.

She put her hand on my arm. 'But you must comb through his teenage years with him. Don't let him be evasive. Don't let his own . . . toxic experiences stop him . . . experiencing things with you.'

'Thanks, but I don't need relationship advice from someone who hasn't had a relationship since the nineties.'

'Well what do you call this?'

'What?' I said, confused.

She batted her hand back and forth between us.

'Me and you? Hah! I mean a proper relationship. A romantic relationship.'

'*Romantic*. God help you.'

But she did have a few relationships, years ago – relationships in which she invested enough to be jealous. Are you sitting comfortably? I'll begin anyway.

A long time ago, back in the days when love was still analogue, my mother knew a man named Roger. Roger the Theatre Producer, to give him his full title. And you really must, with men like that, or there's simply no point to them. Like most of my mother's men, Roger was married and lived in London, but he travelled a lot. The first night he stayed I came downstairs feigning a headache, a thirst, I was feverish (with curiosity). I was thirteen.

She was in the kitchen fixing something long and cool. He was short and hot.

He started at the sight of me, white-gowned in the doorway. *Oh, hello! You must be Jenny.*

I nodded and went to sit at the end of the sofa, beside the coiled cobra lamp that was my mother's most beloved possession. I smiled at Roger expectantly. I had things to learn. I liked the way his arms looked in his short-sleeved shirt. I was at an age when I still trusted muscles.

How old are you? I asked.

Forty.

Wow. So vastly, impossibly ancient. He looked smart and rich and like he'd been around all the blocks. I hadn't even been around *our* block. I tucked my feet up and sat, knees making a rhombus – greeting him, and all exciting men, everywhere!

I heard the glasses she was holding tinkle. I didn't turn. I sat there, eyes on Roger's eyes, waiting, counting. Two seconds, three. *What time is it, Mrs Wolf?* Her hands clamped onto my shoulders. She hauled me out to the hall.

You're too old to sit like that.

She wanted me to cry. I wanted to cheer. I suppose because I felt like we were finally on the edge of something real. She wasn't protecting me with her anger – not like when I ran near the road or went missing in shops. There was fear in her eyes along with the anger, I could see that, but there was also a third emotion – one she wasn't comfortable with, but one she couldn't suppress. Aha! Ahaha! Oh, the pitiless epiphanies of the child confronting the threshold guardian. She was my end-of-level boss, the obstacle between me and some higher plane; some outside; and I would defeat her eventually, and she knew it. Those spurts of golden growth – they come like sailors, giving everything, taking everything.

And then one day, Roger stopped coming.

'What happened?' I said.

'It ran its course,' my mother said. 'As all relationships with men should.'

I looked in her eyes for the lie. She stared back, like she always did, with her eyes folded. I'd looked into her eyes so many times, in real life and in photographs, trying to do a sort of past-life regression on myself. And what of my mother's childhood?

The McLaine Sisters were four redheaded sisters, my mother being the eldest by three years. Even my grandparents saw their children as a novelty – they made them sing together in competitions on holiday in Rhyll, Blackpool, and other such seaside towns. My mother said they lined up in a row on stage, like the von Trapps. They wore black jodhpurs and white blouses and grey waistcoats, like four little horsewomen. ('Not my first rodeo,' my mother says, every time she's about to go on stage.) They usually won, but when they didn't it rather ruined the holiday. My mother still throws out a tune when she has a drink in her. She's what you might call a loose karaoke cannon.

What does your mother do? the kids asked at school.

She's an actress, I said.

She did still her vocal exercises every night. She rewatched her appearances in obscure soaps (*Under the Doctor*) and low-rent biopics (*Shelly's Shame*). She had a bedroom that was more of a boudoir. When my friends came round she tried to correct their pronunciation and gave them instructions on voice projection and vocal preparation – *Breathe deeply from your lower lungs, imagine a rubber ring around your waist and try to push the ring outwards as you breathe in. Shoulders down, breathe in through your nose, out through your nose and mouth. Bend your knees – not THAT much, you look like you're on the toilet . . . Relax! RELAX!*

We had hot holidays. A 20-inch TV. I swanned around school in my Clarks Magic Steps with the hidden key in the heel. I used to drive with her on the ring road, to and from the satellite towns where she performed: Sale, Altrincham, Eccles, Weaste. Me, riding shotgun, solemn as a priestess. I used to saunter into those clubs and pubs, those half-done places that smelled of stale beer and freshly sawn wood. I saw the staff and punters nudging each other. *There, look, it's her. The Daughter. The One.*

And so that night at the restaurant, I watched her carefully with Art. The way she straightened his napkin for him, pleased on a helpless level, and it was like seeing her smooth the tie of someone who'd never existed. She was relieved. She didn't have to worry I was going to be left stranded. I'd met a man, a socially mobile, upward man, and she, for all her old feminist foot-bones, could relax on account of the fact I had safely – finally (that shelf was getting dusty!) – entered some version of adulthood.

INT. YOUNG JENNY'S BEDROOM

Night. A single bed with a rainbow-patterned duvet cover. A rug. A full bookshelf. A bedside lamp on. Everything small and infused with hope. Jenny is in bed. Carmen is pacing the room, reading from a book.

CARMEN (over-emphasising): *Never do anything by halves if you want to get away with it. Be OUTRAGEOUS. Go the WHOLE HOG. Make sure everything you do is so completely crazy it's UNBELIEVABLE.*

Jenny picks at a patch of loose paint on the wall. Carmen stops reading.

CARMEN: Right, that's it.
JENNY: What?
CARMEN: You're not listening!
JENNY: I am!
CARMEN: Do you know how much people pay to come and see me these days?
JENNY: A million pounds.
CARMEN: Seven fifty with booking fee.
JENNY: Wow.
CARMEN: Look. I've worked a long day after a long night and I'm off to work again as soon as Aunty Bev gets here and I'm trying to make precious time for my daughter and she could not care less.
JENNY: I was listening.
CARMEN: You weren't! You couldn't give a monkey's. Here I am, giving it my all. TO THE WALL.
JENNY [*quietly*]: You're overdoing it.
CARMEN: What did you say?

29

JENNY: Again.

CARMEN [*huffing*]: It's drama, darling. It requires voices.

JENNY: It's Roald Dahl.

Carmen throws down the book and storms out of the room.

Jenny sighs, rolls over, switches her lamp off and goes to sleep.

IN THE WINGS

We were at the Mind Body Spirit show at the Birmingham NEC. I stood behind the partition wall, watching her doing her thing on stage – plucking people from the audience and giving them messages from beyond. I was drinking a cup of lemonade. She was grand-standing. She was majestic.

She says she'll see you for the dancing, pet, can you accept that?

She said you were there by her side the whole time, and your love let her know she could go. Can you accept that, my love? You can. Thank you. Bless you . . .

When she'd finished, the applause was deafening. The crowd demanded an encore. At one point she looked to the side and winked at me and I got a thrill so electrifying it made me judder. I blew bubbles into my lemonade. Lemonade spilled over the rim of my cup, onto the grey top of the temporary stage block. The stage manager told me off and sent someone for a cloth, but I didn't care, I was too busy watching my mother, in mid-flow, bowing and smiling and saying thank you, soaking it all up. I wanted to capture that sight of her, preserve it forever, that scene. I remember thinking that sentence to myself: *You are mine, all mine.*

When she got off stage, we walked around the festival together. It was a goblin market. We stopped at a stall called 'The Horned Goddess' selling dream-catchers, angel cards and gemstones. It stank of joss sticks. My mother was wearing her full regalia. A child jumped away from her. 'Mummy, that lady's scaring me!'

My mother affected a look of horror. 'I'm not a lady!'

We stopped by a small gypsy caravan. *MADAME AURACLE: AURA READINGS AND MORE* it said on the side.

'Do you want your aura reading?' my mother asked.

'If it's all right I'd rather have a jacket potato with coleslaw,' I said.

'Come on,' she said. 'After this.'

In the caravan there was a photo studio of sorts set up in the lounge: a Polaroid camera on a tripod. A sectioned-off area under a curtain.

The madame was sitting on a tasselled stool. She was as wide as she was high, and dripping in turquoise. 'I am Madame Auracle,' she said.

I sat in the electric chair, awaiting my execution. The assistant was wearing a baggy olive-green T-shirt. She instructed me to place my hands on the metal plates either side of the chair. I obeyed her because she looked like Christina Ricci, and I would have done anything for Christina Ricci. She stood in front of me with the camera. 'Smile!' I obliged.

A few seconds later, the photo chugged out of the camera. I peered at the picture. I looked startled and stern, like a constipated headmistress in an Adidas T-shirt who had farted a rainbow.

'Now for the reading.' Madame Auracle took the photo in her hand and raised her eyebrows. 'Lots of red . . . You are an enthusiastic and energetic individual, forever on the lookout for new adventures. You are quick to anger and can lose your temper over the smallest thing. You are generous with your time and energy when called upon for help. You are easily bored.'

'She won't even sit still to watch a film,' my mother said.

Madame Auracle continued. 'And so now we come to the other

side of your personality — we have lots of yellow here. The yellow part of your aura represents the highly critical part of you. But those who have high standards, that exacting voice inside that is so harsh on the world and others, that same voice is even harsher when it turns on you, isn't it?'

'Yes,' my mother said, 'definitely. She has VERY high standards.'

I nodded.

'And if you were easier on yourself, then you might find it easier to allow others to love you for who you are.'

'Too true,' my mother said.

Madame Auracle nodded sagely. 'Your main fault is that you can be overly analytical. And this creates a fear that makes you unable to communicate openly and freely.'

I said, 'Sounds like a lot of people I know, to be honest.'

Madame coughed. 'That concludes the reading. Most auras stretch three feet around the physical body; however, if you're a trauma survivor your aura stretches fifty feet around you — which means people around you on the bus will be sitting in it. Your mother will be sitting in it. We'll all be sitting in it, right now. Your aura mess. I can clean it up for you for an extra £5.99.'

I shook my head.

'You should have a quick clean,' my mother said.

'I'm not traumatised.'

THEY SAY

you should never look at the comments. That to go 'below the line' is to open the portal to death and damnation. BTL = the Gateway to Hell. I say, that kind of self-control is one for the healthy of mind and heart. Meanwhile, you'll find me shrieking and wallowing in the lake of digital hellfire with all the worst people on the internet. Waving, drowning, backstroke, who knows what I'm doing – but I'm not for being saved. Come on in! The water's . . . excruciating.

My column goes up around 4 p.m., for bored souls on the homeward commute. In that way, you could say it's asking for trouble. I sit at my desk and refresh the comments over and over. Nice, nice, nice, nice – my brain trips over these like they're just air, like they're nothing, like they're fuck you what are you trying to do *be my friend?* – then – Ah!

A mean one.

I read it over and over, savouring it.

OVERPRIVILEGED VANITY PUFF PIECE – DOUBT MUCH OF THIS IS ACTUALLY TRUE

I feel the words like holy fire. I am vanquished, but also victorious. They are right! This person understands me completely! (Maybe they're the secret love of my life??) I knew I was heinous and here is the proof! Let me burn! Let the flaming be righteous! I deserve it. I deserve it all. Moar!

Three times you mention your weight in one article. Seek help.

MOARRRRRR.

I hope you die

Oooh! Old school. Satisfying on a basic level.

Another, somewhat on theme:

Maybe you should start writing something more appropriate like obituaries

I ponder this. I do like thinking about death, so it's not a terrible idea. I think about my own death approximately once a day. I don't think about the actual moment of dying; I think about my own autopsy. Or I think about the person, or people, who'll discover my body. I hope they will be beautiful, and weep tenderly. I think beautiful people weeping tenderly over your dead body is one of the very loveliest thoughts a human can have.

A little way down the thread, I see a comment from Sid. She has written:

How could you do this?? Do I get financial recompense for this exposure of details from my private life? Great piece tho babe! X

I panic. What if Mia sees the comment and deduces that I am no longer living with Art and in actual fact living with AT LEAST ONE WOMAN? My palms sweat. Could I go over to the tech woman and ask her to delete the comment? Or would that make things too obvious? I should have access to my own comments, surely! I'm wide open here. It's not right.

I call the lift, but when it arrives there are a few people in there, so I smile politely and walk away because the last thing I want is a conversation. As soon as I am on the stairs I am on my phone again.

I sit on the Tube, scrolling – harried, fraught and febrile.

Nicolette is waiting for me outside the Yoga Shed, sucking on her vape. Nicolette looks like a Russian supermodel: rail-thin with puce-tipped hair. She always smells of applemint. She is a new friend, even though I swore off those when I hit thirty-five. We met at a fancy dress party a few months ago – a friend-of-a-friend's thirtieth. The theme was 1988. I went as Garfield and Nicolette was Jessica Rabbit. My costume was sweltering and I'd just had a Brazilian so was doing neat, dry, rasping farts. I was timing them admirably with the music. I saw a woman who looked like she was concentrating, too. What secrets did she have in her pants? I moved towards her in stages, casual, doing a humble smile when she caught my eye. I stood next to her and it was like slotting into a puzzle I'd been trying to finish for a while. I asked her how she knew the birthday boy and she said: *Oh, I'm just staying here taking coke until I despise myself sufficiently to leave.* I knew then that this was a person I could really learn from. Not least because the times I have taken drugs I've immediately lost my cool. I have no discretion. I get too agitated. One time when I was with a group of people in a pub awaiting a delivery of pills, when the man with the baggie arrived, I shouted 'PILL!' across the pub, instead of his name, Chris. Like I said, super cool. You all want to go to Ibiza with me.

The night we met, Nicolette instantly started following me on everything, even Pinterest. She didn't slide into my DMs; she galloped. Talk about chutzpah. 'Reply All' should really be an adjective, and Nicolette is very Reply All. I'd had a few drinks and liked her energy so I didn't even do the wait-an-hour-to-look-casual thing (the equivalent of waiting three days after a date before you contact them): I went Full Fast Follow Back. I wanted her to see how fast I could love her, too. She was mine and I was hers and we both sensed it. We've had to talk, though, about the way we heat up and cool off on each other's needs when we've been in physical proximity, because sometimes it does get intense, like we're trying to bridge some sort of divide we didn't feel when we were actually together.

Nicolette used to write for lefty rags but now she writes interior-design features mostly. I guess it's true: we all get more right wing as we age. Over the past few months, our friendship has worked its way past desperate cordiality to a place of real assault. She's wearing an antique wedding dress festooned with lace, teamed with tracksuit bottoms and leather boots. It's a look that screams Sporty Loyal Cossack. We hug. 'You look crackerjack.'

'I was unsure when I left the house, but you know when you want positive affirmation on the things you're wearing? Go to the *old girls*.'

'Define old?'

'Sixty or seventy yah. If I get a wink or a nod off an old girl on the street, I know I'm doing it right. And I got about six on the way here, so.'

Nicolette lines up the angles of her face with the outside of the building. 'Come in,' she says, beckoning me towards her without moving. 'Come in with me.'

'I'm not looking so hot.'

'Black and white makes it all all right.'

I stand next to her and smile, lips no teeth because that's how I feel. I look at Nicolette's fingertips gripping the phone – her grown-out gel manicure is pleasantly prostitute-y. She takes the shot and posts it. I wonder whether to do one too, but my hesitation – as always – costs me momentum. Nicolette and I have discussed social media – being, as it is, a major obsession within both our lives. We have categorised users, ourselves included: likers, non-likers (stealth users), tactical likers, and the Truly Sound of Mind. I am more honest with Nicolette than I am with anyone else, even Kelly – which is strange for someone I have known a relatively short amount of time. I suppose it's a different kind of honest. I just let my mouth run. In my lighter moments, it is because I adore her. In my darker, it is because I know that I have nothing to lose by her disapproval.

'Gimme a mo,' Nicolette says. She dabs at her phone.

My own phone pings. I look at it. Kelly.

Hey, can you chat?

Nicolette looks up from her phone. 'Did you cut your hair?'

'Yes.'

'I mean that literally, babe. Did YOU cut your hair?'

'Actually, I did. But then I got it professionally tweaked.'

'Are you having a breakdown?'

'No! I don't think so.'

'It's not a criticism. Maybe psycho is the way to go. I almost rugby tackled a charity hijacker to the ground earlier. Do you know what he said to me? *Mate, you just dropped your smile.* I wanted to end him. More than I wanted to end cancer.'

'You should have. I hate those harassers. I hate the way they try and teach you how to be a good human. The guilt trip of it, you know? Like they're responsible for the fabric of society.'

'Yah. I don't have time for it, either. I've not stopped since 5 a.m. I ate a sandwich on the toilet at work, to save time. Then I remembered that was how Elvis died.'

'We'd better go in.'

'I suppose.'

In the studio, we take our positions on our mats.

'Be non-judgmental with your breathing,' Natalie the yoga teacher says.

I try to not judge my breath. Hey, breath, just do your thing. Lately, I've been focusing a lot on stabilising the water in my inner bowl. Natalie said to think of my pelvis as a bowl full of water and to keep my tailbone tucked in and my pelvic floor engaged to keep the water steady. I knew Natalie was a good person the first time I walked into her class. She's small and nervy, which I find reassuring in a yoga context. It lets you know she's been through it – spiritually, I mean. She says my Warrior Two is really coming on and I could be as fierce as the goddess Durga if I put my mind to it, so whenever I'm standing anywhere I try and be mindful of my inner water. I am aware I sometimes look a bit odd at the bus stop.

The inner water would be a lot easier to manage without the

memories that invade as soon as I take my eye off the present. A door opens in my mind, and in they surge: a procession of people who don't like me; people I have wronged in some way, Banquo after bastard Banquo – that friend I kissed, that woman who shouted at me on the cycle path, the *YOU HAVE NO INTEGRITY* man (who in my mind looks like my old French teacher, who I had a crush on). Another spasm at the thought of a meeting with three PRs the other day where I used the word 'groovy'. Which all takes me back to the croissant, its pathetic tally, my fundamental unlikeability—

'Move your arms in time with your breathing, Jenny,' says Natalie.

'I am.'

'You're breathing that fast?'

At the end of the class Natalie asks us to imagine we are trees, rooted into the ground down our backs, but all I can think of is *The Human Centipede*, which makes me feel hurlsome. That film cannot be unseen. Once I start thinking about it, it's like there's literally a rod up my arse. Or a Rod up my arse, depending on who the scientist might have abducted.

'Concentrate on your breath, Jenny,' Natalie says. 'There is nothing but your breath.' Is she giving me more advice than anyone else in the class? Surely I'm not the worst in the class. Dear sweet Christ, just when your day can't get any worse. I breathe in and out and try and listen, but it sounds like a ventilator in a hospital, like someone being kept alive, possibly against their will. It's not a tranquil thought. I'm not sure I've ever been good at being tranquil though, in all honesty. I've never seen a hammock and thought, that looks relaxing. I just think, that's going to tip up, with me in it. Kelly bought me a session in a sensory-deprivation pod for my birthday last year and I got out after five minutes. It was so dark in there! The woman giving me the induction told me there was a button on one side for the lights and an alarm on the other side in case I got into trouble. But once the lights were off and I was floating, I couldn't tell whether

I'd spun right round and so I didn't know which button was the lights and which was the alarm, so I didn't press anything out of fear. She also told me I'd know my hour session was up because five minutes before the end, a 'small wave' would ripple through the tank, emerging from the top of the pod, behind my head. Well, I was on tenterhooks anticipating that small wave. How small is a small wave? Would it flip me over? I got out after five minutes because the tension was so unbearable. I told Kelly it was great, and I really fucking hope she doesn't buy me another.

After class, Nicolette and I walk together to the end of the street. We pass a skinny woman walking her Italian greyhound.

'You know that thing about looking like your dog?' I say to Nicolette. 'Do you think it could work the other way around? So you get a dog you want to look like and you become as one, shape-wise? Or is it that you're attracted to things that look like you, in a cloning sort of way?'

'I don't think anyone would want to look like *an actual dog*, would they?'

'I wouldn't mind the physique of a Staffie. I might try it. I might get one. Maybe it makes you morph like any relationship, except physically not psychologically.'

My phone pings. Kelly again.

Hey – did you get my last message? Could do with a chat x

I'm thinking of what to reply and start scrolling before I know it and then Nicolette says bye and I put my phone back in my pocket and try to find my bank card and what was I doing? And how is it already dark? I zip up my jacket and hurry on. The street is littered with leaves, like the remains of a parade I've missed.

I POST

a video of my feet going through the leaves.

No sooner has it gone up than Nicolette likes it and comments with a line of hearts.

I message her:

> You are doing that thing we told each other to be aware of and promised to tell each other about

> What thing?

> After we've seen each other in real life, remember? You don't need to prove our closeness to anyone else on there or the ongoing elevation of your feelings towards me. No cord has been cut. Same way if we haven't seen each other or spoken for a while you don't have to NOT like anything I put on there to make me notice you like you're withholding affection from a lover

> I am not doing that! I felt those hearts

> Nicolette I know a real line of hearts and you know a fake line of hearts and that was a fake line of hearts

> Okay

As soon as I've finished messaging, I go and see what Suzy Brambles has been up to. Not much. Which is rather remiss of her, I think.

I catch the Overground to Dalston Kingsland, and from there walk to Stoke Newington. I like the walk down Kingsland Road, past the meat market and cocktail parlours. Old locals sip bitter outside the last few traditional boozers. Unhinged newspapers scud across the street into coffee cups and cigarette ends.

When I get to the house I open the front door and shuffle in past the day's pizza leaflets and taxi cards. This hallway is getting darker, and it's not just the year; it's the clutter. It used to feel spacious in here. Just after I moved in, Kelly came round and ran down the hall in her boots shouting: *Is this your house? Is THIS your HOUSE?* I said it was, for now. We have a plan, you see, Kelly and I. A plan that has withstood years, relationships, jobs, everything. We envisage spending our dotage together as an elderly couple in a manor house somewhere on the moors. 'The Commune', we call it. *When we're in the Commune . . .* we say:

We'll drink martinis at 9 a.m.

We'll try all the drugs we were scared of taking when we were younger, like crack and smack

We'll Whac-a-Mole each other's haemorrhoids

We'll have the highest quality mattresses money can buy*

*And employ a person specifically to put duvet covers on

We'll go out in each other's arms, freebasing — with Alanis Morissette's Jagged Little Pill *on repeat*

For now, alas, me and this dark hallway must find some way to coexist.

I walk through to the lounge. Sid and Moon are in there, encrusted on the sofa, drinking Sid's homemade probiotics.

Fuck. I forgot to buy an avocado.

Frances must be in her room. She's the only one I can really endure for more than five seconds.

Sid has artist's hands, scabby and ink-covered. She works as a receptionist at a recruitment agency and spends most of her time doodling. Moon works in PR and is rocking neon knitwear and an erupting beehive. They are having a conversation about intestinal flora.

'There's a convincing argument that we are composite organisms rather than individuals,' says Sid. 'I don't know which way round I work sometimes – whether my brain leads my stomach or my stomach leads my brain. If it's the latter, that means I am ruled by billions of bacteria.'

'I know what you mean,' says Moon. 'I've often wondered whether I have a personality or whether everything I've ever said or done has been a response to *eating or not eating bread*.'

'So true,' says Sid. 'Sometimes I think the word "gluten" sets off a chain reaction in my body. I think it's only a matter of time before they ban the word, too. And quite right . . .'

'Listen,' I say, 'would you guys mind tidying up in here if you get time tonight? Just, you know . . . the footbath and the bagel slicer.'

They stare at me. 'I don't suppose you remembered the avocado?' says Sid.

I shake my head. 'I'll get you one tomorrow.'

'No avo and calling me "Stephanie" in your column. It's practically abusive. Lol!'

'I changed your name out of respect for your privacy.'

'And then you wrote about our personal habits.'

'It was for other women to learn from.'

'What's to learn? There was no conclusion in the piece. Nothing in it was of any consequence whatsoever.'

'The conclusion is if you honestly share then you feel less alone.'

Moon snorts into her ginger ale. 'You said it was twenty years ago. That's not very honest.'

'Again, protecting you.'

'I think talking about your friends' bodies in public is a pretty garbage thing to do.'

'It's an online feminist magazine. And you're my lodgers.'

'Well,' says Sid, 'that's put us in our place.'

My cheeks are hot. I turn and walk out of the room.

I am thirty-five, I am thirty-five, I chant as I walk to my room. I pass Frances's door – the door to what should have been a different room altogether. I can hear her practising her latest one-woman monologue. 'Call me, Adolf!' she's screaming. 'Call me! *CALL ME!*'

She gets funding for this shit. It's all a bit much.

THEY SAY

screens at bedtime are bad for your brain, but the sensation of holding a phone is, I find, therapeutic. I find the shape of it re-assuring. Soothing. I press it to my chest like a bible. Every few minutes I lift it up and look to see what has changed in the world. I feel the weight of my thumb. My heart pounds. My veins thrum. I am in every way alive and progressing. My brain is lit up like the Earth from space at night.

I have a couple more likes for the croissant. I think it's reasonable to conclude now that it wasn't worth it. I squandered an entire morning on that. I can't keep building these cathedrals out of crumbs.

I scroll.

A friend of mine, a semi-famous scriptwriter, has posted a picture of herself in a lift. She isn't smiling. She looks like she's in a perfume ad. Like she's thinking: *Look at me, don't look at me, who are you, I don't trust you* . . . It is very effective and confusing. I comment:

Looking reflective

We're real-life friends but she doesn't follow me on here, which has always been a point of hurt. I know she seldom uses social media and she has a strict sense of how she is 'seen'. But why don't I fit in with however she is seen? Why am I not perfect follow material? Also, cuttingly, she follows some truly trashy vloggers, which is a real kick in the teeth. Now I've posted the comment I start to worry. It's like I forget this stage of the process; like I set myself up for it. She might not reply. She hasn't in the past. So why does that boil down to a failing on my part? I have to ask myself that, because it does. I didn't use to have this – this innate distrust of myself. I feel like I have lost my pace. It's like everything has been speeding up and up and up and I reached my own terminal velocity. I thought my twenties felt like rush hour, but no. My twenties were just pleasantly hectic. The thirties are the real rush hour.

She replies, three minutes later.

Miss you Mac

Well now follow me back and you wouldn't have to, is what I want to say. *Then you could see me regularly. It is within your grasp!* But I don't have the gall.

I don't know when all this started feeling like . . .

Like . . .

I see a picture Mia has posted of her dog.

I decide to have a think about whether to like it. A like is never just a like.

My phone beeps. I look.

It's a text.

From my mother.

I am supposed to pick 12 women who have touched my life and whom I think might participate. I think that if this group of women were ever to be in a room together there is nothing that wouldn't be impossible. I hope I chose the right 12. May my hugs, love, gestures, and communications remind you how special you are. Please send this back to me. Make a wish before you read the quotation. That's all you have to do. There is nothing attached. Just send this to 12 women and let me know what happens on the fourth day. Did you make your wish yet? If you don't make a wish, it won't come true. This is your last chance to make a wish! Quotation: 'May today there be peace within. May you trust that you are exactly where you are meant to be. May you not forget the infinite possibilities that are born of faith in yourself and others. May you use the gifts that you have received, and pass on the love that has been given to you. May you be content with yourself just the way you are. Let this knowledge settle into your bones, and allow your soul the freedom to sing, dance, praise and love. It is there for each and every one of us.' Now, send this to 12 women (or more) (you can copy & paste) within the next 5 minutes. In addition, remember to send back to me. I count as one. You'll see why xxxxxx

I instantly feel harassed. I stare at the text for a moment. As I'm staring, another text from her arrives.

How r u? xx

It doesn't feel right that someone older than me abbreviates more than I do, but this is the way it is. She texts me approximately once a week. When I ignore her, she turns up in my dreams. The other night she was in the doorway of my room, wearing a pair of wings – fine-boned and iridescent, like a dragonfly's. They glistened in the moonlight. When she turns up like that I have to remind myself that the visions are only my version of her – the real her is three hundred miles away.

I close my eyes and see it. That house. Mock Tudor. Mock everything. Our street was adjacent to a big-dog housing estate and the kids would come and chuck crab apples at the garage doors. I'd look down from my turret bedroom window, feeling quite the oppressed royal. Someone wrote 'WITCH' in chalk on the wall and my mother looked at it proudly while I burned. *Thousands of years ago, witches were respected as healers,* she said. *They were wise women in the community.*

And then we got doctors, I said.

Did we, though, she said, *did we ever really 'get' doctors like we got witches? What I'm talking about is a gift, not a career choice.*

In the garden there was a huge laburnum tree where caterpillars grew in the buds and dangled down on invisible threads in late spring. She liked bright plants. Pinks and yellows, for good energy, to ward off evil spirits. Lupins, azaleas, bleeding hearts. She dug up the pampas grass after I told her it was code for swingers. In the middle of the front lawn there was a monkey puzzle tree, its base beaded with grey stones, Japanese-style, after something she saw in a magazine. Other things: the crack-spangled patio, the planters polka-dotted with moss, the eternally unoccupied bird box. I've been back a handful of times. Birthdays. Christmases. Odd times off the slingshot of another failed love affair.

A WOMB OF ONE'S OWN

I lived in Stepney Green, Kentish Town, Streatham. I saved like Scrooge. I wrote for fourteen hours a day. I was in some kind of rocket mode, blazing a way, trying to escape an old atmosphere. I walked home down the worst of roads in a knitted hat, trying to look mad (un-rapeable), with my Yale key between my first two fingers. I had a contact – one, from a kindly teacher at school. I followed up on it. A trade magazine for a supermarket. It was a start. I ate a lot of sautéed vegetables. I had love affairs with men whose guitars were as badly strung as their sentences. Oh, to be fearless in terrible shoes again, oh so fearless and able to tolerate the cheapest of drinks and the cheapest of shoes. Outlet pleather and bad designs but all that time ahead, all that time, to wear terrible shoe after terrible shoe and wake up on another floorboarded, guitar-lined attic room with a leisurely hangover and all the hope in my heart. I'd leave before they woke, leaving a calligraphic note, and I'd go home and close my own door and feel joy when I saw the pictures I'd hung on my walls. The chairs I'd arranged. The carpets I'd chosen. The paint I'd painted. I started to feel what could be a kind of love of creating my own space. A love that could be nurturing and proud, as well as utterly romantic. A love that felt accessible and, if not quite democratic, then self-made. Empowering. All mine. To share with people I might have round, in varying contexts. I was romancing myself. I was also looking after myself. This was progress.

The first day of my first job, I texted my mother to tell her. She replied:

Good luck xxx

Good luck! Have you ever read a less motherly text? Good luck! I thought about her at least once every three minutes. I scratched my scalp and sniffed it; it smelled of her. I'd come into my flat and feel her energy there, latent somehow, in a place she'd never been. I missed the North: its winds and mosses; its cool, thirsty cities. I'd look at the weather reports for Manchester and feel glad when the weather was good. I had it as a location to slide past on my weather app. *My little darling, I'm glad you have clear skies tonight*, I'd think. I sang 'Don't Look Back in Anger' so loudly on the Tube once, drunk, that someone gave me a pound. I thought about our old living room, telly and lamp on; a cube of light in the vastness of space. I was an astronaut out on the arm of the mothership, umbilicus stretching, stretching, stretching.

THERAPY SESSION #1
(DRAMATIC MONOLOGUE)

Hi, yes, here? Okay. This is a nice office. Plain, but I suppose that's so I focus on the task in hand, which is no mean feat! What do I think that is? Sorting out my mental state haha. I should probably do more exercise. That would probably make a big difference. I noticed you had a kayak strapped to the top of your car outside, do you like to kayak, or do you have children? [Pause] Oh, I see, well I was just making conversation, I ramble when I'm nervous, I suppose that's music to your ears. It's like I can't stand silence and that's possibly because my mother was loud at home and when there was silence it meant there was a problem. [Pause] No, I've never had therapy before – does it show? I hate sounding like an amateur. Do you know how long it took me to choose what to wear today? Days. Literally. I was thinking about what might make you like me the most and I settled on something plain but with a few flourishes and I'm glad because I see now that's very much your vibe. I'm not judging you, I barely know you. I know this is meant to be a socially pure zone but I don't believe in any space you can hurl things into without consequences – that's just me. Everything has consequences, doesn't it? Every act of communication is an act of translation. I should probably have done Philosophy rather than English and Communication Studies. I don't even really know what Communication Studies is, other than a chance for the lecturer to talk about his days on the broadsheets. He's no use for magazine contacts. [*Pause*] What's my relationship like with my mother these days? Desultory. Can I say that? It's not like she was the worst in the world. She didn't molest me or anything like that – and sometimes I think it would have been easier if she had. If I'd had something concrete to work with, you know? [*Pause*] How's it going at uni? Good. Good, I think. Apart from the Communication Studies. It was definitely the right decision to move down. It's a great uni – and the fact they organise things like this – what do they call it? Pastoral care. Some universities might be embarrassed they'd attracted a load of loonies, but not this one – and I respect that. [*Pause*] Do I have a relationship with my father? No, I don't even know his name. She'd never tell me. Which gives her clairvoyance skills some credibility, because it's like she predicted the internet. You know if I had a name I'd have Facebooked the shit out of him. People at school used to tell me he was in prison. Aren't children delicious? Freeloaders, that's what my mother calls them. It's what she called me. It was fucking work, being her daughter. I put a fucking shift in. [*Pause*] I sound angry? Yes, I think I am angry. So that's the thing to work on, I suppose. The anger. That's the thing I want gone. [*Pause*] No, she never heard from him, or she never told me if she did. All I know is he called one night when she was pregnant. She was in bed and she answered the phone and he didn't speak but she knew it was him by the sound of his breath. Sinister, right? In my worst nightmares my father is a perv. You know, an old Rat-Packer. *Come over here, princess, and give ol' Daddio some sugar.* I can imagine her going for a creep like that. Allow me a blowsy moment: sometimes I see things – the undersides of sycamore leaves, oily puddles in tarmac – and I'm reminded of a father I never knew. A cellular memory, perhaps. An amino acid residue. I don't even know how memory works; I suppose no one does – it's one of the things your lot are working on. When he called that night she was so shaken that her adrenaline surged, and she said she felt me stir, inside, awoken. I often think about that moment. My first encounter with the anxiety the world had in store. I had no protection in place. I mainlined her anxiety like alcohol. But that's not the worst thing. The worst thing she ever did was leave me to go on holiday to the Bahamas one Christmas. Worst Christmas of my life. I was sixteen. I vowed I'd never let her hurt me again, and I haven't. She sent me a postcard. I still have it. It's what you might call a prized possession because every now and then when I feel my resolve weakening, I reread it. I didn't take it lying down, though. I had my revenge. [*Pause*] How? I staged my own suicide the day she got back. You've never heard someone scream so much. It was magnificent. I wrote a note and left it downstairs and then I got in the bath with a razor and some fake blood. I'd say she's probably seeing her own therapist about it but she's quite anti-therapy. Gin is her therapy. I hope she rereads the note. It was a really fucking good note. But then, I am a lot better educated than she is. [*Pause*] No, that is no thanks to her. She paid for my education and then she partied all night. What kind of self-sabotaging showmanship is that? Her problem – and she has a whole catalogue of problems, believe me – but her main one is she doesn't have any true friends. She's a loner. And that means she has no one to set her straight. It's not that she lowers the tone; it's that I don't think she realises there *is* a tone . . .

MY DEAREST DARLING JENNY,
I hardly know what to tell you – other than Roger and I are having a marvellous time and it's not as hot as I feared, which you know is a relief for the likes of you and I who suffer with the dreaded frizz. You would not believe the beaches – I have taken lots of photos so as soon as I get back I'll get them developed so I can show you and with any luck they won't just be of my sausage knees or half a palm tree. I hope you are having a very merry Christmas and you found the money in your card under the tree – get yourself something nice in the sales. No one seems bothered about the millennium bug here so I really think try and keep your panic under control darling (you do worry!) although poor Roger did suffer another type of bug when we first arrived but that seems to have mostly evacuated now and certainly hasn't put him off the lumumbas. See you in the new year – and the new millennium! I hope it will bring us both many great things. I really do feel so positive about the future and just know you're going to make me so proud.

Take care.

Your loving mother XXXX

LIKE OF DUTY

I don't reply to my mother. Instead, I go back for another dose of Suzy Brambles. But lo, what's this? A new post! I devour it.

She has been out in Soho. She has imbibed too many shots. She has succumbed to a falafel kebab. Soho . . . So . . . close, and yet so far. I give it a *Deep Like*. You really feel likes like that. Everyone must. And then I comment:

LIVING YOUR BEST BAB LYF

With no kisses, to look nonchalant. Then I wonder whether I should have put Livin' with an apostrophe rather than Living, to sound more youthful. Then I go through Suzy's follows again just to check I am still there. It makes me feel strong to see myself amongst her chosen people. I know she is seeing what I'm doing, even if she doesn't feel the need to reach out. I notice that she has started following Art, which is odd because he hardly ever posts anything, just the odd nice coffee or cool job he's been on.

Music strikes up from the living room downstairs – which means Sid is DJing again. I did once tell her that those decks are strictly a weekend-only activity and then I felt so old I instantly relented and brought home a load of shit-maddening frenetic dance records, just to disprove my own point. It's like when I left a bad Airbnb review – the only bad one I've ever left – and the host replied so viciously that I left another review on another site that was completely complimentary and over the top and I got so carried away writing it that by the end of it I was convinced I had been wrong and was actually madly in love with the place, so I booked another stay there. They declined my booking.

I send Kelly a message:

> Okay I'm dying here. I can't stand these people in my house. I'm trapped, terrified of the future and sick of pretending. Send help

Kelly doesn't reply, which isn't like her. I hope she's not in some way trying to manage me. I thought we'd made an agreement to not do the passive-aggressive thing with each other. We just save that for everyone else in our lives. I look at her Instagram and like her two most recent pictures, out of duty. She is my friend, after all.

My favourite rental flat was above a furniture shop. It had a shower-head in the bath I had to trap under my foot while I soaped my armpits. When I sat on the toilet at night, silverfish scooted around my toes. One time, a cockroach made a cameo. The saving grace was a grubby little balcony, complete with two upturned buckets where I could sit with a friend and smoke. Over the road was a wicker warehouse. The first time Kelly came round I said: *Don't ask me who would want to live in a flat like this because I have no idea.*

She replied: *Someone who wants to assassinate a wicker salesman.*

I said: *Kelly, comments like that are why you are the love of my lifetime.*

She said: *Well, it's not like I had much choice about you being mine.*

I don't know what she meant by that. She's funny, Kelly, sometimes. She fights her feelings. It's like on some level she isn't satisfied with the way things have turned out. And I wonder whether that's just motherhood or something else inside her.

I try and relax by looking at the page of someone I was mildly obsessed with for a while when things started getting bad, @ Virginiaginia. She's luscious, and I don't use that word lightly. She's a cultural commentator married to a pop scientist. I go to her Twitter. I realise I am secretly hoping she has split up with the pop scientist. I am looking for evidence of this. Why? Schadenfreude? Solidarity? I start looking through HIS photos to see if SHE has liked them, to work out whether they're still going out. I'm fucking cracked! But I can't stop. The compulsion is all-consuming. I require the 360 on this. I deserve the 360 on this. They have liked each other's posts, but maybe they'd like each other's posts MORE if they're not together any more, in that generous, fake way exes do. It's looking hopeful – there's no mention of him otherwise for weeks and weeks . . . I click through to her blog. The most recent post is called 'Starting Over'. Aha! V. promising! I read, ravenous. Drat, the post is about some recent foray into watercolour. Ah. So disappointing. They're dreadful paintings, too. And prove nothing. I slide back to her Twitter. There – I find it. Ten weeks ago.

A picture of them at a barbecue.

I console myself with the fact that they could have split up within the past ten weeks.

As I lie waiting to fall asleep I listen to Father John Misty's *I Love You, Honeybear*. I wonder whether I will ever love anyone like that.

Like I love Father John Misty, I mean.

(I wonder if he's still with his wife?)

PICTURE THE SCENE

An eco lodge on the edge of the Sahara. Sounds awful, right? I mean, you could fall in love with pretty much anyone there, even a camel. It was a press trip. Art was some sort of trainee travel photographer on his first junket. I was doing a feature on sustainable lodges for *The Nonspecific Nerd*. I was seeing three men, one of them the editor at a poetry publishing house, the second the UK's foremost Alexander Pope critic, and the third ran an indie music label in Brighton and had DJ'd at the BAFTAs. All of them were divorcees. I'd run around Soho with each of them in turn, sometimes two together, hoovering up the summer.

When I first saw Art I wasn't instantly attracted to him. He bounded around – I mean *bounded* – snapping away with his Leica camera, the brown leather case dangling proudly. I recall his khaki shorts, his hairy legs, his designer-shabby vest, his blister pack of stomach muscles, his luxury gadgets. There he was: White Male Gonna-Make-It.

He came up to me as I stood reading the itinerary in reception. He said later that when he tried to make conversation with me, I looked at him like he was asking for money. I used to be like that. Measured. Poised. Gilded.

'Amazing, isn't it?' he said – giddy, lucky, asinine.

'What, that it's 11 a.m. and they haven't given us *coffee*? Yes. Quite.'

He was taken aback. I smiled and said: 'I know, I'm an entitled bitch, right? But that's what this is: the Age of Entitlement. That's what they'll call it, years down the line. There'll be a marble statue of a woman like me with an empty cup and a face on, defining the era.'

He laughed, and I felt my wings unfurl. And why not? I was a woman in my twenties. The whole world was mine to kill.

That first night in Egypt, the hotel laid out paper lanterns on the paths, leading the way to dinner. I noticed him at his table, sure, but there were other people to notice, too. I wasn't limiting myself. I was infinite with possibilities.

It was a glam gig. The backdrop of the cliffs, the hotel carved into the soft sandstone; we were off on a jeep ride over the dunes the following day. The Michelin-starred chef had made a vegetarian dinner from the lodge's sustainable, irrigated garden. It was so nice it felt dirty.

After dinner I took my mint tea to the quiet garden and Art followed me.

We got talking. Initially, our conversation took the tone of jousting. We were teasing each other, nudging each other, showing off, retreating, peeking back. That was my natural way, but I see now for him it was because he was coming from a point of hurt – albeit misguided, self-indulgent hurt. It didn't take him long to tell me that he was contacting his most recent ex regularly to 'take her temperature'. Otherwise, he said, 'People become saints or monsters in your memory'. He'd been unfaithful to her, and she'd ended it.

I noticed he had a tattoo on his bicep. The trishula. 'Are you Buddhist or Hindu?' I said, keen to change the topic.

'Neither.'

'Just ethnically confused.'

I was pushing him in every puddle. But he deserved it. All white men you meet deserve it. He smiled. 'The trishula means something to me. It symbolically destroys three worlds: the physical world, the past, and the mind.'

'Handy.'

He sighed. 'I feel like I've destroyed a few worlds lately.' Another sigh. 'I've been thinking of working in a soup kitchen, or something like that, to try and redress the balance.'

'Noble.'

'She won't talk to me,' he said, and looked genuinely hurt. 'I can't stop feeling bad about it. She's crazy, but I want to help her.'

I said, 'Can I level with you?'

'I insist.'

'I detest the whole *I'm such a bad guy* spiel. It's all about keeping "You" – the man – as the all-powerful, controlling pivot of the universe.'

'But I feel so guilty! Can you understand that?'

He annoyed me, then, and I almost went, *Naaah. You know what? Naaaah. See ya.* But I sat. And I stayed. And I said: 'You've got to watch guilt. It's a tricksy one. Too often it's just narcissism incognito.'

Why did I stay? To educate him? That's what Kelly said: *If you have a relationship with a white man you are basically running a correctional facility every fucking day, mate.* But Kelly had been single longer than my mother.

Art looked at me more sadly than he knew. 'But I worry about her . . .' he said. 'Eliza,' he said. 'That's her name.'

Eliza. I know what she looks like, the particulars of her CV (downloaded as a PDF then shamefacedly deleted) (oh god would she be able to tell??). It's funny how close you get to someone's ex via the internet and the sexual hangover. I knew from the way Art and I had sex, at the start, the things Eliza liked. Before we made our own impressions on each other the impressions of the past were there, like muscle memory. The tweaked nipples (SO not my bag);

the *I really want to fuck you*s. There is something meaningful, some kind of growth, in that historical cross-pollination. He had her name tattooed across his heart. I never asked him to remove it, but it was like she was there, every time he was naked. His body said her name. She was an echo in the room. A tracer on the light of our love.

Back to Egypt.

I said: 'Have you considered the small possibility that Eliza is actually fine, and you might be using the whole "guilty" thing as a way of continuing to feel powerful?'

He said nothing to that.

'You terrible cad,' I went on. 'You rotter, you rogue. Leaving a poor helpless woman all alone in this krewl world. And no, no, don't tell me, you've done it hundreds of times before, haven't you? There's a frothy wake of broken hearts behind you, trailing around the globe, isn't there?' His mouth was half open and he was shocked, shocked-laughing. He pushed his fingertip into my shoulder, but I wasn't deterred. I was on a fucking *roll*. 'Go visit a prison, or even better, a bank,' I said. 'Then you'll meet some truly bad men. You're just some middle-class pusskin who's watched too many box sets.'

He looked at me like he wanted to kill me. Then his face changed. He said: 'I see you, hipster.' He smiled sweetly. 'I see you, with your piecemeal personality and your dietary restrictions and your General Pinochet T-shirt.'

'Do you think you are upset by these things because you secretly want them for yourself?'

'I see it all for what it is. I would guess you've never been loved as much as you thought you deserved. I think if you really wanted to change the world you'd find a way to stop being so furious and so quaint.'

I tried to think of Oscar Wilde. Of Aristophanes. *To be insulted by you is to be garlanded with lilies.* I tapped my cigarette on the sandstone floor and looked back at him. 'Well well. Don't we have all the undainty revelations.'

He was a gun, I was counterfeit. The expectation up until that point might have been that we'd sleep together that night (we didn't), but with those two admonitions, we fucked each other good. I don't think we had ever felt our sex as much as we did in that moment.

Well, maybe one other time.

He smiled sweetly again. 'Do you think there's one person for every person?'

I shook my head. 'No. I have never thought that.'

'I'm scared of not meeting the right person.'

'I'm scared that not meeting the right person, over and over, might be the point for me.'

He nodded grimly. 'Same time tomorrow?'

And that's how it went. We drank mint tea and smoked together every night in the garden after dinner. 'Hey, movie star,' he'd say, when he saw me. I cringed at that. I ensured my cringing was visible. Still, I sat there, waiting for him, Movie Star Me.

On the last day, we swapped email addresses.

He emailed me as we travelled in separate cars to Cairo.

INBOX

Subject: YOU

ARE SOMETHING ELSE.

That was it.

I have to admit, it excited me. The boldness. The way he used the subject bar as part of the message. The lot. I read it and I thought – *Okayyyyy, maybe we have something here.* I had never been emailed like that. It was like seeing my own brain pinned wriggling to the page. Delightful! And moreover: undeniable.

I didn't reply. (Hahah. Mine to kill. Mine to kill.) I stared at the email. I sat back in my chair. I watched two pale yellow butterflies twirl around each other. *Are you dancing? Are you asking? I'm asking. I'm dancing.* I clicked my phone off and then clicked it back to life and stared at the email again. I wanted the feeling to last forever.

I messaged Kelly:

What do you make of this then?

I was milking it, I know. But I felt like I deserved a bit of milking after such a drought. And there had been a drought, certainly on the sexual-banter front. I'd been having a lot of sex, but not so many sexy verbal high jinks.

Kelly replied:

Sounds like an alpha male. Good luck

GOOGLE SEARCH

'how to attract an alpha male'
'how to seduce an alpha male'
'is it possible to be truly loved by an alpha male when you are an alpha female'
'alpha males throughout history'

I SAID

You are very sweet.

Cool. AF.

I'd waited until I knew his flight had left (he was off to Paris, an hour earlier). I was careful to use a full stop as he had done, and I realised I respected people far more when they punctuated properly. They were to be taken more seriously. He replied, from the air (imagine that!).

You have blown me away. All the way to Paris.

I didn't reply. I boarded my flight. I drank a Grey Goose and Fever Tree tonic and felt thoroughly international.

When I landed, I had three more emails.

I just got back to my hotel room and expected you to be in my bed but you weren't.

And:

I was standing on the Metro on the way home and thinking about how people are just bunches of cells, radiating off into smells and sounds.

And:

That thing you said to me about guilt really struck a chord. You are the wisest person I have met in forever.

Kelly said:

> Jesus Christ. He talks in hyperbole – sure sign of a narcissist
>
> Wait a minute, I talk in hyperbole!
>
> Wellllll
>
> I LOVE narcissists. They're so . . . covetable
>
> As soon as you reciprocate he'll go quiet, trust me

But it was too late. I was coveting. I thought hard about his 'smells and sounds' remark. I tried for irreverent. And when you 'try' for *irreverent* . . .

I sent:

We are all just filthy little beasts underneath

Immediately after I'd pressed Send, I started to worry. We'd known each other all of five minutes. It felt too early to get away with the suggestion that I was unhygienic. We were still trying to impress each other with our arthouse knowledge, and here I was . basically saying I stank like shit.

Argh!

He didn't reply for a few minutes. He had gone off me. It was a despicable thing to write. And me, supposedly, a professional writer! What must he think of me? Oh god oh god. What if he thought I had some kind of bestial fetish? It was too much. I didn't know what to do. I was panicking, panicking. It strikes me now how rapidly I changed. From cautious and in control to anxious wreck. How? Why? He'd got to me, this one. Aggggggggggraaaahhhhhhhgggggggggg. It's almost as though there's not room for romance in modern life, what with feminism, work, social commitments and anxiety.

Kelly wouldn't help.

> You could ask me how my day is going or how Sonny's
> first sleepover went

I misread her irritation as envy.
It's romantic! I protested. But she wouldn't have that, even.

> It's not romance. It's mania

> Well you have basically stalked people, so

> That was ONE TIME, I was at a festival and I was high,
> so it doesn't count

> Forgive me for just wanting some basic reassurance from
> a pal

> Manic

> Romantic

> Romantic mania. You are in ROMANIA mate

> Look, don't shoot the messenger. Of The Truth

> *Hermes has joined the chat*

Then Art sent back:

You're adorable.
X

Adorable! Moi!
I sent Kelly:

All fine! He replied!

And I dashed off, to Art:

Well, if you say so, squire!
X

He didn't reply to that.
Kelly sent:

Sweet

Whatever, Kelly.

Round I went again, on my spiral . . . *Squire!* Just the thought of the word made me feel nauseated. I hoped he didn't think I was someone who was into reenactment societies, although he HAD said in Egypt that he liked antiquing, I reassured myself, so maybe he liked old-fashioned language, too . . . There was so much to ponder. So much to google. But there's only so much you can glean from someone's cousin's Facebook page. If I could have found more on the Dark Web, I would have gone there. I would have gone anywhere. Even a Wetherspoons.

Looking at it critically, retrospectively, I was laying some kind of claim, I suppose. I thought I was adoring, but I was actually . . . well, invading. I was storming into his past and present desires. I'd never taken someone like that. I don't know what came over me.

Some kind of pioneering urge. Obsession seeks possession. Just ask my mother.

A whole day later, I sent a simple:

How's it hanging?
X

Friendly! Breezy! Brief!

It was just a lovely friendly email from one lovely new friend to another.

And then . . .

He didn't reply.

And then . . .

I started to worry that he would think I was referring to his penis. I was freshly distraught. How could I expect to be a creature of mystique whilst referring to someone's penis as 'it'? Oh god, that he might think that!

Then:

I've just bought a cocktail cabinet that's too big for my flat. Mid-century modern. It means you have to come round for cocktails, Foxface.

My fingers were typing before my brain could even scream NO WAIT A MINUTE WHY THIS DETERMINATION TO PUT YOURSELF BACK INTO TORTUROUS PAIN, WHY NOT SAVOUR THE SWEET ABSENCE OF FEELING—

I can't wait to see your cock
Tail cabinet
Oops sent too soon!

Well, *I* thought it was funny.
Everything.
In me.
Tensed.
Then, the blessed relief of a chime, a name, an *I-see-you*.

Hahahahahahahahahahhahaaaaa

I went all hot and happy inside.
Then he wrote:

I am going to destroy you.

You try keeping your pants intact when things hit that height. I replied:

Promises, promises.

No kisses. Just pure raw come-and-get-it. Oh yeah, mufux. The cracks. The verbal ping-pong. You'd never heard anything like it! They were publishable, our email exchanges. They were sublime.

But all that effort. The waiting, the trying, the wanting, the joining-the-dots in between. The pretty pictures out of something and nothing. My brain was – *is* – too good at spotting patterns. It's not a million miles away from a certain kind of madness.

I tried to stay in control. I even sent him an email to Kelly accidentally on purpose one time.

Can we meet a bit later tonight? I have to file next week's column early because of Christmas break XX

I wanted him to know I had an exciting work life.

Then I sent: Whoops sorry, not for you!

My stage management, my timing, was seamless – or so I thought.

He sent back: I figured. Good luck with the column x x

Years later, he told me he'd seen through it. That it was 'a bit exposition-y'. That it was 'the kind of thing he'd have done, years ago'. I was furious. I was fucked. It was acid. It was tragic. Because I know, deep down, beyond where it hurts, that I will never have that kind of frisson with anyone, ever again. It was like kissing a mirror – when the mirror starts kissing back. It is an invitation to drown.

For now, back to the salad days. The proses. The roses.

THE PATATAS BRAVAS

On our second date we went to a tapas place in Victoria Park. We sat outside and drank too-sharp cherry-red wine out of beakers. We discovered we were both trying to eat less meat, and were both scared of wasps. It was too romantic. I told him I was buying a house. He sat back in his chair and whistled. He said I'd done good, that he should probably buy a house, that his career wouldn't last forever. *I came from nothing, like you.* I said: 'My mother has money.' I used her like a doubloon in my pocket, then. 'She matched me for the deposit. We went fifty-fifty.'

'Nice.'

'She's done very well, doing what she does.'

'What does she do?'

'You and your trishula will soon find out.'

He'd been taking photos of birds and butterflies. I remember those pictures, hung in his tiny flat, and later, in my house. The stained glass of a butterfly's wing. The hard black crescents of swifts. He photographed bower-birds and the extravagant nests they made to attract a mate. The males collected coloured objects – usually blue – like magpies did, and made little gardens, *bowers*, to lure in a female. I suppose what surprised me the most was that I found them beautiful, and Art found them beautiful. So humans shared an aesthetic with birds. How odd, for two species to share an idea of beauty. I said as much.

'Are you luring me into your fancy new bower, with these jewels?'

he said. I sat back. 'Oh, you have a mean face when you turn your smile off! For a pretty girl. Are you going to look at me like that for much longer? Wow. I feel like taking a picture so you can see for yourself!'

'I'm not trying to lure you anywhere,' I said, insulted. 'You can do what you like. I have no desire to mate or marry. I am a busy woman with plans. It is not in my nature to surrender.'

(Baby me, oh baby me. I want to fly back in time and tell you you're wrong and hug you and tell you everything's not going to be okay.)

When I went to the loo he emailed me:

What if I adore you?

I sat on the loo and typed back:

What, then?
What if I do, though?
Well, this IS a conundrum . . .

Someone knocked. I hitched up my pants.

'Are we . . . categorised, then?' Art said, when I was back at the table.

'Is this', I said, 'a hoary little question about exclusivity?'

He laughed at that. He told me I could call the shots. Ha! I laughed, then. I was a 28-year-old woman. I was taking the shot-calling for granted. I looked at him in a way that told him so. I revealed . . . an amused scowl.

'What are you going to do about them, then?'

'Who?'

'The other three? Your three amigos. The curly-haired one in particular needs to go.'

Ah, so he'd looked and found them. He had made deductions. Course he had.

'Is this an ultimatum? I don't respond well to ultimatums, I should warn you.'

'I wouldn't dare.'

'I am completely honest with all of you. I have everything I need. If you want to come along for the ride, be my guest, but I'm driving.'

'And what about the teatimes?'

'What about the teatimes?'

'Are they not lonely? The endings of the days? Do you not long for that nightly family feeling? Decompressing at the dining table.'

I couldn't answer for a long time. He'd hit a nerve all right. He was wily, this one.

'There are other ways of getting that.'

'You might not need the other ways forever.'

You know what it is? The light does it. Every time. You'll buy anything – a house, a situation, a feeling – if the light is right. That night, the light was right.

'Just know I'll do everything in my own time.'

'Of course,' he said. 'Of *course*. But – in the interests of transparency . . .'

'In the interests of transparency, I suggest you take off your shirt and your trousers.'

Ha! What a sailor. I was epic. Randy Crawford's 'Almaz' comes to mind. It's strange how a lot of people hear that as a tragic song.

KELLY HAD SAID

You're like a deranged Victorian

I just want my missives to be as good as they can be!
Help me be the best me I can be, friend

These are EMAILS, not missives. Wake up and smell the
technology. Also why aren't you texting each other? Email
is a bizarre choice of medium

It's romantic. It's the closest we've got to letters

Apart from actual . . . letters

Too slow

I think the slowness would do you good

There's a lot to be said for spontaneity

No there isn't. Spontaneity ruins lives

At least in the olde days they understood the true power
of the written word

That was all they had! It was fucking years between
dances! They might be dead before they saw each other
again! It's not like that now. You're going to Nando's next
week so chill the fuck out

I AM CHILLED, I EMBODY CHILLED

I'm going to ask you this once, just once: what are you scared of? It's like I've never seen this side of you. Where has it come from?

Hahahahahah I really do not know what you are talking about, mate

Okay. Did you start the emailing or did he?

Him. Why?

Just asking

It was a very complimentary email

It's still his choice of medium though, isn't it? You're in a safe little box. That's all I'm saying

You only don't like him because he makes you feel morally inferior in your food choices and I know that's true because you've started buying RSPCA-approved salmon

Very surprised you have time to analyse the contents of my fridge these days given how much time you're devoting to being online

Do you think I'm quirky enough for him tho? He shot Patti Smith the other day and he knows a LOT about films

Look, just because he owns a copy of Battleship Potemkin and has a few tattoos doesn't mean he's not a mainstream twat

But then I think she warmed to him.

SOBER SEXTS

WHERE

Are you and what are you doing?

This was a regular line of questioning from Art in the early days.
I relished it. I took my time replying. I cracked my back and waggled
my fingers, magician-like. I crafted my responses.

Kelly told me off for it. I suppose she was getting annoyed at
this point by how many emails I was getting her to proofread and
suggest better jokes for.

'These are emails, Jenny,' she said. 'Not TV comedy scripts.'

'But they *matter*,' I argued. 'There's no way I'm sending substandard
communication.'

'But they're too laboured. They're . . . overwrought. You're better
when you're fast and unconsidered.'

'Hush. Now – do I use the word "mystery" or "mystique"?'

I started running drafts of tweets by her, for her approval.

'I'm not doing this,' she said. 'I'm not feeding the beast.'

'What beast?'

'The beast of your digital anxiety.'

'As a friend you should give me what I need. I would give it to
you.'

'You need help.'

'That's not funny.'

'I'm not joking. Do therapists not specialise in this yet? Is there not social media rehab? There should be.'

'It's called motherhood.'

Kelly was silent for a moment and then she said, 'You're making more and more digs like that, I do hope you realise.'

Art said:

Why the changes in font sizes?

It was because I made notes in my phone and then cut and pasted them to create the perfect work.

I mailed back:

I have no idea! Life is full of mystique

I stared at the message for hours, lamenting the fact I hadn't used the word 'mystery'. Mystery was indeed the far superior word. Sometimes the simpler word was the more effective word. Argh! Why was it always necessary to *actually* fuck up before you saw your gravest fuck-ups?

The first time he tweeted me, it was his first tweet in two months.

@thejenniferMcLaine YOU.

That full stop. That full stop had me in A FURY OF PLEASURE. It was a hard black sun of decisive cocklonging.

He continued

Are a goddess. I am a drunk loser on a piano stool.

78

I fired off:

Get a grip, Tom Waits

I gasped after I'd sent it. I kind of couldn't believe my own gump-
tion. I'd sort of done it without thinking. Even though I was getting
into him, that sort of *I'm such a loser* shtick pissed me off, you know?
It's like all those people who make out they're 'such geeks' (*I'm such
a geek!*) online, as though they're wearing braces aged thirty-two and
gawking around in striped tights. What they're really saying is, 'I'm
clever even though I'm stylish. Do not be fooled by my attractiveness!'
And what Art was really saying was, 'I'm cool even though I'm commer-
cial!' I still listen to Tom Waits' music. And all those other sad old men
with their self-indulgent songs. Anyway, Art fucking loved my disdain.
He replied:

I have so much respect and admiration for you, Jennifer.

I *mean*.
How the mighty fall.
I started emailing him every day, whether he replied or not. I
sent him links to songs and playlists he might like. I sent him my
funniest YouTube videos, decades in the gathering. I gave him advice
on how to host his first cocktail party, an email that took me six
hours and three drafts to write. It was one page long, with pictures
and links. The effort!
He didn't say he'd made the cocktails. He did say:

I have been looking at pictures of you online to while away the
time.
X
A

I replied quickly – not because I had to, you understand, but because it got it out of the way and then it wouldn't disturb my sleep for the rest of the night thinking about what to reply.

I have been looking at pictures of you too.
Jx

Which was a falsehood. I had been looking at pictures of his ex. I texted Kelly:

I've found her online. Art's ex. She's a shoemaker called Eliza. Now I can no longer enjoy shoes or the BBC Pride and Prejudice box set. Great. Two major pleasures banished from my life.

A shoemaker?

See even seeing the word shoe is making me feel sick

So what? She's his ex.

Do two big kisses mean the same as three small ones? Emotionally I mean. I want to look like I'm not too obviously reciprocating by being utterly repetitive, but I also don't want to diminish the feeling

I think you're overthinking it

WELL DEAR GOD FUCK YES QUITE INDEED. But do they?

Jenny, there is no way he will be paying such close attention to all this

Lucky him

It's not luck

It's unlucky to have my brain right now, I know that

You can conquer this. You can. I believe in you.

Can I send you a photo of his ex?

Negative

Just WhatsApped a screenshot. DISCUSS.

HOW MANY TIMES

Can I send you our last few emails to analyse the vibe?

This friendship is barely passing the Bechdel Test rn

He hasn't replied to my last one!

When did you email him

Seven minutes ago!

COOL YOUR JETS, MCLAINE

Help me Obi-Wan, you're my only hope

[. . .]

Jenny?

Jenny?

I've been thinking about our bodies and the way they fit together.
A.

He has just replied! A MOST EXCELLENT REPLY. All
good xxx

Mate, you are so deep in Romania you can't see the
Romanian wood for the Romanian trees

Yeah xxxxx

Okay, well see you next time some chump ignores you for 8 minutes I guess

They were a pretty good fit from what I can remember.

J.

What are you thinking about?

I am thinking about my cock in your mouth.

Shit – sorry, I mean your cock in my mouth!

I don't have a cock, obvs

Okay I really don't want you thinking about the fact I might have a cock

Unless that is your thing? But I don't think it is!

RRRAAAAAAAAAAARRRRRRGGGGGHHHHHHWWWW AAAAAAHHHHHHHHHHH

What now

WHEN SEXTS GO BAD

Do I want to know?

Kelly, please, please, please, please, please can I send a few emails to you?

No no no no NO

It's unethical

UNETHICAL? YOU TOOK COKE IN THE CRYPT OF ST PAUL'S CATHEDRAL

You bitch – we said we'd never speak of that again

QUID PRO QUO, CLARICE

SEND ME THE MAILS THEN YOU DICK

Thank you!

ABSOLUTE CHODE

Just sent them. Also why won't he give me his phone number, do you think? All he has given me is his email address and he doesn't have wifi in his home!

What kind of weirdo doesn't have wifi? I hate him already. It's like those twats who don't have TVs. Sad bastards, trying to make a stupid fucking point. I would never date someone without a TV. I find it positively offensive. People without TVs are pseudo-intellectuals who are too fucking stupid to realise that shit looks better when you watch it on a TV

I think he has a TV

As for those without wifi? They are addicts in remission

ABLUTIONS

The first time he stayed at my place he turned up with a paper bag. He shuffled in with it and hid it behind the umbrella stand as he slid his shoes off.

'Been shopping?' I said.

'Just grabbed a quick shirt in the sale.'

I caught a hint of it, then: his anxiety. I'd spotted the pills in his bathroom: Diazepam. A little something-something. Why not? My mother had her gin, and I had my work ethic.

He stood in the hall, looking around, reading my life but also girding his confidence, I knew. 'I have wondered so much about the details of this place,' he said. 'You're going to have to give me a moment to savour it.'

'Okay.' I thought of how, a few hours earlier, I'd been in the shower washing my body in preparation for him, and while I was doing so I thought of him washing his body in preparation for me, soaping his penis while I sponged my vulva, there we both were, separately preparing. I'd giggled at the absurdity of it – the futility of it, too, perhaps. It's one of love's greatest losses, every time, I think, that kind of fastidiousness.

Later, we kissed beautifully, awkwardly, our heads turning like sunflowers by teensy degrees, in front of the ten o'clock news. The best new love makes you feel fifteen again: clumsy, electric, conscientious.

I said: 'Where are you working tomorrow?'

'West.'

'You could stay. If you like.' It was Sunday. Teatime. I didn't want to be alone at Sunday teatime. Suddenly.

'Okay.'

'Okay!'

We kissed some more. Then I said: 'That's why you bought the shirt, isn't it?'

He went pink. 'Well I didn't want to turn up with a . . . So I bought a shirt, just in case. But then it was also *just a new shirt* – so, no pressure!'

'It's okay, I don't want you to worry. Shall we both just agree to try and not worry?'

He grinned awkwardly. 'That sounds good.'

'I know it's probably not possible, but it feels like a good thing to try and do, don't you think?'

'You are my dream girl.'

'You are my dream boy. Let's enjoy our youth while we can.'

I looked in his eyes. It was as though we had shown each other a card – our most secret card – and as we did so, simultaneously (3-2-1, go!) we realised it was the same card. Hey presto. And like that, the fear was gone. It was nothing short of (much as I like to avoid the word) . . . *magic*.

He went to use the bathroom. I imagined him seeing my things laid out in there and making conclusions. I'd arranged a few things, like a stage set. Left a few labels angled in a certain way. I'm sure he saw through them all, but knowing that was almost as delightful as the possibility of deceiving him.

MY BATHROOM SAID

Bathroom of a woman who is busy but takes care of herself
Bathroom you can have a bath in with her someday maybe
Look at that big shower. You could have sex in that shower
The shower is very clean which also probably means her vulva is clean
Smell her products. You know you want to
STOP SMELLING HER BATHROOM PRODUCTS I'M CALLING THE
* POLICE*

TIPPING POINT

The next time we were in a hotel it was in a spa town where he was shooting bathroom suites. The sex was rough and fast and he was more dominant. I guess he felt as though he had some ground to regain, and that makes me sad, now. (Did he know I'd seen his benzos?)

At the end he pulled out and came on my chest.

I was just about to tell him what to do when he got up and shot around the corner in the direction of the bathroom – I presumed to fetch a towel. Towel scrubs are a real feature of modern hotel-based sexual encounters. We should make more of them. It's so impossibly romantic, having your abdomen scoured with a hotel towel, don't you think?

Art returned, towel in hand. I felt like a stain on something. The moment had more than passed. The moment had got on a flight to Rio.

'Did you come?' he said, suddenly realising.

'No, but it's okay.'

I looked down at my tits, at the spunk sliding down the sides, off my nipples.

'Did *you* come?' I said. Which I thought was pretty fucking hilarious.

Later, we took valiums and lay on the bed watching *Stargazing Live*. Modern love.

MY MOTHER SAID

'A boyfriend? Who on earth has managed to tie you down?'

'No one. We're just dating.'

I didn't particularly want to introduce them. It never went well, when my mother came down. Lingering ignominies included a book launch (with the Pope scholar) where Mother necked so much free wine that she read all the bookshop staff's palms, unasked, and toppled head first down a spiral staircase. I was beyond mortified. (*A psychic*, Art howled, when I told him, *who can't see a staircase coming!* I said: *It was obscured in the floor!* God knows why I defended her.) When Kelly's mother came down, she made her pies and cleaned her house. She was the same woman every time you saw her. She had her feet on the ground and her grandson on speed-dial.

But Art begged to meet my mother, and my mother begged back – out of curiosity too, I think.

We met in an Italian place. She and Art hit it off with Campari spritzers and talk of Italy. Wasn't pappardelle the true pasta lover's choice? Weren't people who used the phrase 'a mean spag bog' the perfect morons? I sat on the other side of the table, marvelling. I'd thought I'd have to smooth things, you see, like I did with my old friend and her father, whom she hated. That was a tough gig. (When he died she unfriended me, so my purpose had been clear.)

Anyway. Art. My mother. I thought I'd spend the night passing the metaphorical salt. But no, my mother and Art were *off*. So much so that I found it hard to get a word in. They shared a sharing platter. They matched each other drink for drink. They liked the same music, the same flowers, the same shitty reality-TV shows. It was like watching twins reunited. A part of me thought – still thinks, age-gap notwithstanding – they'd make a better couple.

At the end of the meal, Art said: 'Tell me a story about Jenny when she was younger.'

'She was possessed, one time, in Reading.'

Art spat out his drink. 'Were you?'

I said: 'There was fuck all else to do in Reading.'

(I actually did think I had a demon, years later, but it was after I'd watched *Paranormal Activity* and I think directly related.)

My mother said: 'Jenny's never respected my gift.'

Art said: 'What else do you do? Tea leaves? Crystal ball?'

My mother laughed. 'You can find out everything about my services on my new website, *Medium at Large*.'

I said: 'Never knowingly under-advertised.'

'But really it's whatever people want, dead or alive,' my mother continued. 'I just get messages. Things like cards can help build a clearer picture. A story, if you like.'

'Human beings do so fall for a narrative,' I said, pouring myself more wine.

My mother said: 'I'll tell you about the time she won first prize at the swimming gala. A red ribbon for front crawl. She dived in and tore down the pool, light years ahead of the rest. You should have seen her go! Like a jigsaw through a sheet of metal. Dukdukdukdukduk!'

Art smiled.

My mother continued: 'But the reason she won was because she didn't breathe! The whole length she just stayed under and held her breath and went like the clappers!'

'She's saying I didn't do it properly,' I said. 'That I didn't deserve it.'

'No,' my mother said, 'that's not what I'm saying at all.'

Art went to the toilet.

My mother said: 'I have a very good feeling about him. A very good vibe.'

'It's early days.'

'But you must discuss why, for him, the fear is often greater than the love. You must discuss that, because that might become . . . problematic for you down the line. He lost someone recently, didn't he?'

'Just . . . please. Stop it.'

'Do you want my opinion?'

'Do I want some hackneyed psycho-babble instead of what I know? No thanks.'

'I thought you wanted my opinion. I thought that's why you invited me.'

Her question terrorised me then. Why had I invited her? To please Art? Or was there some old lizard part of me still seeking my mother's approval? Either way, it was primitive.

Art came back. She and I paid the bill. When Art tried to leave a tip, my mother leaned forward, brandy in hand, and said: 'You're going to hurt my daughter.'

'Right-oh,' I said, 'we're off.'

Art stared at her. He didn't try and move. 'I love your daughter,' he said.

'Who passed recently in your family?' my mother said.

'Mother,' I said.

'My uncle,' Art said. 'Last year, just before I met Jenny. My mother's brother.'

'Your mother, Deborah, who Jenny tells me is quite a woman. Quite the cultured Londoner.'

'She is,' I said.

'Yes,' said Art. 'My uncle and I were very close. I'm named after him.'

I looked at him. 'You never mentioned an uncle.'

'Love does not advance by weddings; love advances by funerals,' my mother said, and took a long, satisfied sip of her brandy.

'What does that mean?' Art said.

'She always says that,' I said. 'It means precisely nothing.'

'It means that fear drives love,' my mother said.

'Do you believe that?' Art said, to me.

'No,' I said, to my mother, who was looking at Art.

Art smiled. 'I'm sure you taught Jenny a lot about love.'

'She did,' I said. 'She taught me you should never go to bed on an argument. You should STAY UP ALL NIGHT ARGUING.'

Art laughed.

'Pisces?' my mother said.

'Oh dear sweet Jesus,' I said.

Art nodded, amazed.

'Mm,' said my mother. 'Indecisive. Slippery. I knew one of those.'

'Hometime!' I said.

'Well, she seems lovely,' Art said, in the cab.

I looked at him. 'For real?'

'Yes. She's a bit extrovert, but I found her wacky ways endearing. Reassuring, almost. It's like she's plugged into a deeper plane, you know?'

I stared at him. 'Oh god,' I said, 'you're a believer.'

'I'm open-minded.'

'You're just another millennial looking for meaning in all the wrong places. You know she does all that shit by micro-eye-movements? She only decided to become a psychic when she failed as an actress. She's a mutant. She preys on grief and fear.'

91

Art shook his head. 'There's just no way she could have known. I have never, and will never, talk about my uncle.'

I retreated from him then, ashamed almost. 'Maybe she planted the suggestion.'

'She's not that devious.'

'Want to bet? My childhood was ripped through with her ambivalence. She alternately smothered me and wounded me. She was all over the place. She was crazy.'

I realised I was describing her in the same way most men described their exes. The way Art had described his.

I WAS EIGHTEEN

the day I left home and I'd made her drive me to the station. The car was new. The cars were always new. Rentals or benevolent benefactors. This one was a blue Jag. I remember the way her leather jacket creaked as she turned the corners. At the station, people stared as we pulled up. I went for the door lever.

'So you're leaving? Just like this?'

'Daughters leave,' I said. 'It's normal. This break-up was inevitable.'

I got out and slammed the door. The slam of it. I could have done it harder.

'Is this about my choice of vocation?' she said, through the open window. It was a normal question but I felt her anger and violence, too. That layer of red under her looks.

'It's about all your choices. It's about your fucking *chaos*.'

I didn't look back as I walked into the station but I did hear the Jag vrrrrooooomm away.

What was it really about? So much, so many things, over the years. A granular resentment that grew into a plaque around my heart.

ART SAID

I would like to take some photos of you, if you don't mind.

What kind of photos?

Nothing pervy.

I'll be the judge of that

I would like you to be naked.

Fuck off

They will be photos that define romance and womanhood.

I was thrilled. Deeply, problematically thrilled. I pressed him for more details. It would be tasteful, of course. Politically right-on. And, a week later, I was on my back on the kitchen floor, holding some roses over my bush and staring up at the black circle of Art's lens as he stood on two kitchen chairs over me, balanced like a bridge. Part of me billowed at being his subject. I wanted scrutinising, I did. I wanted someone to look and look and look at me and not stop looking. The roses were meant to symbolise menstruation – that's what Art said in interviews. Hahaha! Who WAS this guy?

'I am going to buy you a present every time you get your period,' he also said to me.

94

'That's quite a commitment.'

'So be it.'

Before the photos were released I used to sneak down to his darkroom in the cellar, flick on the strip light, and ogle myself. I was overjoyed they were going out into the world. That anticipation was mine and mine alone. I knew how well they'd do. I felt my own proximity to heat, to warmth, to . . . almost-love. I couldn't wait. Could not *wait*. How did they make me feel? Adored. Seen. Validated. I wanted all those girls I went to school with to see. I felt as though I had that in my eyes as I stared out, lethal. *Bow down, bitches* . . .

Kelly said: 'Do you not feel a bit exposed?'

I said: 'Are you making a photography joke?'

'No.'

'He's an artist,' I said defensively. 'It's his job to expose things.' A fudge! Similar: 'Would you love him if he wasn't an artist?'

Oh, but (I took my time with this one, pre-prepped): *'Art wouldn't be Art if he wasn't an artist.'*

He loved me, and I loved him. We did. We assuaged each other's fears for as long as we could. But once the pictures were out, and people talked over me when he tried to introduce me, I saw myself for what I was: the silent partner. It was a legacy, but not my legacy. Half of me revelled in the glory of being seen; the other half felt undermined. But Art still saw me. Still saw right through. Didn't he?

Like when he found me in the kitchen that Halloween – our third Halloween party in a row. We'd invited so many people – it must have been close to a hundred in the end. Pumpkin lights and cobwebs were strung along the bannisters. The lounge was full of hags and zombies. I was in the kitchen, tipping pineapple juice into a pan of hot rum punch. A tower of vintage teacups teetered by the hob.

Art came up behind me silently and put his arms around me. 'You okay?'

'Yeah!'

He'd moved in by then. I was still adjusting. It takes time – the rearrangement of your innermost parts, making space, accommodating. I rearranged myself, and my house, for him.

He said: 'Stop stirring a sec.'

I stopped stirring (outside. I was still stirring inside).

'You know you've been in here since everyone arrived.'

'I'm busy making things.'

He turned me around. 'Are you? Or are you hiding?'

I laughed. 'Hiding! Why would I be hiding, in my own house, from my own friends? Hahahah!'

'Why are you making *four* hot cocktails?'

'Because it's a party!'

'Are those . . . canapes?'

'Yes.'

'You look insane.'

I felt insane.

He whispered: 'I don't really want all these people here, either. I like a lot of them, but I'd much rather we were relaxing in front of the TV.'

'It's a party! Parties are relaxing! I love parties.'

'Do you? Or did you just want a houseful, and then you created a chaos to remove yourself from the situation?'

Fucking hell. That enquiry seared me to the bone. Here he was, slicing through my carefully curated kindness. I wondered how many other times he'd seen through my little charades: when I crossed a room to talk to someone who was on their own, knowing he was watching. I wanted all those people there because I wanted to be liked. And I liked a lot of them, really I did. But did I actually want to talk to them, all at once? Did I actually think I could talk to them all? Or did I fumble introductions, panic when more than one person tried to speak to me at once, make excuses to go to the toilet too many times, plan extravagant cocktails that would keep me in the kitchen until I was sufficiently liquored to blunder through some two-inch small talk with the equally liquored? All those exhibitions I smiled through. All those parties I hosted. All those dinners I presented. All that I was, I was not. I was a lie. The antisocial party girl.

He smiled – the archaeologist moving from hammer to brush. He said: 'You know no one gives a shit? Everyone's happy with wine. Calm down.'

'Are you telling me to calm down? As a man, to a woman?'

'No, just . . . Yes. Calm down. Calm the whole fuck down, is that better?'

'Nope.'

He tried some cocktail and winced. 'You know when you asked me about my worries? You know how you *still* ask me about my worries?'

'Yes.'

'Well, this is me, doing that. Checking in. Taking your temperature.'

I thought of the thermometer by the bed. I said, 'Okay. Thank you.'

'Now, what *is* this?'

'Hot rum punch. My mother's recipe.'

'How is Carmen?'

'Oh she's good. It's Halloween. Busiest time of the year.'

SOMEONE SAYS

'Excuse me, can I sit down, please?'

I look up from Suzy's *Good morning from me and my oat cortado!* to see a woman standing, holding the rail. She looks troubled. Faint, almost. Everyone else around me looks up from their phones, too. A voice! A human voice in the vacuum! What can this mean? The end times?

The woman is directing her voice to a woman sitting in a priority seat. Faint Woman is wearing a Baby on Board badge. (What was it that bastard said to me, the time I wore one? *Did you lose your baby?* Because he couldn't see my bump, presumably. I felt too sick and embarrassed to question him further, on a packed train. Prescient, though. Prescient fucker.)

To my surprise – to everyone's surprise – Priority Woman says No.

'Sorry?' Faint Woman says.

I look down, hard, at my blind phone.

'I'm tired,' says Priority Woman. 'I've had a bad night and I've got a busy day. Why are my needs not as great just because I'm not pregnant? Pregnancy is not a moral agent; it is a physical state. By giving you my seat I am perpetuating the idea that pregnant women are more valuable – and this does none of us any good.'

I look up. Faint Woman looks flummoxed. And tired, really tired. I look down again.

I want to speak up. I want to be that person who speaks up and punctures her bubble of harmlessness for the sake of what is right. No – actually, I want this situation to end, right now. Why am I in this situation? It's not fair. I don't deserve it. Why am I under pressure like this?

I might tweet about how outrageous this is. I could do a phenomenally wrathful tweet about this, believe me.

I remain quiet.

'This is for the good of all of us,' Priority Woman says, 'me sitting here and you not. Think of it as taking one for the team.'

I look up. Faint Woman is staring at me. The train moves off and she steadies herself.

JENNY, GET UP. A voice, from somewhere inside me. A deep, old, serious one. The voice of someone I don't even know. GET UP RIGHT NOW.

I stand up and offer Faint Woman my seat. She accepts with a pointed 'Thank you', sits down and immediately looks out of the window. I walk away, down the Tube.

Priority Woman is furious. She stands up and stomps after me, accosting me by the next set of doors.

'What was that about? I was making a point for womankind. It's not progress, politeness, you know.'

I don't know why or how, but I say: 'The pregnancy was a red herring. I'm afraid it's about kindness. If someone asks for your seat then you give it to them, because they probably need it.'

'How do you even know she's *telling the truth*?'

I look at Faint Woman.

'She really is.'

'Prove it.'

People – everyone – are looking at us. We are the best entertainment available right now. I don't care.

'What, you want me to go and buy her a pregnancy test and make her piss on it?'

'If you have to.'

'Fuck whether she's telling the truth. The truth has nothing to do with what's right.'

'You're a fucking idiot.'

She's seething, Priority Woman. She's seething at me. And I bow my head. I cower a bit, waiting for the next blow, but she just seethes, like a malevolent spirit.

I look out, at the spark-lit, scraggy walls of the tunnel. I pray to the spirits of trains and journey destinations that this woman gets off first or I get off first and we don't have to walk with each other to the barrier. She gets off at the next stop. I thank the spirits.

I get off at King's Cross. There's a message from Kelly.

Hey. Not sure if your phone's working but I see you've been on WhatsApp – can you give me a bell when you get the chance? Know you're busy

I suppose I should text her, although why hasn't she replied to my cry for help? I go to the toilets and sit down and breathe, expecting to cry, but I don't cry. I wait for the notes of myself to hit my nostrils; to reassure me I'm alive in some small, low, semi-fragrant way. When I'm done, I wipe and check the tissue.

A REALLY BAD SIGN

Behold the new creative elite of Soho! That's what I think every time I walk into Café Monocle. It's bristling with pending influence. Café Monocle takes up the entire top floor of WerkHaus. In the very centre, there's a pool surrounded by striped loungers. I have a recurring nightmare where I end up in here by mistake with my mother and she skinny-dips.

I head for Gemma and Mia, who are by the main bar as always, working their way through a pile of Negronis. I tried to drink Negronis for a while to be in their Negroni gang, but I had to revert to Aperol Spritz. I just can't do bitterness without fizz, and if that makes me primordial, so be it. I'm not even that fussed for drinking much any more. I think, what's the point? It will only turn warm in my mouth and then break down to acetone and other chemicals in my system within six or seven hours, which will only exacerbate my anxiety around 3 a.m. I'm a real gas.

A drone lands on the bar, almost toppling my drink. It looks like a patent white clutch bag.

'Tell me that doesn't give you a wide-on?' shouts Mia. 'Accessory of the season. The paps could make a killing with it. Up a skirt faster than a presidential hand.'

'Ugh.'

'Aperol Spritz?' says Mia. 'In October? Are you trying to shift some kind of paradigm?'

'Nice hair!' says Gemma.

I touch my hair. I wanted to look like a youth. A boy, even. I had to go and get it put right by a professional. I shuddered as the hairdresser gave me a head massage, cursing myself for wearing an un-padded bra, hoping she wouldn't notice that my nipples had gone erect. It was the most aroused I'd felt in months, and I hated it. Still, I was relieved she didn't speak English. It takes the pressure off when there's a communication barrier.

'Very short,' says Mia. 'We'll need to get more byline pictures, but maybe we should wait until you stabilise. You keep changing . . . shape.'

I take comfort from this, in that she's not going to fire me if she's suggesting fresh byline photos. It's like when she asked for a breakfast meeting and I turned up nervous and then she ordered eggs. I relaxed because there's no way you fire someone over eggs. You do it over coffee. Or yoghurt, at a push.

Vivienne is drinking champagne. Vivienne only drinks champagne.

'Good evening, all,' I say, and find myself putting on a hint of a Yorkshire accent. Sometimes I put on my friends' accents as a way of acquiring their special strengths in certain situations, like a superhero choosing from a set of skills.

'Hardly,' she replies. 'There's so many other things I'd rather be doing.'

'Like what?'

'Oh, I don't know. Faecal vomiting.'

'What's that?'

'Apparently a really bad sign.'

I turn and try to make conversation with Gemma but it's too loud and effortful. I crash around. A few years ago, at a party in Dalston, Kelly and I met a man with a taxi meter hung round his neck. He had adapted it to run off time not distance. He kept the meter running while he was talking so that everyone could see how much his time was worth. Kelly had a conversation with him (more of a row, really) worth £26.42. He was a web designer. We thought he was a twat. Now, here, I can see where he was coming from. I should have a sign across my forehead that reads: *Sorry, Not In Service.*

'What's your star sign?' Gemma says.

Ah! Star signs. I can do this. If I concentrate. Let me totally get into my now. Although the other day someone asked me which Hogwarts house I was and I said 'Blacksticks' before I realised that's a type of cheese.

'I bet you're something watery, aren't you . . . like Pisces,' says Gemma.

'Scorpio.'

'Apparently, Scorpios make the best journalists.'

'Do they?'

'Yes. They're excellent at research.'

'I only really write about my life.'

'But that takes the most research. In your *mind*. I really loved your piece about co-habiting with women. Ignore the haters, that's all I can say. I thought it was great.'

'What haters?'

'The comments.'

I swallow. 'Below-the-line is my cardio,' I say, weakly.

I look around the bar. On the chalkboard menu is a dish that makes me sad whenever I see it: *Squid cooked in its own ink.* It strikes me as callous to serve up an animal in its own defence mechanism. I take a picture and post it, with the caption:

Talk about kicking a cephalopod when it's down *#THESQUIDSARENTALLRIGHT*

I've barely posted it when Mia motions me towards her. 'Where is he?' she says. 'Art?'

103

'I don't know,' I say. 'Does it matter all that much?'

'Yes it does, actually,' Mia says. 'I want to offer him a job, if he isn't too busy.'

'A *job*?'

'We need another house photographer.'

'I thought it was company policy to only employ women.'

'We also need to think about our profile. Feminism will understand. Besides, we'd be fools not to capitalise on our unique access. And if there's one thing feminism hates more than the patriarchy, it's fools.'

She looks at me. I drink some more of my drink and take a breath.

'Art might not make it,' I say, 'because even though we do still hang out together a lot of evenings we are not super officially together-together any more if you know what I mean.'

Mia looks at me. 'Sorry, what?'

'We are together in every way apart from the technical way.'

'Technical way?'

'It's an intense modern friendship.'

'What?'

'We broke up.'

'Oh dear god! Why?'

'It was very amicable. Zero animosity. No one did anything bad to anyone. That's why we're still able to be close.'

Mia stares at me. She doesn't believe me, that much is evident. She says, 'You must be *devastated*.'

'No really, I'm not.'

'It was seven years!'

'But I look on it as the perfect length, really. Relationships should not be judged by their continuation but by their quality. Also, why do things have to last forever in order to be deemed a "success"? Things can come to an end and not have failed. My relationship with Art was a complete success. But it had a sell-by date. And now it's over.'

'Good lord! You're a gibbering mess!'

Someone comes over to talk to Mia and I stand there, useless, tensely curled, like a prawn, as my mother would say. I get out my phone and check my likes. One hundred and counting. I should get back to doing the animal ones more often. I could borrow a cat for a day.

Mia is talking about me to the person she is with. '*Devastated,*' she is saying. '*Dev-a-stated.*'

And then I do my regular thing: I go through Suzy Brambles' follows to check she is still following me. It's just a habit, really. A formality. It's the extra dopamine kick I need tonight, seeing myself there, amidst the . . .

Wait.

No.

I am not where I usually am.

My heart plummets.

My thumb panics.

I go out of the app and go in again.

I am still not there.

I turn my phone off.

Turn it on again.

I go through her follow list twice — no mean feat, there are over six hundred people on there. But, it would seem, I am no longer one of them.

I bend my knees and do some heavy breathing.

MIA SAYS

It's clear you're heartbroken, Jenny.

She pulls me upright and takes my drink.

'I'm really not that bothered about Art.' My voice is a pip-squeak.

'You've gone ashen!'

'It's all the Aperol.'

'You've only had two. You seemed like the perfect couple. Those first photos he took of you! The ones that blew up. They captured AN AGE. They characterised an *entire summer of my life.*'

'What we always had was a solid friendship, and that is what we still have,' I say, measuredly. 'So it's not really a break-up, more a . . . change of definition in terms of our relationship. Who needs to label things in this day and age anyway? It's much more progressive to keep things loose. We're just as close, we just don't have sex. But we weren't having that much sex anyway. So in terms of the day to day, nothing has really changed.'

Mia puts her arm around me. 'I think you'll get back together,' she says. She looks reassured. 'It's just a blip.'

'Maybe,' I say. 'Would you excuse me, Mia? I have to go now.'

'Of course.' She pulls off her arm. I exhale and move away.

'See you Wednesday.'

'Take the time you need.'

'See you Wednesday.'

I WALK

through Soho – awful, extraordinary Soho, teeming with the weekend-drunk and lumbering tourists. I slip into the M&S off Oxford Street, go to the booze section and buy two bottles of white wine with Renaissance paintings on the bottles. I always feel better about buying wine when the bottle has art on it. It's classy bingeing.

I drink one bottle on the way to the Tube, necking it in tepid gobfuls. I stop outside the Tube where a homeless man is sitting with some Marvel figurines laid out on a bed-sheet. I hand him a pound.

'Thanks love,' he says, readjusting Spiderman. 'Have a nice evening.'

'No chance of that,' I say. 'The worst thing has happened. I have had the most horrific day.'

'Sorry to hear that, love,' he says.

'If someone likes you for months, what makes them suddenly stop liking you?'

He looks at me. 'Fella left you?'

I shake my head. I think I might walk off but I stay there. 'Are you on social media?' I ask.

'Facebook,' he says. 'Now and then. For arrangements.'

'Well then you'll understand. Although I have to say I find Facebook quite suspicious.'

'Suspicious how?'

'It listens. It's listening to us right now, on your phone. If I say panini maker you're going to get loads of ads for panini makers next time you log on.'

'Don't say it, then.'

'Panini maker! Panini maker!' I shout towards his phone. 'That should do it. Just you wait.'

He turns his phone off quickly.

'My mother's on Facebook and that's part of the reason I avoid it. It's hard to see her interacting on there. It gives me physical pain. It's like watching her dance. She started putting all these passive-aggressive memes on there directed at me, which was the main reason I left. I still have actual PTSD about it. Facebook is pretty much my Vietnam.'

He stares at me. I drink more wine.

'Facebook,' I say, 'is a data-collection agency dressed up as a chummy get-together but geared towards fuelling insecurity and pain. They do that to maximise the power of the ads and keep people coming back. Then they can all keep selling the same shit back to us more effectively.'

He says, 'It makes it easy for me to meet up with people.'

'You think that, but the one thing Orwell didn't predict was that we'd put the cameras IN OUR OWN HOMES. IN *OUR OWN FACES*. You know? We're like our own fucking Big Brothers. It's all worked out so perfectly I bet even the social media bosses can't believe it. Do you know the kids of everyone who works at social media HQs in California all go to this school that's ringed off from the internet behind a massive firewall so they can't get online until they're sixteen because their parents know it will ruin their lives and minds?' I stifle a sob. 'Like it's ruined mine.'

I tell him all about Suzy Brambles. He keeps looking around, unable to concentrate, but I can tell he gets the gravity of what has happened. Maybe he's on that Spice stuff that makes people unable to focus their eyes. I'm glad I can focus my eyes on him when I concentrate because if I couldn't I would worry that I looked just as fucked. I unscrew the second bottle of wine. People pass, heading into the Tube; some of them hand him money and he says *Ta, yeah, nice one*. Another homeless man comes and stands nearby; he looks at the man on the ground and then at me. He smiles, I can only presume supportively, as I fill him in on what has happened. 'I don't come from anywhere and I'm not going anywhere,' I conclude 'This is the curse of the liberal elite.' When I've finished, I start to cry, and he wanders off. Probably to ponder the deeper meaning of my plight as I've just relayed it to him.

As I'm leaving, I give the man on the ground another two pounds. I say, 'You have a wonderful little set-up here. And a community you can trust. Cherish that.'

He smiles but he doesn't look as though he really appreciates what I'm saying, the savage.

I stand, swaying with clarity, outside Oxford Circus. I feel saturated with my own fight, like the squid on the menu. I guess that sums me up pretty well as a modern woman: a creature cooked in her own ink.

DRUNK TWITTER

@CissyGreenModel:
As a mother I couldn't just sit around and watch refugee children die

@jenniferjenniferMcLaine:
@CissyGreenModel as a non-mother I love watching refugee children die. It is one of the great pleasures of my life

@CissyGreenModel:
@jenniferjenniferMcLaine I didn't mean it like that

@jenniferjenniferMcLaine:
@CissyGreenModel How did you mean it then? Because it sounded as though you were suggesting motherhood generates new levels of compassion & empathy

@jenniferjenniferMcLaine:
@CissyGreenModel which I can assure you is bullshit of the sloppiest order

@jenniferjenniferMcLaine:
@CissyGreenModel CASE IN POINT: Rose West

You have been blocked from viewing @CissyGreenModel's tweets

DRAFTS

To: Suzy Brambles

Subject: Why?

Dear Suzy Brambles,
Was it because I was leaving too many comments? I know I might have been a little overbearing. Five under one post is perhaps a tad OTT – but the jokes worked better as individual lines, do you ever find that? I admire you greatly – your output and your work. Sometimes I like your pictures so much I can't bring myself to 'like' them because it feels like it almost trivialises the intensity of the emotion, and also – I sort of hate you for making me like something so much. I feel too seen.

I have consumed some alcohol but this is honestly the truth of how I am feeling, and I know that because I have been thinking these exact thoughts since before I was drunk so it's sort of like a lucid dream in that way. You mean so much to me. Whenever I post anything you are one of three key people I look to see whether you have liked what I have posted. The other two are a famous comedian who follows me quite randomly (possibly mistakenly, but I'll take it) and the editor of Italian *Vogue* who I met once on a press trip and followed me when we were both drunk and I was sitting next to her in a bar at midnight telling her to follow me. Anyway, you are my Number One because you are the most like me – you are my digital support animal. (Actually I'm not sure that's PC any more. You are my digital support animal.) Anyway, sorry if I got too much, I didn't mean to. I was just being appreciative.

I wonder, did you see that comment about my integrity

underneath that column? That would put me off me. That DOES put me off me. Daily. Sometimes hourly.

Or was it the picture of the croissant? That was annoying, I know. I know *now*. But you never gave me the chance to redeem myself. I'm so much more idiosyncratic than that. I'm actually quite gothic beneath this modish veneer. I wish you'd given me the chance to show that side of myself to you. I can't tell you how it feels to see that you have gone. It almost makes my online endeavours pointless. In fact, I might give up. I'm sure you wouldn't like to think of someone abandoning their (online) life for you, would you? This betrayal has been so dislocating that I don't even know where I end or begin any more, personal brand-wise. I thought you liked the cut of my jib. But how shall I cut my jib now? To be honest I just feel like slaughtering it. And maybe I will. Maybe I'll slaughter my jib.

Consider yourself the murderer of my jib.

Sincerely,

Jenny McLaine

KNOCKKNOCK

At first I think it is my soul, pounding for release from its prison.

Then I wake up properly and hear it again.

KNOCKKNOCKKNOCKKNOCKKNOCK

It is someone at the door.

My brain starts screaming instead. My brain! Blaaaarrggg. It is too big for my skull. It is coming out through my eyes. I need painkillers as a matter of urgency. I have a thirst a thousand crystal reservoirs could not slake. I also dropped my phone on my face while I was using it in bed and I think I have a black eye. Help me. Who is here to help?

My bedroom door opens. 'Jenny?' Sid sticks her head around the door. 'Are you okay?'

I sit up. I think I might hurl. 'No. What is that noise?'

'There's somebody at the door.'

We look at each other.

'Somebody at the door? Who would be at the door?'

'I don't know! But there IS somebody. AT THE DOOR.'

'Dear god! Are we to have no privacy? Why are people so determined to intrude all the time? Who would come to a door and *knock on it*?'

KNOCKKNOCKKNOCKKNOCKKNOCKKNOCK

We both jump.

I get up and grab my dressing gown. I open the bedroom door to see Frances and Moon peering over the bannister.

113

'Who is it?' Frances shrieks.

'I don't know! I'm not expecting any callers!'

'Whoever would? Who knocks on a *door* in this day and age?'

'It's outrageous!'

'So rude!'

'Such an affront!'

'I need a lie-down.'

'You know I read they're developing an email system,' says Sid, 'whereby you get an email when someone is at the door, and then you reply to them, via email.'

'We need this in our lives.'

KNOCKKNOCKKNOCKKNOCK

'I peeked through my blinds,' says Moon. 'It's a woman.'

'A woman?? What does she look like?'

'Sturdy. Middle-aged. Lots of jewellery. Sort of . . . fancy and tough, like a celebrity sportswoman.'

Oh my sweet dear god Jesus. My heart pounds in my chest. My head pounds in my head.

'It might be Amazon,' Sid says. 'Looks like there's a van. Have you ordered anything?'

'No . . .' I pull on my dressing gown on and tie the cord tight. 'I mean, I don't know! Who ever knows? I can't be expected to keep track of all that! That's what the tracking link is for!'

I tiptoe halfway down the stairs.

The letterbox flaps open again. 'I know you're in there!'

'Is it that smackhead again?' says Moon.

'It might be a bailiff,' says Sid.

'It is not a bailiff,' I say. 'Things are not quite that bad.'

Moon says, 'Well, whoever it is, let's just open the damn door and ask her what she wants.'

Sid starts to pass me on the stairs. 'No!' I shout. 'No.' I pull her to one side. 'Do not answer the door. She might go away.'

But I know that's not true. This is the woman who read my diary every day and replaced the hair trap on top – I caught her, tweezers poised, tongue-tip poking out. She is relentless. She is alien blood.

Frances looks at me, confused.

The letterbox flaps again. 'Who is that? I know someone is there! I can see SHAPES.'

Frances joins me flat against the wall.

A hand comes through the letterbox and waves. 'This is my daughter's house and I demand to be let inside!' The hand stays there.

Frances gasps. 'Jenny, is it . . . your *mum?*'

I stare at the hand poking through the letterbox. It is the hand of a dame. Long nails painted pale blue, gold rings, an impatient flutter of the fingers. The hand retreats.

'JENNIFER, DARLING! OPEN THE BLOODY DOOR!'

'Hard to tell,' I say.

'Hadn't we better let her in?' says Sid. I see my mother's power has worked its way under the door and into their hearts, like fungus.

I look up to Sid and Moon.

'Let her in,' says Moon.

I move towards the front door. I hesitate just before opening it.

Oh god. Can I do this? If I allow her to step over this threshold I don't know what it will mean. I should never have given her an address for Christmas cards, that much is evident now. I never felt obliged to invite her here. She almost ruined my education. This is my house.

I unlock the door. Open it.

A punky feather cut, cheap platinum. Tight jeans and a little frou-frou top. Bangles up her arm, loose then lathed, her skin goose-fleshed in the October air. Gold earrings. A hologram eye pendant round her neck, winking as she moves. Mascara, liner, gloss and froth. A laugh like a splat.

My mother, everyone. Everyone, my mother.

'Jenny! I thought you were going to leave me there all day. Are you compos mentis?'

'I *was*.'

'What have you done to your hair?'

'It was an impulse thing.'

'Is that a black eye?'

'Sorry, what do you want here?'

She motions to a man on the street, next to a large hire van. 'It's fine. Just give me five mins.'

'Who's he?'

'A driver.'

'Five mins for what?'

'You not going to invite me in?'

I step back and she walks through. 'Well, look at this little place! It's even smaller than you described!'

'I've sent you photos.'

'Those tidbits are never the full story though, eh?'

I watch where her hands go, what she touches.

'Oh!' she says, looking up the stairs. 'You must be the lodgers. Who knew so many people could fit in such a small space.' She looks around the hallway, assessing. 'Well, I hope you've all made alternative arrangements.'

'What?'

My mother looks at me. 'I came as soon as I could.'

'What do you mean?'

She looks at the walls. 'You know,' she says, 'I've got my whole hall covered with her articles. That first piece she did for that supermarket magazine. They put her on the cover.'

Budget Wedding Dresses – Happy Ever After or Just a Disaster? ran the header. A question immediately answered by the ill-fitting dress on my torso, and also, unfortunately, by the magazine's red masthead, which leaked, and bled into my face, making me pink as a ham. I left the magazine soon after. I couldn't face the canteen.

'A wedding dress?' says Sid. 'She's a radical feminist who writes for a radical feminist online magazine.'

'It was from a supermarket. I think that's pretty radical actually,' I say.

'Shame it'll be the only time she gets to wear one, though,' says my mother. 'You know, it's as I suspected. There's not a single photo of me up here.'

I say: 'There's not really a photo of anyone.'

There isn't. There's just a few gaps and lost nails, where Art took his pictures.

'We hardly ever see her with anyone,' Sid says. 'No one comes round.'

I shoot her a hard look. 'I'm really busy, actually. I have an active social life. And anyway, you're all always here. That is basically a society.'

'This is Sid, Moon and Frances,' I say. Frances steps forward, like she is about to be knighted. My mother takes each of their hands in turn. 'Very strong energies. Very raw. Especially you.' Sid steps back.

'Mother,' I say, 'what's going on?'

My mother widens her eyes and looks at me meaningfully. She lowers her voice. 'Your text, darling. Your . . . predicament. I am here to help you sort things out.'

My stomach plummets. That's why Kelly didn't reply. I sent that dumb, pathetic yelp to . . . my mother.

'Oh god!' I say. 'That wasn't meant for you! And I was being all late-night and dramatic.' I look at my lodgers. 'There has been a miscommunication. It's all good.'

'No,' my mother says, 'it's not all good. You are evidently not all good. Look at this lightless tomb you're living in.'

'This house cost . . . is worth more than yours. As you know.'

'That's London for you. A city of discontented idiots in expensive houses.'

I look at Moon, Sid and Frances. 'It's going to be okay,' I say. 'No one is coming or going anywhere.'

They look at each other nervously. Then Frances says: 'Thing is, Jenny, we were just having a meeting earlier this morning, when you were still in bed. We have decided we don't want to stay here. When we are so . . . misused.'

'Misused?'

'In your "journalism". We're not paying this month's rent, and we're leaving. We're going to an Airbnb until we find somewhere else.'

'That settles it!' says my mother – domineering, genial. 'This is what you call good old-fashioned serendipity. I am a big fan of Serendipity, and all her sisters.'

'No,' I say. 'No. Just . . . no.'

Frances says: 'Personally, I can't bear to stay in one place for more than a few months. It cripples me, creatively.'

Sid says, 'I don't want the treasure of my life to be the silver drawer for your magpie claws. You are twisting my real. You are junk mail.'

My mother stares at her.

ONE-LINERS

I'd gone round to a friend's house and her father had made me cry because he'd said: *Well, I bet they don't have to worry when they run out of fuse wire in your house.* Incidentally, this same man later said to another friend, who dropped a peanut down her top: *It's good to see Victoria is finally developing a figure.* Appropriateness was not the man's forte.

My mother came to pick me up in the car – a Mercedes, I think it was then – and she looked at my face and just *knew* (it wouldn't take a psychic . . .).

'What's happened?' she said.

I told her.

She put the car into Park and got out. 'Wait here,' she said.

She walked up to the door. She rapped. He answered.

'You seem to think my daughter's hair colour is amusing,' she said. 'Which I think is troublesome, if not pathetic, for a man of your age.' I could hear every word, even though she had her back to me. What can I say, the woman could project.

He said something, probably sarcastic.

She said, 'Don't pick on the remarkable people. Go back in there with your ordinary-coloured hair to all your ordinary-coloured-hair family and live out your ordinary little lives. Meanwhile my daughter and I will be over here, being extraordinary.'

'Is that why her father's never been around?' he said. (I heard that part.) 'You were too extraordinary, were you?'

'No, he was too dead.'

My friend's father's face dropped. 'Oh god, I'm sorry, Carmen, I had no idea.'

'That's your problem,' my mother said, her parting shot. 'You have no idea.'

She got back in the car and started the engine.

'My father's dead?' I said.

'No,' said my mother, shifting the car into Drive. 'But it was a great line, don't you think?'

I stared at my friend's father as we drove away.

I SAY

'Look, Mum, that text was a mistake, and even if it wasn't, even if it was on some level some weird Freudian cry for help, it just would not work you staying here, even for one night. I'm sorry.'

I say it quietly, like I'm not sure whether I believe it.

My mother is nodding, yes yes, in that way she does, after which she just does whatever the fuck she wants. She is staring at Sid.

'The treasure of your life,' my mother says, 'is everyone's to steal. Because she only steals from her point of view. It's her experience of your treasure, so it cannot be stolen.'

'It's a garbage thing to do,' says Sid. 'It's not the truth.'

'The truth doesn't exist. Now, go put your lady balls in a bag and skedaddle.'

Sid says: 'I bet you voted for Brexit.'

'Goodbye!'

As I watch Moon, Sid and Frances, one by one (in that order), leave the hall and make their way to their respective rooms to pack, glad to be going, I feel creeping sureness that I might want my mother to stay, even if just for one night.

Don't let her in, says a small voice inside of me. *Remember.* Always remember that Christmas.

THE OUTRAGE

Christmas, 1999. The thick tinsel was coiled around the bannister. The angel chimes were motionless on the sideboard, their candles unlit. She was by the front door, her Louis Vuitton case packed, her make-up pageant-perfect. Around her head sat a halo of framed qualifications to impress clients as they came into the house: her certificates from the Institution for Mediumship, Orange County. Healer of the Year 1997 from the Spiritualist Church of Great Britain. Photos of her with soap stars . . . The overall effect was of a try-hard pizzeria wall.

I called her a gold-digging slut and she called me *cold, hard* – the usual things she said when I had her over a moral barrel of some kind or other.

'I know you're practically a grown-up now,' she said. 'And you have your friends.'

I didn't really have friends. I had lots of people I stood with in school, lots of messages on my yearbook page, but no one I could really talk to.

'Why the Bahamas?'

'Roger is taking me! Well, he's already there, so I'm meeting him!'

Everything was exclaimed; she was so excited, I wanted her dead. I looked at the opposite wall, where there was a dreadful photo of the two of us; dreadful of me, anyway. The two of us at Disneyworld, three years earlier. I hadn't put enough sun cream on and my face burned so badly I got blisters that joined up across my nose, like the scales of a snake. You can't really see at the distance of the shot, the photo's only saving grace; what you can see is my forehead and my shapeless Aztec-patterned shorts-and-T-shirt set. I was yet to discover the power of belts. My mother is next to me, wasp-waisted in shorts and a vest, sporting a pair of inexplicably cool aviators. Not even the men of Tinder would choose the younger woman out of that line-up.

'Two weeks is a long time.'

'The freezer's full.'

'What if the millennium bug happens?'

'There's long-life milk in the cupboard under the stairs. Come on, darling. Do I not deserve a bit of happiness? Can you allow me that? Please?'

I watched the taxi turn the corner and then I cried my heart out. I couldn't say it. *Stay.* What was the point? Her bag was packed. She wasn't one for unpacking once she'd packed.

I'm not saying I'm wise. That would be a stretch. But I know that the above scene is the ghost that walks through all my rooms. This Heartbreak 1.0 is a loop I cannot cut, no matter how much therapy, how much distance, how much steel. It comes back, and back, and back again for my heart and my happiness.

What are you scared of?

Of being left behind.

Of not being wanted.

Of coming second.

And the disappointing utter fucking childishness of that.

BABY ELEPHANT

My mother and I sit, gin-loosened, in the lounge. There is a nature programme on the TV. African elephants trekking across the heat to find food and water. A small baby at the back of the herd is slowing. It desperately needs a drink. The narrator tells us how just a small amount of water would save it from near-certain death.

'Dear god!' I cry. 'Whoever is filming this, do they not have a bottle of Evian in their knapsack? This is unbearable!'

'It's Nature,' my mother says. 'You can't interfere.'

'Of course you can! That's what makes us human! GIVE THE BABY ELEPHANT A DRINK, YOU MONSTROUS FUCKS.'

'Elephants are matriarchal,' my mother says, 'they're smart. They won't let it die.'

'So why don't they stop?'

'Because they have to get to the watering hole to save the whole herd. She knows what she's doing. That big old one at the front. She knows.'

The baby elephant collapses. 'I don't think she does. Turn it over. I can't watch. Whoever made this should be thoroughly ashamed of themselves.'

My mother shakes her head. 'It's like what I do. I can't pick and choose what might be painful for someone to hear. I just channel. I am a conduit. That's all they're doing. They're presenting life as it is.'

'TURN IT OVER, A BABY IS DYING I DO NOT WANT TO SEE A DEAD BABY.'

'The baby is not dying. See, the older elephants have spotted the watering hole and they're going to bring some water back to it in their trunks.'

'They won't be quick enough. TURN IT OVER.'

I close my eyes and stick my fingers in my ears. La la la.

'Jenny, they're saving it!'

'TURN IT OVER!'

She turns it over. 'Nature, red in tooth and claw.'

'Fine! Sure! Over there somewhere! I don't have to see the horrors of the world to know the world is fucking horrible.'

She flicks back over quickly. I scream.

The baby elephant is prancing around, spraying water out of its tiny trunk, in the watering hole.

'THERE!' my mother says, standing up. '*TOLD YOU.*'

'Well I still think whoever made that needs to do the psychopath test. How could you just "channel" when something needs you and you have the power to help it? Does your integrity only stretch as far as your sense of what's right?'

She shrugs, and then goes to the kitchen to make more drinks.

When she comes back, she stands in front of the painting of herself and says: 'Do you think I still look like that?'

'Mum, that painting was done twenty years ago.'

'I felt old then. You were fifteen.'

'I remember.'

'I think I stopped at twenty-five, in my mind. I think my personality set at twenty-five and I've never got a day older. That's why the outside catches me by surprise sometimes. I don't feel like I look.'

'You look great.'

'You're a love.' She sits down, still looking at the painting. 'So,' she says, 'how are you doing?'

'Fine.'

We look at each other. As always during these mandatory catch-ups, I imagine her thinking of my life as a museum through which she is being selectively tour-guided by me. *What's in that room? Can't go in there, Ma. What about that one? Sorry, not part of the tour.*

'Still working at that womany website?'

'Yep.'

She sips her drink and says, 'And you're . . . still in touch with Art?'

'Of course. It's perfectly amicable. We speak regularly. Emails, mostly.'

'Still lovely long emails like before? I loved hearing about those.'

'Yeah.'

She waits.

'So what happened? I haven't seen you since and it's – well, it's such a shock, darling.'

'We wanted different things.'

She sighs. 'Have you considered the fact that sometimes relationships need work, darling?'

I stare at her. 'I've had longer relationships than you.'

'Have you considered that your fertility halves at the age of thirty-five?'

I look surprised. 'Does it? Surely not. I thought women's fertility INCREASED the older they got, no? Tell me more.'

She laughs. 'You know you can tell me anything.'

I laugh.

'What happened exactly? I'm trying to process it. He meant something to me, too.'

'Look, do you mind if we don't talk about it?'

'Whatever you want, darling.'

'What did you get up to today?'

'I just called in on a few old London friends.'

'Who?'

'You won't know them. Before your time.'

She lived in London, a few years before I was born. She had a few small parts in the West End and almost got a big break. Then she met my father. *Another actor?* I asked her, hopeful. No, she said. That would have been even worse. She said she did his tarot cards the night they slept together.

And what did they tell you?

Well, I wasn't really paying attention . . .

'And I brought some champagne. Shall we open it?'

'What for?'

'Our new chapter.'

She gets up and goes to the kitchen. I watch her go.

What do I remember about living with her, before? Her warmth. Her violence. Her loyalty. Her barbs. Her largesse. She always had to have the last word. Her moods were riotous. Every now and then over the past twenty years I have felt, suddenly, how far apart my mother and I are, and a wash of cold has flooded over my entire body. Then I remember that this happened when I lived with her, too. Sometimes I'd make myself look more scared than I was, just to guilt her. (Later, I did this a few times with Art, too. I cowered. I shrank from him; or rather, from his fear of himself. Worse: his fear of the *fatherly* part of himself. I must admit that, now. I was aware of that sly leverage.) I knew that what I felt for my mother was, long-haul, in danger of distilling down to the purest of feelings – a feeling that, after her death, would feel like the bleakest, most pointless seclusion.

ART SAID

'Are you *crying*?'

I was. I was openly weeping, in front of the TV.

'What is it?' he said, his face open, his hand on my hand as he dropped to his knees. 'What?'

'This,' I said, weakly gesturing to the screen. A manatee was swimming in a school. A smaller manatee was swimming behind it.

'Oh, babes, you know you shouldn't watch nature documentaries!'

'No, it's fine! I'm not sad. It . . . makes me want to have a baby.'

Art's face changed. He stood up. 'What?' he said, laughing.

'IT MAKES ME WANT TO HAVE A BABY,' I bellowed.

'A great ugly sea cow?'

'I don't know why. Order amongst the chaos? Blame Darwin. David Attenborough. I don't know!' I wept more.

He looked around my feet. 'Have you had . . . wine?'

'No!' I said. I noticed him notice the empty glass. 'Well, not to a traumatic degree.'

He put his arm around me. 'Why don't you put some comedy on? Leave these delightful creatures to it.'

He turned over. It was *Frasier*. Daphne-supposedly-from-Manchester was affectionately abusing Niall and he was affecting not to love it.

'What do you think?' I said. 'About babies? I hate to be prosaic but I am approaching my mid-thirties and once you hit thirty-five you're technically a geriatric mother. They actually call you that.'

'Yeah. Maybe. I mean yeah! I haven't given it loads of thought.'

'So what should we do?'

'I was thinking we could order a takeaway and demolish a box set.' He got up. Canned laughter erupted from the TV.

I said, 'You like hanging out with Kelly and Sonny, don't you? You enjoy that dynamic. That . . . role.'

'Yeeeaaah. Kelly's a tough cookie sometimes but I don't mind seeing them the odd weekend. Let's just relax and try and be creative right now? That's the life we said we wanted, isn't it? I don't want us to lose the mystical parts of ourselves.' He said, 'I'm really hungry, are you not hungry?'

He had been eating a banana in the bedroom that morning, standing there by the window, his back hairs striking out a coarse aura. I had felt a stronger sexual attraction than I have ever felt, before or since, to any human; any ape. Was this raging oestrogen? It was a valid question. My desire for a child. Where had it sprung from? Was it a desire for a lifestyle upgrade, or the wish to do what my mother couldn't? It was an autumn feeling, that's the best way I can describe it. That joy. That terror. That rush. That silence. That peace. That fear. Everything in a puddle and a pile of leaves. Everything dying and coming up gold. You know when you see a beautiful view and you sort of surrender to it – you feel yourself slacken and weaken, and you slouch a bit like you're broken down. Reduced. Mortalised. Remembered. And it's awful but it's also . . . a fucking relief, you know? I want to be reduced by my biology, sometimes. I want the pressure of my higher understanding switched off. Does that even make sense?

Later, we lay in bed, our faces inches apart, breathing each other's breath.

'I suppose I would like to create something I didn't have, for someone else. And myself, by proxy,' he said. 'But I'm scared I don't have the necessary skills.'

I said, 'Me too.'

'What else do you want?' he said.

Sometimes I think I want to walk down a school corridor in autumn-time and see sugar-paper drawings tacked to walls and recognise them. Sometimes I want that more than anything. Other times I just want to be alone with my imagination. Mostly though, I just want to not care what every single person thinks of me all the time, and I want to not have so many people's opinions whirring round my brain, and I want to share my life with someone and not get bored, and I'm so scared that isn't possible, because that is a lot of boxes to empty and sort. And sometimes I just want to have a shower and put on a clean pair of jeans and eat a sandwich in a café and feel like a normal fucking person.

I can't even remember what I answered in real life.

MY MOTHER SAYS

'Wait for it! Ooh!'

She is straddling a bottle of Bollinger. The cork pops out and we both smile in shock. She pours out two coupes. She says it as we cheers:

'Champagne is a verb.'

Her credo. She used to say it the evenings when she had people round. The séances and tarot nights that descended into social orgies. She didn't just have people round. She hosted, like a gigolo on a yacht. Those parties. All those people down in the lounge. There was Alan with his mesmerising tracheotomy, Donegan with her granite stare, Glynn with his glowing pate, luminous as the nose-cone of a rocket on re entry, and old Miss Lunt who used to teach Latin and still came out with the odd phrase when she was startled (or possessed). It sounded like Hell itself. A gabble of voices. Catastrophic singing. I'd sit on my bed, trying to read, willing them all to leave. One time I got up and yelled 'SPOONBENDER!!!!' down the stairs. She shot up two flights like a rabbit, mojito muddler in hand. Other times, when they wouldn't leave, I used to go to the bathroom, take her toothbrush out of the cup, pull down my pants and dab the bristles on my anus like it was giving it a little kiss. Mwa mwa mwa.

'So, how is Unton?' I ask cordially, to move things along.

'Still the happiest small town in the world.'

131

Small town is right. After Hiroshima happened, the local rag, the *Unton Chronicle*, ran the headline: *UNTON MAN INJURED IN JAPANESE BOMB BLAST*. Which tells you everything you need to know. Unton's other claim to fame is a tall black pole in the town square. I showed it to Art on one of the few times I brought him up to visit. 'Is it a maypole?' he said, eyes wide. Oh no, I explained, this was the 'Meat Pole' — so-called because in ye olden days it was the custom to annually grease the pole and fix a large piece of meat to the top, then watch members of the community attempt to scale it. Sort of like the Wicker Man, but without the craftsmanship. If the climber reached the top they could take the meat home as a prize. That's my cultural heritage.

My hand grips my glass. I look at the folds of skin around the stem. In my teens, two separate psychics (friends of hers) told me I'd have four children because I had four creases on the side of my hand. Hilarious. And what did she want for me? A career as a doctor or a lawyer or, as she put it, 'even a fucking accountant would do, Jenny.' What was it she said? 'An English degree will only deepen your female disadvantage. You'll end up a teacher, or something else entirely that you'll get into quickly, untrained. Something lowly. Women are expected to nurture and teach. We are the so-called *architects of society*. You know what I say? Fuck that. I'm shit at relationships and I'm proud of that. I am an ideas woman. An entrepreneur. And I didn't work my arse off for fifteen years for you to become a cardie-wearing woodland creature.'

(Becoming a cardie-wearing woodland creature was my rebellion, you understand.)

I text Kelly:

Hey

She texts back:

SHE LIVES!

Get this for a curveball: my mother has come to stay

I knew there had to be some crisis or other

It is a crisis indeed

Is she dying?

Possibly. Will ask

'Are you dying?' I say. 'Is this a situation that's going to end in me wet-wiping your backside and reading you passages from *The Little Book of Calm*?'

'No,' she says, and then she sighs. 'I want to help. I see you're not yourself. And I can help. Beverly's staying in my place and paying me rent.' She sips her champagne. 'And I might as well tell you, darling. I've enrolled on a course to train as a death doula.'

'A death doula? What the fuck is that?'

'Someone who guides a person out of this life and into the next.'

'Right-oh.'

'I already have transferable skills. I can offer the full package, so to speak. My client list is . . . well, it's *healthy*, but it could be healthier, darling, you know. It's almost as though the *unhealthy* might be key to my future success, if that's not too tasteless a thing to say. I didn't come this far to plateau. There's a thirty-day training course starting next week in Balham. So you see, your text arrived at the perfect time. I've been meaning to get down and now . . . well, I'm like you all those years ago, aren't I, your regular Dick Whittington.'

'You can't stay here for a month.'

'I know! What a notion. I'm sure you have plans, help with money, all that sort of thing. Who are you texting?'

'Kelly.'

'How is she?'

'Fine, I think.'

'She must still be so grateful to you, even all these years down the line. He must be a teenager now.'

'He is.'

'Still, you never forget when someone has done something for you; you do right by them, don't you? Forever.'

'Hm.'

'There's a bottle of Amaretto in my suitcase.'

'I don't have more than two drinks per night. For my sleep hygiene.'

'Sleep hygiene? Makes me think of sheep dips.'

'My phone tracks my sleep and I've been coming in short lately.'

'They're all trying to be our friends now, the phones, aren't they, like the banks. The sleep tracking. The health data. That's how they get us sucked in and make us need them so they can make us miserable again.' She chugs her drink.

'Know what I heard? If you have more than two drinks then your body has to spend more time breaking down the alcohol than looking after you.'

'You know what I heard? If you have more than 3.5 units of alcohol per week, you are 85 per cent more likely to be judged by society.'

HOW I MET KELLY

I was coming home from a press screening. It was rush hour (it was always rush hour). My cab driver was nice, and Magic FM was playing 'If You Leave Me Now' by Chicago. I'd made my excuses for the afterparty, but I was dreading getting home, really – to another lounge full of flatmates. I was sick of all the flatmates by then; round after round, their demands and needs and petty thievery. I couldn't wait to be alone with my imagination. I was so depressed at the prospect of going home that evening I'd taken a £40 cab to cheer myself up. It was only half working. I was mostly thinking, *I could have put this in my savings, and been an inch closer.*

The weirdest thing was, a black balloon bounced across the road in front of the cab about five minutes before, and the driver swerved and we both said *Oh!* and I suppose it made us both pay attention a bit more, that standard portent of doom. I certainly had my eyes on the road. We drove on another few minutes and that's when I saw him: a tiny kid, toddling across the grass verge at the side of the carriageway, heading for the road.

'STOP THE CAB!' I yelled, surprised at the sound of my own authority.

The driver stopped. 'I see him!' the driver said.

'I'm going!' I shouted, flinging open the door. 'Call the police!' I still don't know where this person in me came from.

The child toddled on, picking up speed. I headed for him, fast – my shoes slipping as I accelerated. I have never felt adrenaline like it. I ran and ran, and when I reached him, in the wet grass, he was a few feet from the barrier. He was wearing green pyjamas and little monster slippers streaked up with mud. He stopped. I didn't. Cars were beeping. A few other cars had stopped. He stopped and pointed at the road. I grabbed him, and he did not want to be picked up. 'No!' he said, kicking me with his dirty slippers. 'No, no!'

I gripped him like a prize. 'Shh,' I said. 'It's okay, okay, okay.' I don't know where those words came from. Another random voice inside me. Another past life or future life seeping through the cracks. He stopped struggling. I felt accepted, strange and warm.

I turned my back to the traffic and saw Kelly running towards us. She was monochrome with fear. She barked two barely decipherable syllables in an animal panic – a name I would later come to know. I walked with him towards her.

INBOX

Hi Foxface how are you? X x

Great! How are you? X x

Awesome! Question: do you want the vintage cups and saucers? I packed thom by accident and just realised! X x

No thanks x x

Are you sure? You spent ages collecting them from charity shops. You were obsessed with putting mulled wine and hot punch in them at parties x x

Obsessed is a strong word! I was just zestful, as I recall x x

Okay well if you're free next Friday come to my exhibition launch! Would be so great to see you. X x

I might do. Where is It? I've got a few things going on at the mo x x

From 6.30 p.m. at the Hexagon Gallery on the South Bank. Bring a friend x x

Okay thanks I usually have work drinks on a Friday but will see xx

I'll be wearing a red carnation. Holding a bag of crockery x x

Seriously don't worry about the crockery x x

My mother is asleep in her chair, her bottom lip drooping. I've never seen the resemblance. I look back at my phone and then I go into the contacts and add Art's surname to his name – So formal! So distant! He isn't just Art – he is *an* Art. He is *Art who?*

I only wish I knew more Arts.

ART SAID

'Listen, is this still a good thing for us to be doing, do you think?'

'How do you mean?'

'I'm just aware that it's becoming . . . stressful.'

We'd been trying for four months. I was pissing on jumbo bags of mail-order ovulation sticks. I was taking my temperature every morning before I got out of bed. The fucking had gone. In its place was a fever. It rots the crops, that kind of monomania. It curdles the milk. I felt passive, waiting. I hate waiting. Waiting creates too much thinking time. I thought about it a lot, during that time: how I was shrinking into a wench while he was still growing into the adventure of himself.

'Is it?' I said, chewing my thumb.

'You're getting pretty . . . obsessive about it. Like it's the be-all and end-all. It's so much pressure to put us under. And I don't want that. I don't need it. You know, I need to be in a good headspace to do what I do. To do it well, I mean.'

'Yeah. I just – well, it's a project, isn't it. I don't like to fail.'

'Fail?' he said. 'This is not a competition. Come on, let's go and relax. Only beauty!' he said. 'Only beauty in my house!'

'It's my house.'

'In this house! Our house! Let's have a beautiful life, and enjoy ourselves, can't we?'

He was still taking my picture, now and then. I posed for him.

139

I stood. I sat. I lay. I smiled. Even when he was just snapping for fun, just for him, he'd say, 'Smile!' Like that. Like a fucking *catcaller*. But no one wants to smile all the time, do they? No wants to look like their heart is too soon made glad.

And then (are you ready?) I started posing alone, in the front room, by the bay window. I held my arm rigid, finger in mouth, pressing. I was waiting for him to come home – knowing that he would go straight to a bar after a job; knowing that I would eat another dinner alone; but still, I stood at that window, staring through another screen, waiting for love to show up.

Nevertheless.

We got pregnant. At least, I think we got pregnant. So many things happened to make me doubt it, I started to feel like Queen Victoria by the end with her succession of uterine phantoms.

But there it was, in blue and white.

In November, I sent him an emoji of a cross.

Turning Christian?

Guess again.

Woah.

Yep.

Wow.

Innit.

How do you feel?

Like I'm awaiting transformation. How do you feel?

Five.

Minutes.

Later.

Excited!!

ART SAID

'Are you sure? Like, really really sure?'

He'd come home with presents – big cartons of juice and boxes of pre-cut fruit. I gave him the test for his own perusal.

'Well, there you go.'

'Yes. I don't think these things are often wrong.'

'I kind of wish you'd waited for me to do the test.'

'I was just so impatient, and I didn't really believe it could be.'

(This was only half true. I'd wanted to manage the potential shame myself. I'd decided that if it was negative, I just wouldn't tell him.)

'This is my thing now, too,' Art said. 'Scary!'

I wondered if he'd rest his hand proprietorially on my stomach or, anything else gruesome and cheesy like that. But no. We sat there, each holding a large Tetra Pak of juice, looking at each other, and the juice, and the room, alternately, incredulously – unsure whether to hug each other in celebration or whether that would be too self-congratulatory or inappropriate given the ambivalence of feelings (fear / joy, nervous / excited, panic / satisfaction). Personally, I was paralysed. It's hard to do anything with a big carton of juice in your hand.

Months later, at the hospital, the nurses made me doubt myself all over again. *There's so little of the HCG hormone in your system, it's really surprising that you were—*

That I was ever actually pregnant? That's what I wanted to say. But I was all out of chat that day.

Sometimes I think I just made it all up. It was part of my perfect personal brand at that point, curated by myself for myself. Put out there to make me like me. Or some twisted shit like that.

WHAT LASTS?

I said to Kelly, the night after Art moved out. We were in her kitchenette on the cocktails and coke – brains wired, hearts stretched and pinned. 'What actually lasts, over time?'

'Passion.'

'Not sex?'

'Not usually. But they can be connected.'

'Art asked me to "milk" him a few weeks ago.'

'What?'

'Yes, I found it quite disturbing. Why would a man want to be milked?'

'Maybe he was trying to spice things up.'

'Bum steer.'

'Well, that's another option.'

'Not for this cowgirl.'

Kelly speared a maraschino cherry with an acrylic nail. 'Sex is a funny one. It always changes over time.'

'Says who?'

'My va-jay-jay.'

She's no Schopenhauer, Kelly.

BAD STAND-UP

Hi where are you?

On my way home from work, why?

You were meant to meet us at the movies at 6 for Sonny's
bday

Oh shit, I'm so sorry. It's been a tough week. Totally forgot.
So sorry!

You were meant to bring the cake as well

So sorry! Like I said, tough week

It's okay. Forget it. Just don't say you can do it if you can't
do it. It's really important that, with kids

Are you having some kind of go at me in that 'as a mother'
way you do sometimes because we did talk about this

Just forget it, Jenny. Say hi to your mum. See ya.

GHOSTESS WITH THE MOSTEST

When I get to the end of the street I detect the unmistakable whiff of burning sage. My heart takes a nosedive. It can mean only one thing: she is bothering the ether.

Sure enough, as I snick open the front door I hear them. *Is there anybody there? Is there anybody there?* A terribly random endeavour, don't you think? Sort of like Chat Roulette, but with ghosts. You've literally got a one in three chance of getting a wanker. I always thought of the afterlife as being like an airport waiting lounge, filled with impatient spirits, with one phone at one end, that would occasionally ring and be pounced on. *It's for Kevin! Kevin?* And a spirit would sprint over, pushing through the crowds, hand raised. *That's me! I'm Kevin! Wait, don't hang up!*

My mother would be sitting on a table to hold the room. She always made sure her head was higher than anyone's, like Caesar. I remember the nights I couldn't revise because the caterwauling was so loud. My French listening test was a disaster. I arrived late and said I'd run over a dog on my bike; an unconvincing lie, I see that now. The tutor looked at me woefully. I sat down. I had missed half the test. French was my only B. When I got the results it was like a pair of soft breasts sitting there, jiggling, mocking me, among the strong, triangular As. I could not function in that house.

This is my house.

Her head darts out of the lounge. 'Jenny! Come join us!'

I step forward and say in what I hope is a hushed tone: 'What are you doing? You know I don't like being around this.'

'The spirits live amongst us, Jenny.'

'Christ knows where they find the space, with all your coats.'

'It's just a few people, connecting.'

'Getting drunk, more like.'

'Alcohol is the safest choice in the capital. I forgot how the water makes tea taste like a goat's arse-pocket.'

A huge man comes out of the lounge. He has earlobes like medallions of beef. 'Carmen,' he says. To me, an enforced and dramatic, 'Hello.' To Carmen again: 'I'm just worried we will run out of time to make contact.'

He looks stricken. This is the unsavoury part. The wounded and hopeless, the lost. Preyed on.

'Just a moment, Benjamin, love,' my mother says.

I look down and see an open cardboard box, filled with A6 flyers. I pull one out.

Carmen McLaine – Spiritual Healer and Psychic-Medium. Specialist advice on Love and Relationships, Family Matters, Exams, Careers, Jobs, Luck, Death and more. 25 years' expertise in dealing with Spirit. Pay after results. 07876 211560. Facebook: Carmen McLaine

'What are these?'

'Flyers. I decided to try and drum up a bit of business locally.'

'You've put these through people's doors? Around here?'

She nods energetically.

'No,' I say. 'This isn't that kind of neighbourhood. There's a Facebook group about the bins that people are too busy for. They don't want intruding upon in their own homes.'

'Well, the response has been very positive. Come in!'

Benjamin nods and sits down.

I take a deep breath. With no idea how much of my reputation is left, I hold my inner water steady and follow her into the lounge. There are six of them in there, three on each sofa. Caroline from over the street, Raoul and Leonie from next door, and two other people I recognise from down the road. The table is covered with bowls of tortilla chips and half-full tumblers. My mother's crystal ball is uncovered and sits on top of the TV cabinet. The lights are low and there are tea-lights shivering on the mantelpiece. This is not my lounge. Its strangeness is shocking, yet comforting.

'Hello,' I say. 'I'm just saying hello.'

'My daughter is a non-believer,' my mother says.

'I'm not. I don't really have a label for what I am. Spiritually curious. Open-minded.' I say this to her specifically: 'Sensible.'

'You don't believe?' says Benjamin. He looks sad for me.

'I believe that all this is a valid social framework for processing grief, or something like that. I don't mind it as a support group. It's the money-making aspect I object to.' I say it pleasantly.

Truth be told, when it came to mediumship, I had often felt quite moved by the mumsy delivery – the platitudes, the reassurances. *There's light at the end of the tunnel, pet . . . When one door closes, another door opens . . .* In a way, it was a lot like therapy. And marginally cheaper. Marginally.

'Well, I'll be off so you can get your money's worth.' I nod goodbye. 'Cheerio!'

I make to leave the room.

'I'll be with you in a moment, Benjamin,' my mother says. 'I just need to go and rinse my crystals.'

She pulls me towards the kitchen. There's fancy finger-food on the counter tops. The toaster is unplugged.

'I know you have issues with what I do,' my mother says, filling a gin balloon with ice (where have the gin balloons come from? I do not own gin balloons). 'Just as I have issues with what you do. Your preaching to the choir.'

I see a stack of notes in the wine rack. She sees me staring at them.

She continues: 'What I do has its place. It is worthwhile, you know. In the modern world, textual and verbal knowledge is prized above other kinds, and that's not right. What I do is intuitive. Not everyone is academic.'

'Don't compare this to a lack of plumbing apprenticeships, Mother. I'd rather you were an arms dealer. Seriously, I'd be more proud.'

'Do you think this is easy for me? All these voices, all these years? I have no peace, no privacy.'

Benjamin walks into the kitchen. 'Carmen,' he says, 'I hate to hurry this clearly intense personal situation, but Toby won't hang around all day. He's faster than you might think.'

I look at Benjamin. Poor love.

'Yes,' my mother says. 'I will be five minutes. Please just give me time to recharge.'

He nods and walks away.

'Son?' I say. 'Husband? Brother? Lover?'

'Tortoise.'

'Oh god. You're doing animals now.'

'It's an increasingly tough market.'

I turn around. I help myself to a glass of water and then realise I am helping myself to something in my own kitchen. I feel like I am trespassing in my own life.

'They'll be gone in an hour,' my mother says. 'I'm doing this for us.' I don't reply. 'I won't do this again when you are likely to be here. We can set up a schedule, on the fridge. So there are no clashes. I am . . . sorry, Jenny. Let me take you out tomorrow afternoon, make up for it. I'll buy you dinner. A matinee.'

'Maybe.' I start to leave the room. 'And stop unplugging the toaster,' I say, on my way. 'It's insane-making.'

I have a few superstitions I've inherited from her. Don't put new shoes on the table. Don't sleep with your feet facing a doorway.

Or a mirror. Don't cross someone on the stairs without saying 'bread and butter'. Spells to keep the house safe. From what? From falling apart.

Too late.

I pass Benjamin in the hall, waiting outside the living-room door. 'I am . . . sorry for your loss.'

'Thank you,' he says, tearing up. 'It has been agony. Toby was my constant companion.'

I go outside to the garden. I light up a cigarette and as I smoke it I watch the moths mob the porch light.

I WOKE UP LIKE THIS

a) Suzy Brambles has left me
b) My mother is in my house and
c) I left my tampon in, and it has leaked. The sheet looks like the
   Japanese flag.

DRAFTS

Subject: Not Fit for Purpose

Dear Womb,
I want my money back. Not just for that, but for all the periods.
Literally a quarter of my life. All that time, all those mood-swings,
all those sanitary products – and for what? NOTHING.
Bests,
Jenny McLaine

THE MIND CREATES THE ABYSS

Hey, how are you?

Hey! I'm okay. On my way to meet my mother in some weird shabby pub she likes in Soho. How are you?

I'm okay but listen I've got a bit of an emergency and I wondered if you could help – really sorry to ask but there's literally no one else – my mum is away and the trains are screwed tomorrow and Sonny needs picking up from his dance class at 7 – can you poss do it if I send the address, again sorry to ask

Sure!

Thanks so much – I know he's 14 but it's dark and not the greatest area and there was another stabbing just last week

No sweat

I walk up to the French Horse, a dark, brash pub with flags outside and a smoking galley cordoned off with a stretch of vinyl that says *Stella Artois*. I've walked past it plenty of times but written it off as a little too local. I take a picture of it as I approach. Now, how to caption this . . .

PUB LOLZ! #WOO

No. I am not fifty.

LIVING MY BEST LIFE IN SOHO! #WOO

Nor am I a tourist. Delete delete delete.

MAKING WEDNESDAY MY BITCH

Ooh. That has allure. I post it, and take a quick look at Suzy Brambles. Nothing. That's two days she's been off it. What's the deal? Is she writing a goddamn novel? Maybe her account has been hacked. Maybe her phone has been stolen. Maybe she's broken a limb. I would just about accept a broken limb. If she were to post, tomorrow say, or the day after, a hospital-bed selfie with her shapely leg in a white cast, I would like it deeply, privately.

'Jenny!' My mother has spotted me through the doorway. 'Come in and meet my friend Linda.'

I walk in and up to the bar. My mother is holding a dainty-small glass of white. She is leaning on the piano like Amadeus Mozart in the film *Amadeus*. A mad-eyed dog with a bouffant do.

'Hiya,' says the woman behind the bar. She has piercings all the way up the sides of both ears – little studs and hoops and chains – and peggy front teeth which show a laissez-faire attitude in this dentistry-savvy age. I suspected this place was run by vagabonds.

'Wine?'

'I don't suppose you do coffee?'

'Machine's off.'

'Wine's fine.'

My mother laughs. 'Linda, this is my daughter, Jenny,' she says.

The woman nods, turns and bends. Her bracelets jangle as she opens the fridge. My mother leans towards me. 'We used to be lovers,' she says, not quietly enough. Still, presumably Linda is aware of this fact. If it is a fact. My mother continues: 'In my youth.'

'Excellent.'

I walk up to the bar. The woman hands me a small glass of white wine. 'We only do one size.'

'This is the perfect size for me.'

'You can have ten,' my mother says. 'You can neck it like a shot.'

'How long have you been here?'

'Half an hour.'

'An hour and a half,' says Linda.

'Grass.'

'She came in all flustered, like she'd been at a casting.'

My mother goes red. I look at her.

'I thought you were at your course?'

'Oh, I couldn't hack that in the end, darling. Or rather – I feel I can do so much *more*. It's too limiting to pigeonhole myself completely. I have things to offer the wider world. Besides, I don't want to end up morbid, do I?'

She waltzes over to the piano and starts to play 'One Moment in Time' by Whitney Houston. Linda rolls her eyes and goes to clear a table. I sit at the bar, on one of the tall stools that always make me feel cool. I get out my phone and start scrolling. Just before the first chorus my mother breaks her tune and shouts: 'Come on, Jenster!'

'Don't call me that,' I say, still scrolling. 'It makes me sound like an off-road vehicle.'

She does the song to the end, screeching over the music like a banshee. I barely notice because the pub post is proving popular.

'What's that? I'm not on the square photo one. I just do the Facebook.'

She is suddenly at my shoulder.

'Stop creeping!'

'I didn't look *purposely*, it was just there. You know how we're trained, as humans, to look at a screen. Our eyes are drawn, helplessly, to the lit opportunity.'

'Is that right?'

'That's right. No phone at the bar!' barks Linda.

'Yes, no phones at the bar, Jenny, godsake,' says my mother. 'Have some respect for the old days.'

Linda rattles a cocktail shaker. Ratatatatatatat. She pours violet liquid into two martini glasses and garnishes each with a blackberry and a mint leaf. She places the two purple cocktails in front of us.

'What's this?'

'A Bramble,' my mother says. 'I asked Linda to make them up specially. I have a feeling you'll like it.'

I flinch. 'What made you order that?'

'It looks nice. Why? Is it terribly gauche or old-fashioned or something?'

'No, it's just . . .'

'What?'

Her head is close, so close. Her eyes – like the snake from *The Jungle Book*. I shake my head.

She picks up a glass and hands it to me. 'Okay,' she says. 'Bramble for your thoughts.'

I look at my mother and go through all the possibilities in my head of what I could or could not say and how she might receive it and—

Oh god, what is even the point.

I sigh, exhausted. 'There's someone on Instagram with the same name as this cocktail and she stopped following me recently and I don't know why but I know the possible reasons make up a large proportion of my daily thoughts. You could say I am quite distressed about it.'

My mother shakes her head quickly. 'Come again, darling?'

I tell my mother about Suzy Brambles. As I tell her, she sips her Bramble and looks occasionally at my phone. When I've finished telling her, I exhale and take a sip of my drink. My mother is studying me carefully.

'So let me get this straight,' she says. 'You're upset because someone you don't know might not like a version of you that doesn't really exist.'

'I assure you, it's far more complicated than that.'

'The trouble with your generation, darling, is that you think you invented the internet.'

'We . . . did. You're thinking of cocaine and blow jobs. Although I never thought you were too au fait with drugs.'

Linda raises her eyebrows. I recall an incident, I was thirteen or fourteen, when my mother found a twig in my blazer pocket that had fallen off a tree on the way home from school. *JENNIFERRRRRRRRRR*, she'd shrieked through the house. I sloped downstairs and found her in the kitchen, with the twig held aloft. *Is this DRUGS?*

No, Ma, I'd said coolly (I was the master of teen exasperation by then). *It's a twig. Is the menopause making you this insane?*

'So smart, aren't you,' my mother says. 'Well, you might have invented the internet but you didn't invent all the feelings that come with it. The mind creates the abyss and the heart crosses it. Can I give you my honest opinion?'

'Can I say no?'

'This is all about attention, Jennifer. You cultivated a twitch when you were eleven, remember? She did, Linda. She sat in front of the TV night after night, practising a facial twitch, until it started happening spontaneously. She changed her handwriting every year for the start of the September term. My little chameleon. Now, how am I supposed to think this time you're not just finding some new way of getting people to look at a version of you?'

'Because I feel all this deeply.'

'But *why*? What do you want from her?'

'Jack Nicholson has been described as "a very social loner". I feel much the same way. I am happiest in my own company against a backdrop of general adoration. I want to be adored in my absence.'

My mother laughs. 'Sounds a lot like death, darling.'

'Yes, it does, doesn't it.'

'Drink your drink.'

'Stop looking at me.'

'Show me her, then,' my mother says. 'This fabled Suzy Brambles.'

'Don't say her name.'

'Why?'

'It makes me uncomfortable.'

I don't want it in the air.

My mother nods slowly, staring at me.

'Don't give me shit about this. You're the one who talks to ghosts.'

'Yes, I do, don't I? Now, show me this enigma who is tormenting my daughter! I command it!'

I show my mother Suzy Brambles' feed. 'Now, don't whatever you do touch it. NO! You almost touched it. Do not touch the screen. Hold the phone at the edges. That's it. Okay, now carefully.'

'*So delighted and excited to be at the launch of Brigitta's new photography book!*' my mother reads from Suzy's latest post. 'No she's not. She's just saying that to look like a person who knows someone who's having a book published – note the first-name terms, I bet she's met her once – and is going out doing things. She's lying.'

'She is not lying,' I say. 'They're great friends. They went to WerkHaus FarmHaus together a month ago. Suzy's not a member, but she knows a lot of members. She's never in the WerkHaus itself. That would be too much.'

'It's a pitch. She's a hustler, darling. Is she over the age of twenty?'

'She's twenty-eight,' I say. 'Just. She celebrated in France. Look.'

I scroll back and show my mother the pictures from Suzy's birthday celebrations in a petite gite near Dieppe. *Quelle belle vue!* The baguettes were to die for.

'*What better way to see in the last year of my twenties with wine, cheese, good company, and so much gratitude,*' my mother reads. 'Hahahahahahahahhahahah!'

'What's funny about that?'

My mother selects another post. '*Every time I read a French novel I think of what a marvellous job translators do and how important it is to acknowledge them* . . . "Every time"! Know what she's really saying there? *I READ FRENCH NOVELS*. Hahahahahah!'

'You're being very harsh! Stop phishing her!'

My mother looks at me. 'All these posts, Jenny, are not actually about any of the things they say they're about. They are all about *her*. She's selling herself. And you're buying it, darling. This is like when I used to take you to the theatre and you became fixated with individual actresses onstage, a different one every time. You'd stare at them during the applause, trying to catch their eye.'

'Did you touch that, then? Did you tap it as you made that insulting point?'

'No!'

'You did. You double tapped it. Oh my god.'

I look at the heart. It has gone from empty to full. It is bright red. I have liked an old picture of Suzy's, and now she will know. She will know I have been looking back through her profile. Like a weirdsome loser creep worm.

'You liked it you liked it you liked it you liked it you liked it.' My head is in one hand. I am rocking slowly on the chair.

'What's the big deal?'

'WHAT'S THE BIG DEAL?'

'She won't know it was you.'

'She will! That's the point of all this shit! This is like when I accidentally liked one of Art's ex's pictures and I had to change my whole handle and profile name for a week so she didn't know it was me and I still worry about the fact she will have looked back and realised at a later point. I have inherited your incriminating sausage fingers!'

I take my phone back and click it to sleep. I drink my Bramble, severely anguished.

'Don't worry,' my mother says. 'Seriously, darling. Your so-called Suzy Brambles is one big construct.'

'*Don't* say her name.'

'Come on,' my mother says. 'Sup up.'

'Where are we going?'

'*All* my old haunts. Some fresh air. Some perspective. You wonder why you're anxious – when you constantly stare at a device that beams nightmares into your eyes. Enough 2D.'

'It's not what it was, Soho,' I tell her, as we walk.

'What, sleazy and dirty?'

'Affordable.'

'I don't think it was ever that. But I did go to some great parties in flats around here.'

Then, 'Slow down,' my mother says. 'Slow down.'

I slow down.

'Have you ever strolled around Soho?' my mother asks. 'I don't mean dashed between meetings – I mean just allowed yourself to dawdle, on these streets? Have you ever really looked up at these buildings?' she says, raising a bowled palm to the sky, like Hamlet.

'I don't know. I suppose not.'

'Have you had a cigarette in Soho Square and not spent the whole time looking at your phone? No? I thought as much.'

We head for the square, find a bench and sit in silence. The square chatters and tinkles around us. I itch to look at my phone, but I resist.

'Should have got Linda to do us a carry-out,' my mother says.

I look at the almost-bare trees. The last leaves flutter in the wind. I'm not normally an alfresco person but I think you can occasionally commune with nature if the conditions are right and you're miserable enough. I've had a few 'moments' with rats, foxes and squirrels: eye contact, each other's focus for a brief second. I even had a mini-thing with a Canada goose once, but I think it was possibly brain-damaged.

Straight after our moment it flew into a railing.

When we get home, she runs me a bath. Blobs of lavender and rose oil bob around the top. I sit and try to let my body soften in the water but then a big gob of period comes out. I watch it unfurl between my legs, like a brown fern. It turns the whole bath brackish.

My body feels like a city I have been defending vaguely, and selling off, piece by piece. I remember the first bra I wore – triangular and stiff – the first chunks of me portioned up into shapes to be sold. I was rainforest, razed for cattle. There's a block of new luxury flats just behind my right ear. The boundaries of myself depress me because they are meaningless. I'm ravaged inside. I have been invaded by a Trojan horse full of Time.

After my bath I head downstairs. My mother is in the kitchen drinking her nightly eggnog that she swears by for strengthening her already strong voice (a green smoothie every morning to regenerate her liver). She sings a sudden line of Billy Joel and I am reminded of how she does this in her own kitchen – in our old kitchen – to 'soften the atmosphere and dispel the spirits'.

'Want one?'

I shake my head.

She pulls a box of melba toast out of the cupboard, extracts one piece and spreads it thinly with extra-light cream cheese. I watch her as I breathe.

'Do you not have it up anywhere?' she says. 'That picture of you and the roses?'

'No. It has nothing to do with me any more really, that.'

I don't even know where it is. I think he must have taken it with him. It was his photo, after all. I was in it – or rather, my body was in it, but now I think if I saw it I'd feel more than I meant to.

'How's Art's mum? What's her name, Deborah? What does she think about it?'

'We exchanged brief texts, all the best and whatnot, you know. I don't really know. I feel like it's not really my business any more, is it?'

My mother raises her eyebrows and bites her toast.

I ADORED

Art's mother. She was splendid – stately and sharp, in her tiny flat by the water in Glasgow. Her name was Deborah (Deborah) (it did, actually, suit her) but everyone called her Debs. My mind often returns even now to those Friday nights when we caught the sleeper train to her place. The duck pond. The red bricks. The hallway tiled with tasteful art. I'd walk through the dappled lounge out to the veranda and she'd rise from her sunbed, warm and musky, and pull me close with such a sweetness I felt as though *she* was *my* daughter – that was the level of delight. When she cooked for us – invariably a roast chicken – all the condiments came out: mustard, horseradish, peanut butter, mango chutney, the lot. She was like that. Generous. I got to a point where I was scared of saying I liked anything in case she gave it to me. One time she packed me off with a thin, sinister wooden statue of the Virgin Mary (I thought it was a decorative shoehorn!), Art rolling his eyes as I trotted dutifully out of the door with it in my hand. I still had that, somewhere, in a shoebox, along with a silver St Gerard pendant she gave me when we said we were trying.

DRAFTS

Dear St Gerard,
Fat lot of use you were.
BR,
Jenny McLaine

ART SAID

'Don't take this the wrong way, babes, but you're not very maternal.'

I stared at him.

'It's not a bad thing!' he said.

'It sounds like a bad thing.'

'You're just very conscientious and neurotic, delightfully capricious and contradictory – and hilarious of course.'

'What's that, Art?' I said. 'The fucking feedback sandwich?'

'Ha! There – you see?'

'NEUROTIC?'

'Sorry, that's the wrong word. You just think too much.'

YOU

You are not maternal, said the blood.
    You are not maternal, said the tobacco.
    You are not maternal, said the overtime.
    You are not maternal, said the overdraft.

TERMS OF ENDEARMENT

The next evening I wait outside Sonny's dance school near Tower Bridge. I watch the lights inside the building, looking for signs of departure, in between checking the comments on my column, which this week is about the benefits of being big spoon for a change.

Sonny comes out. I am stunned, for a moment, by the height of him.

'All right?'

'All right? Did your mum tell you I'd be coming?'

'Course she did. Be a bit weird if she didn't.'

'I suppose.'

He sets off walking. I follow. I wonder whether I should have brought him a drink, or some chocolate. Crisps? A Kinder egg?

He pulls out a pack of cigarettes.

'What are you doing?'

'You smoke.'

'I don't care. This isn't okay.' I take his cigarettes off him and put them in my pocket. 'You can't do this in front of me. You have to hide with your mates in a shitty bus station somewhere. Or even better, don't do it.'

'I thought you weren't like them, but you are like them.'

'Who?'

'The rest of them.'

'I'm sorry I forgot your birthday, Sonny.'

'That's okay.'

'I've been . . . having a bit of a hectic time. I'll bring you a present round soon, okay?'

'Okay.'

'Let me know if there's anything in particular you want.'

'That pack of cigarettes.'

'Very funny.'

He starts looking at his phone, so I look at mine. I loop back round my apps and refresh. As my Instagram feed refreshes I see there's a new post from Suzy Brambles, from a few hours earlier. How did I miss this?

It's a picture of someone's arm. A man's arm. There's a section of tattoo visible. A trident of some kind.

It is Art's arm.

I fall to my knees, phone in hand.

IT IS A PICTURE OF ART'S ARM.

Not only that, but he has commented underneath:

Nice composition, Foxface x x

'Aunty Jenny? Are you all right?'

I cannot reply. All I can do is stare at my phone.

'Are you having a stroke? You've gone a funny colour.'

Forty-six people have liked the Foxface comment.

My mind rises up and leaves my body. I am not myself. I do not know who I am but I am not here and I am not this and I am not myself.

I get up and run off down the street.

I hear Sonny shouting after me. 'Aunty Jenny? AUNTY JENNY?'

I don't know where I'm going but as I'm running I'm checking things against things in my head, calculating, computing, adding it all up. How was I blind to this? I am better than this . . . obscene ignorance. It is inexcusable to have not deduced this earlier. If I could fire myself from running my life right now, I would. This is an act of gross misconduct. Of negligence. A head must roll! Something must die. SOMETHING MUST DIE!

I reach the bridge and push past a group of protesters standing holding signs for something or other. 'MOVE OUT OF THE WAY,' I yell, 'THIS IS A LIFE OR DEATH ISSUE!' They move out of the way. They are unified, momentarily, through fear of me, this madwoman, heading for the edge of the bridge. I find a ledge and climb over the barrier and stand, staring at the river below.

'Call the police!' someone shouts.

'Don't do it!' shouts someone else.

'I have to!' I shout. 'There is nothing else for me to do now!'

'It's never as bad as you think!' shouts another person.

'Don't say that! You're not meant to say that!' someone replies.

I notice a small box of cards affixed to the girder by my head. I pull one out. It is a message. It says: *Things are bad but they will get better. You are valuable. Never forget that x*

I wonder who has written it.

But I've made my mind up. They are all too late. I take a step back (someone gasps) and then I wheel my arm like a bowler with a cricket ball and launch my phone – far far far into the Thames. Then I crouch in a ball and sob.

'Are you okay?' someone shouts.

I raise my head. A trail of snot connects my nose to the concrete floor of the bridge platform. 'NO, I AM NOT FUCKING OKAY!'

I get back to the house and close the door behind me. I stand in the hall.

'Jenny?' says my mother, coming out of the lounge. 'I thought you were going to get Sonny? You're back early.'

I don't reply. I go upstairs and get my laptop out. I stare at the picture some more. Then I go to my emails and email Art.

Why is there a picture of you with Suzy Brambles?

He replies instantly.

Hey. What?

Why is there a picture of you with Suzy Brambles on her Instagram? It's a simple question.

Who?

SUZY BRAMBLES STOP MAKING ME SAY IT

Oh haha that's not her real name. I forgot she has that daft pseudonym! Her real name is Suzanne

I breathe. I exhale and I inhale and I exhale again.

Where did you meet her?

She got in touch via Instagram

Wtf

Then we met at her friend's photography book launch

Are you seeing her?

How do you mean?

I mean are you seeing her shitbird u know what I mean

Okay. I don't want to argue like this so can we talk this through properly on the phone?

NO WE CANNOT

Trying to call

I am not available right now

I am hyperventilating.

Jenny please talk to me

No. I don't think we will achieve anything

Okay. But just let me say this. You and I broke up over six months ago

I can feel hair follicles clenching on my back.

It's not that. She knows me!!!

Suzanne is pretty sure she doesn't know you, Jenny. You must be mistaken x

What, is she there now?

Art?

Is she there???

I hope you're not giving her the fucking speech, Art

Which speech?

The 'my ex is so hurt because I am so powerful' speech
The 'my ex is so crazy' speech
FUCK OFF WITH THOSE SPEECHES, YOU AND EVERY MAN
FOREVER

Take care of yourself, Jenny. Get a spa day! X

My spinal fluid boils loose. I am formicating.

Fuck you hard, Art, fuck you in all the ways and also in ways
they haven't invented yet

I am popping all over, like a carcass in a furnace.
'JENNY,' my mother says. 'Step away from the computer.'
'Fuck off, Mother.'
'Jenny, I'm going to take the computer now, okay.' She does it
like she's defusing a bomb. Like I'm packing explosives in my vest.
'Just – breathe, and stay calm.'
I collapse on the floor. 'He's fucking seeing her.'
'Who? What?'
'Art is seeing Suzy Brambles. I mean, can you believe that? And
everyone tells me I'm paranoid and I overthink – well, you know
what? The paranoid people are *on to shit*.'
'I'm just going to put this down over here.'
Then it dawns on me.
She stalked him on my Instagram. This explains everything.
'OH MY GOD.'
'What?'
'GET ME A GIN, MOTHER.'
She gets me a gin. I am in the same position when she comes

up: calcified. I take the gin without moving my face or indeed any part of myself.

'Okay, darling, there you go. Now, tell me, slowly, what happened.'

I reel off the intel. 'Suzy Brambles has posted a picture of Art's arm and he has commented underneath using a nickname he used to call me. It's an utterly sociopathic act, by both of them.'

'Let me see.'

I open my laptop for my mother and show her.

She sighs. 'Oh darling, that doesn't prove anything. Your imagination is filling in the gaps and joining up dots to create the wrong picture. You were always too good at that.'

'He just confirmed he's with her now!'

'That doesn't mean anything. It could be a one-off. You're over-analysing, as usual.'

'You have to leave.'

'What?'

'I can't do this. We can't be friends. I want you to go.'

IF

you're going to have a miscarriage I can highly recommend doing it during a production of *Macbeth*. It's not only thematically apt but it means you get to exact revenge on an overpriced theatre seat by bleeding all over it.

We'd gone to see some Shakespeare because I was hankering for academia.

Pregnancy made me like that. Nostalgic. Elitist. Sedate. It was January. We were nine weeks. I was thinking, periodically (bemusedly) about August. The whole future had changed. My body was changing. I was being invaded. Realigned. Unutterably. Permanently.

And then, I wasn't.

I'd woken at 3 a.m. that morning, knowing something was wrong. My boobs weren't sore any more and I felt completely normal – the previous abnormal suddenly standing and revealing itself, in all its utter abnormality. I'd forgotten how normal felt, but now I remembered. I felt distinctly un-pregnant. Googling led me to miscarriage chat rooms. I didn't post anything, just read, really. I found a pregnancy message board and a bunch of posts from other panicking women who were terrified, alone, in the early morning, sharing their stories about this terrible unspoken thing that shouldn't be a terrible unspoken thing, but is. *I just woke up and found this . . . Can't get back to sleep . . . Is it blood or is it mucus? It's just a bit pink really, don't you think? Anyone else had this? Anyone out there?* It made me love the internet, briefly. It made me love women, everywhere, protectively. Maternally.

The day passed bloodlessly. I sat tight.

Then, in the theatre that night, beautifully, horribly, perfectly – it began. During a battle scene I felt a hot blip, and. And. I knew it, and it knew me, and it had come. I excused myself and ran to the toilet, checking the fabric as I vacated my seat. Thoughtful of me, don't you think? Aren't women The Best.

I sat on the toilet and stared at the back of the door, unsure how to feel. I was thankful no one knew, but I also had no one to share this with, now. I wanted Kelly. Not my mother. Kelly. I felt as though I had failed on some sort of fundamental level (*YOU HAVE NO INTEGRITY* . . .). Why was I so upset? I wasn't even sure I'd wanted a baby (how can you, intelligently, want something so seismic and unknowable?). Was it hormones? Punctured pride? Or – darker, shall I even . . . yes, yes I must – was it that I was aware on some level of not getting what I'd paid for; what I'd ordered; what I'd felt was my right? Was this the dissatisfied customer in me? The irate little Western consumer? It was puzzling.

I packed my pants with loo roll and went back to my seat. Art looked at me enquiringly and took my hand.

'I think I'm losing it.'

The 'I' then, not the 'we'. It was mine then it was ours then it was mine again. I got both shitty ends of the stick.

'Oh, babes.'

He squeezed. I heard the pity in his voice and I hated being pitied. I felt as though he'd lost respect for me, somehow. That I was reduced by the whole endeavour, and not in the way I expected.

We sat on opposite sides of the taxi, going home. I looked out of the window, watching the rain dance off the low windowsills of the shops. Back at the house, I made us pints of orange squash, like always. Art went to his cellar. I would usually go down too, poke around, pester him, but something kept me upstairs. My phone, I suppose. I looked for advice on when to go to the hospital. That night we slept on opposite sides of the bed. I say slept. I didn't sleep. I put on my eye-mask and even though I could hear Art breathing it felt as though there were miles of silence between us. At one point he farted. It sounded like whale song.

I got up at five, still bleeding. I said: 'I want to go to the hospital now.'

He said: 'Yes. I'll help you.'

ART'S MOTHER SAID

'Is Jenny not coming down?'

I heard her, from upstairs. She'd come round to see us, a few weeks before we broke up. I couldn't muster up the energy or social grace to go down and make conversation. I was also punishing her as a way of punishing him, I see that now. The sins of the son. Something like that.

DRAFTS

Dear Barista,

I did not mean to shout HI! when you handed me my coffee this morning. I meant to say Thanks! like a normal person. I am sorry I made you jump. I am having a bit of a bad time at the mo – although even at the best of times I am not much of a Johnny-on-the-spot. Or a Jenny-on-the-spot, even. (My real name is Jenny, which also might come as a surprise to you because I know I've said 'Suzy' a few times in the past and that is what the cashier has written on my cup.)

You will never see me again, if that is any consolation.

Sincerely,

Jenny McLaine BA Hons.

FULL DESPERATE

What happened??? Sonny just told me you ran off. Did you have some kind of panic attack?

Art is seeing someone I know

So that makes you leave my son in the street?

My son?? Why are you being so motherly and judgmental about this?

Sorry what?

This is real heartbreak, Kelly. I saw them together.

I take photos of my coffee cup from various angles until it looks best. This courtesy phone isn't going to win any awards for its camera, but its saving grace is that it isn't at the bottom of the Thames. It was an interesting chat with the insurance company at the phone store. I said I'd been on a riverboat that unexpectedly swerved. Kelly takes a long time to reply – I watch the grey blobs rippling with promise – and then:

Want to meet at lunch?

Okay

''Sup, gingerest of whingers?' I jump. It's Mia. She's wearing a dress that's like a huge red arrow, pointing downwards. I put down my phone. 'A word!'

'Anything in particular?'

'Something special!'

I pick up my phone and follow her into her office. Something special? Sounds ominous. *This way, turkeys, it's time for your special Christmas surprise!* The main space falls silent around us. Fingers stop tapping keys. Eyeballs stop squeaking from side to side. I sense an imminent axe-fall.

Mia closes her office door. Simone is under the desk, chewing a toy shaped like an iPad.

'So,' Mia says. 'Regrettably [truly, you've never seen someone demonstrate so little regret] I must inform you we're having a maje redesign, and I'm afraid "Intense Modern Woman" isn't going to make the cut for the new-look *Foof*.'

I stare at her. I think about my bank account, plummeting as it is into red below the red. I am probably going to debtors' prison (does debtors' prison still exist?). I am almost desperate. Scratch that: I'm desperate. I am Full Desperate.

'Look,' I say, 'I know they've been a bit vanilla the past few weeks, but I can go full rum and raisin again if you'll just give me one more chance. Just give me another month to turn this around and prove to you I have got what it takes.'

. . . *to be your apprentice, Lord Sugar.*

. . . *to be on your team, will.i.am.*

Mia shakes her head. 'You can work out the week, but then it's *sayonara* at the Monocle. We're having leaving drinks for you! It's all arranged.'

'Oh Christ, please don't publicise this,' I say. 'Give me that at least. Give me my dignity.'

'Don't be silly. People move on. Be empowered by this transition.'

I leave Mia's office and go to a soundproofed booth for a cry. And a look at my phone. For a few hours. Well, what's the point in anything else any more? I post a picture of my hand doing a thumbs up in the empty booth, with the caption:

GREAT TO GET SOME DOWNTIME IN A PEACEFUL SPOT BEFORE THE BLITZKRIEG OF THE DAY #BUSYBUSYBUSY #SENDCOFFEE

And then I put my head on the desk and cry until I am a veritable husk.

MISERABLE PHO

I meet Kelly in the Noodle Hovel for lunch. When she arrives I stand up and hug her. She stiffens slightly. She orders a beer and I order kombucha. We sit opposite each other and look at the food menu. I do not want any food.

'What you need to understand is that I am under siege right now, Kelly,' I say, quietly and emotionally. 'I was blindsided in the street. I was not in control of my actions.'

She looks at me from under her fringe.

I add: 'I also got fired today.'

'What? How come?'

'Presumably because I've not got a famous boyfriend any more.'

'I think that's being slightly paranoid. Are you sure you're not just—'

'Mia's always had the cultural hots for Art. And now my stock's gone down. I can feel it.'

Kelly swigs her beer. 'Fucking Foof Towers. Fuck. Off. S'all bullshit anyway.'

'Shh,' I say.

'What?'

'You're being quite loud.'

'I'm just sticking up for you.'

'But still, you never know who's listening.'

She looks at me the way she's been looking at me since I walked in – like she's trying to see where my face is attached to my head or my hair is attached to my head, or something.

'Yes!' I say loudly, as though I am replying to something else she has said – something else that is a fun brand of conversation, for anyone who might be able to hear or see us.

Kelly shakes her head and takes another swig of beer. 'So you left a fourteen-year-old in the street at night.'

'He's a big boy!'

'He's fourteen.'

'He can take care of himself!'

'But I asked you to take care of him. And you left him. Because your ex is seeing someone new. That's your priority.'

There is a waiter beside us. 'Are you ready to order?' he says.

I shake my head. 'The Art thing is not even the worst thing I'm contending with,' I say.

'Actually,' says Kelly, 'I only have forty-five minutes, so can we order soon?'

'Please could you give us just a few minutes?' I say to the waiter. He nods and walks away.

'I can't think about food while I'm telling you about this. I'm not even hungry.'

'Okay,' Kelly says.

'He's seeing Suzy Brambles,' I say, giving this sentence the delivery it deserves.

'Suzy . . . *Brambles?*'

'Don't say her *n-name*.'

'Is that a real person?'

'As real as the real on my face.'

'Well, it's never nice to find out about these things,' says Kelly, and now she does talk quietly. I am relieved but also slightly unsettled by the sound of her voice. Still, she doesn't know the whole story, so I fill her in. I tell her about the arm picture, the comment, the likes, the messages, the fact Suzy unfollowed me after clearly using me to find Art. We have to tell the waiter to go away again twice.

Kelly looks at her watch and smiles at me in a way she's never smiled at me before, like someone who's about to tell me I haven't got the job might smile at me, a nice person with bad news. It isn't the way you expect a friend to react to this crushing tale of woe.

'What do you think I should do?' I say.

'*Do?*'

'Yes. I don't really care about the job, I can get another job, but the humiliation of Art and Suzy – I just can't begin to process it.'

'Well, it is annoying.'

'*Annoying?*'

My own voice rises then and Kelly's eyes fill with tears. FINALLY, the appropriate response! I hate to see her cry but I'm also glad she's crying. We can cry together about this. For weeks. Months!

She stops crying and wipes her eyes dry. I await her succour.

Eventually, she speaks. 'Look, Jenny, I know you're having a hard time. And I wanted to meet you to talk about it. But we've been together almost an hour and you haven't asked me one question about me. Not one. You haven't apologised for leaving my teenage son alone on the street. I thought I could trust you. You cannot be trusted.'

I halt my inner celebration. 'Er, I'm the one with the catastrophe right now, Kelly.'

She nods and looks at her beer bottle. 'So I guess I should tell you that Paul sent Sonny a message via his mum's Facebook and Sonny got all excited and replied and now he's just ghosting him again, and I could fucking kick myself for not monitoring it all more closely. And it looks like Esther is going to sell the house soon because her kids are pressuring her to, and there's no way I'll be able to find anywhere in London as cheap so I'm looking at where else in the UK to live.'

'Don't even talk to me about money! No one could be more worried about money than me right now.'

Kelly slams her beer bottle down. I jump.

'You own your own house!'

'Which I can't afford any more!'

'You have A NICE LIFE with few responsibilities. You need to grow up and take responsibility for things.'

I whisper-hiss: 'Don't you dare "as a mother" me! I have a mortgage! That's as bad as a child!'

'So sell it and live somewhere cheaper. You have options. My tax credits are fucked. I'll be uprooting Sonny while he's doing his GCSEs. I might not get another job I like as much that's also flexible around school hours.'

'He won't even be at school for that much longer. He's practically an adult. Time he started fending for himself, in all honesty.'

Kelly sits mouth-breathing for a moment. It's not a good look, even for her. Then she says, calmly, almost gently: 'Jenny, can I ask you a question?'

'Of course. Ask me anything you want. I have many more details to share.'

Kelly moves her head almost imperceptibly to the side and back again. She says: 'Do you think we would be friends if that day hadn't happened, with Sonny on the dual carriageway?'

'What do you mean?'

'I've just been thinking a lot about our friendship and how it occurred.'

'I've been a little nostalgic—'

'No, I don't mean nostalgic. I mean re-evaluative, if that's even a word. Have you not, too? It all feels like it's been a bit of a blur until now, but I'm slowing down and taking stock.' She flicks the loose edge of the label on her beer bottle with her nail. 'Have you never thought that day on the dual carriageway forced us to be friends?'

'Forced us?'

'You know how you're friends with people at school because you're in the same class? You're sort of institutionalised. What even makes you make friends with someone when you're older? Would we have found each other naturally? Would we have forged a friendship, naturally?'

'Probably.' A cupboard opens in my mind and I see that day, by the dual carriageway. Then my heart beats and the cupboard slams shut. 'Do you think she's better than me because she's younger? Do you think that's why he's gone for her? I always saw him with an older woman, but he's got a surreptitious agenda – I know it, even if he doesn't.'

Kelly looks at me sadly.

'I love you for a whole variety of reasons, Jenny.'

I swell at this.

'And I think some of them have run out.'

I shrink.

'You haven't always been this fragile maniac. You used to run at things. You used to have everything you needed. You used to not look back. I don't know whether you noticed – to be honest I don't know what you notice any more, other than the way you come across to certain strangers – but I don't have many friends. You're one of a handful of people I can really talk to. *Could* really talk to. All I see of you now is this phony self-promoting person who I don't know.'

'Well, they do say that the people you know the best are the people you end up hating the most on social media. You see through the façade. Otherwise you just think, oh there's that fabulous person having a glorious time.'

'Stop with the theories! You're wasting time caring about all this superficial shit while the world goes to Hell in a handcart. Babies are in cages on the Mexican border. Someone I went to school with just set up a food bank in my hometown.'

'I am very aware of reality. I'm a journalist.'

'You're a fucking child! I have empathy fatigue where you're concerned. And I'm not even sure it's just – well. Maybe we're done. Maybe we're just done. Now. At this point.' She nods to the waiter.

'Don't say that.'

She shrugs.

The waiter starts heading over. 'Are you ready to order?' he says.

'Yes,' I say. 'I think so, almost.'

Kelly puts a five-pound note and two pound coins on the table. She gets up.

'I meant what I said about the way we met,' she says. 'Because right now, I don't think I actually like you. That's the honest truth, Jenny. I don't like you. We've never had a friendship. We had a romance begun by a meet not-so-cute.'

She walks out. I stare at my kombucha. I suddenly remember people might be looking at me. I take a picture of the kombucha.

To all the ferments I've loved before

I post it as I pay the bill.

BREATHING FOR ONE

Towards the very end, Art started refusing to do social engagements as a couple. He started cancelling his attendance at birthdays, weddings, drinks, everything. I was busy with my own preoccupations. I couldn't bring myself to wear anything I'd worn while I was pregnant and charity-shopped most of my cardigans and jeans. I couldn't even bear to wear the same perfumes, so they got shoved in the charity bags, too, even though I wasn't sure whether an opened bottle of perfume was sellable or would be classed as tampered with. I thought I might be being superstitious – feeling like those garments were somehow cursed, or would bring back bad memories. But the truth was, I was tampered with. I felt like a different woman. Nothing fitted me or suited me from my previous life. I was less fleshly. More insect. I had eyes and ears in strange places.

At Sonny's birthday party – a big one, his thirteenth – Art made his excuses ten minutes before we were due to leave the house. I passed them on to Kelly and Sonny. I was the go-between. The middle-woman. The PA to his flakiness.

Sonny said: 'He can't be bothered with us any more, can he?'

Kelly said: 'Not that he ever really could.'

I had a row with Art about it when I got back. I told him what Kelly and Sonny had said.

'I'm not playing happy families on your terms, is that it?' he said.

'I've been there plenty of times. I've ummed and I've ahhed in all the right places. Give me a break.'

'Wow,' I said. 'You were really playing the part for me.'

'Yes,' he said, 'I'm glad you appreciate that.'

'Are *we* a family, Art? Is that what we are?'

'I feel like you're about to trap me with this question. It's a trick, isn't it?'

'Because you're never here. You're always out.'

'YOU'RE always out,' he said, banging his head with his hand. 'The lights are on but no one's home.'

He was wrong about that. Sometimes I closed my eyes at night and it was like there was a light still on at the back of my eyes.

POPULAR PROBLEMS

On the Tube home I listen to Leonard Cohen. Listening to Leonard Cohen makes me feel as though as long as I can be wry and observant about the world then everything will be okay.

An email arrives, from Mia.

Yo! Are you not coming back after lunch? What about your leaving drinks tonight?? We have a hashtag #JENNYSDEFOOFING
MIA

I don't reply. It takes a lot for a person like me not to reply, but I don't. Instead I text Nicolette.

Fancy a drink later? Lots to tell you. X

Yes

I have news too

X.

Good Christ, could everyone stop with the news? I'm all news'd out.

Then I think:

Is she pregnant?

WHY DOES MY BRAIN INSTANTLY THINK THAT?

FUCKING BRAIN. Why is this the automatic news-related question
– the, *Say it brain, say it, you've said everything else* – the worst news-related question. The question that makes my heart feel full of soot.

What? X

Tell you later! X

I text Nicolette a time and a pub and then I put on 'Don't Get
Me Wrong' by The Pretenders and slide into a fantasy where I walk
into a sunny café where the song is playing and my mother and Art
and Kelly and Suzy are all there and I'm all, Oh hi, I just got back
from this brilliant trip where I won the equivalent of an Oscar for
journalism, and they all stand up and hug me and clap and we end
up having a celebratory brunch together and it is ASTONISHING
and inspiring how cool I am with everyone about everything.

A man comes through the carriage with a worried look on his
face. I pull off my headphones and sit up.

'Has anyone lost a black rucksack?' he says.

We all sit up.

'Black rucksack? Anyone?'

I look back down the carriage. Now, I want eye contact. I want
reassurance. We all do. How far away is this rucksack? Has anyone
looked inside it? Will we throw it off at the next station? Could we
not just throw it off now?

Two more people come through the carriage, the same look on
their faces. Plain-clothes traffic police? Plain-clothes Tube workers?

There is an announcement over the tannoy: 'Can the cleaner
report to receive a message. I repeat, can the cleaner report to
receive a message.'

It's obviously code.

'It's code!' I say. People nod at me, thanking me for my insight.
They are glad to be on a train with me, hurtling towards death.

Then nothing happens. The black rucksack isn't followed up.

When I get to my stop, part of me wonders whether I died an hour or so ago; whether the train exploded. And everything since has been some kind of dead-brain dream. I have thought this periodically throughout my life – mostly when I've been on public transport.

I should probably stick to cabs.

It starts to rain, so I wait for a bus at the bus stop. I'm just wondering how to document this – how to make it more exceptional, more meaningful, more like an actual moment in life, when my phone pings with an email and—

You know when you just *know*?

Hi.

Hi.

How are you?

Peachy.

I'm sorry you had to find out like that. It can't have been very nice.

Thank you for understanding. And being patronising. I appreciate it.

Can we please talk on the phone?

No. We barely did when we were together so what's the point in starting now?

To acknowledge our new relationship as friends.

Right-oh. So I suppose Suzanne knows we fucked last month?

I thought we were going to be cool about that?

People change their minds, Art. Often in the most inconvenient ways.

I just wish we could draw a line under the negativity and move on. I want you to meet Suzanne. I think you will like her. She's very kind.

Are you trying to make me feel better or worse, telling me that? Is her kindness testament to your goodness, or is it indicative of my future pleasure in her company?

Haha. I still like how you talk, Jenny.

Thanks?

Let me know when you are ready to talk properly, with me xx

I'll try x

Hope work is going okay? And I saw your mum is staying, hope that's going okay?

Of course

Now THAT I'd like to read about xx

Thanks for the encouragement

X x x x

DRAFTS

Art,
DO NOT LINE-OF-KISSES ME. That does not constitute a
sign-off. Oh thank you for bestowing your almighty kisses on
me – shame you could not be arsed to compose ACTUAL
WORDS, you illiterate blowhard.
Jx

ON THE BUS

I see a kid trying to use the window as a screen. He is two or three, in a little red mac. I watch him pressing and swiping across the misted-up glass, his finger-trails streaking through the condensation. I watch him become gradually more frustrated and confused as things pass behind the window, out of his control. His mother sits staring at her phone, unaware of his predicament. Eventually the kid gives up, and sits staring sadly out of the window as though it is just a window.

I feel his pain.

TABS

I open the front door to see a pile of bills on the mat, stretching up the hall. There are bills on the radiator shelf. How have I not noticed? Credit cards and god knows what. I can't bear to open them.

Nor can I bear to tell my mother I have been fired.

I find my mother asleep in the lounge, the TV on — some awful serial-killer drama blaring towards its denouement. *But nobody could have predicted what she'd find in the garbage* . . . A half-empty gin bottle is on the floor, where it has fallen from her hand. A glass is balanced on the arm of the chair. There are melba toast crumbs on a plate on her lap. The room otherwise is neat and tidy — it's like when they find incidents of spontaneous human combustion and there's a radius of charred destruction and, beyond that, disquieting normality. I found her once on the bathroom floor, unconscious, face down, her fingers flexed, her nails in the grouting, like she'd been trying to claw her way out.

Her laptop is there on the floor. I open it and see there are tabs open — tabs on all my social media. My Twitter, my Instagram, my columns, my practically defunct website.

I turn off the TV. She wakes up.

'Jenny! Sorry, I must have drifted off.'

I nod.

She collects her laptop from the floor. 'I've started to pack,' she says. 'I'll be out by nine a.m. tomorrow.'

I nod again

'Have you had a bad day, darling?'

'I really have nothing to measure that against any more.'

'Do you want a melba toast?'

I shake my head. 'I think I'm going to go out and meet my friend Nicolette for a few drinks tonight.'

She replies almost too quickly: 'Of course! You enjoy yourself! Here,' she fumbles around on the floor for her bag, her purse, and takes out a fifty-pound note – a fifty-pound note! Saints alive – and hands it to me. 'Get you and your friend a bottle of something nice on me.'

I sniff and take the money. 'Thank you.' Then a voice pops out before I can stop it. 'Will you be here when I get back?'

'Of course I'll be here! I'm not going until the morning, remember.'

I nod. I stand there, coddled in this knowledge.

'I took your advice, by the way. I went to see a therapist.'

I look at her. 'No way.'

'Way.'

'You said you didn't believe in therapy. You said you were too old. You said it made people worse.'

'All those things may well be true, but I took your advice.'

'And?'

'It was as I suspected. My mother messed me up but I also owe all my success to her. A poisoned chalice is still a chalice, Jenny.'

'I'll pass on the poisoned chalice, thanks.'

'Shame you don't get a choice.'

'Watch me.'

'She asked me about my worst memory.'

'Full on. No foreplay.'

'I started telling her about the death of my mother, and how I missed it by five minutes.' I look down. 'And then I realised that wasn't it at all. It was finding your suicide note.'

'You can stay a little longer, if you like. If that would be useful to you, I mean.'

'Would it be useful to you?'

'Yes.'

'Then I'll stay!'

My chest floods with warmth. She hugs me from where she's sitting and her head is against my stomach. I think about how when she was a foetus in my grandmother's womb she already had eggs inside her, and one of those eggs would become me. What would become three of us was there, in one body, all at once – like those Droste-effect pictures that show a girl reading a book with a picture on the book of a girl reading a book with a picture on the book of a girl reading a book with a picture on the book of a girl . . .

Mum,

I am sorry to do this at Christmastime, and I know the sight of my body in the bath is going to be a terrible thing to come home from the Bahamas to, I just thought it best to get it out of the way while you were away. I also thought New Year (New Millennium!), New Start – and what better time to have a complete life overhaul than now? Once the funeral's out of the way, you and Roger can crack on with your chic new life together. I just hope his wife understands. Once you tell her your daughter committed suicide she's bound to let you off the hook.

As for my reasons, let's just say I have come to feel desultory about my impending existence, and it's an attitude that is rather incompatible with life. You know what I can't tolerate? Consciousness. Specifically this consciousness. I'm hoping you're wrong about everything and I don't end up stranded in this consciousness for all eternity except with no body, because my body is the one part of me I actually like, apart from my thighs, and the second teeth on either side of my front teeth, and my shapeless feet and lack of discernible eyelashes and brows.

I read an interesting thing the other day about bees. In a honeybee colony, the queen bee rules while her daughters do nothing but work. They forgo the chance to have offspring of their own, despite being physically capable of producing sons. When the queen dies, the workers find an egg of suitable age and feed it royal jelly, resulting in a royal successor, but sometimes they don't succeed, leaving the colony queenless. It's a risk. They give it all up for the good of the hive. Imagine that kind of altruism.

I'm afraid I just don't have it in me.

So, farewell.

Jenny x

GRANMA SAID

'Oh, it's you two again, is it?'

'Hi, Granma,' I said. The day room was beige and maroon, like her nightgown. She ignored me. 'Where's my little dog?' she said. She meant Nathaniel (the spaniel).

'Nathaniel's fine,' my mother said.

This was a lie. The dog was dead.

Granma turned to me as though I was a pleasant stranger in need of advice. She gestured to my mother: 'She lies, this one. You've got to watch her.'

'Yes,' I agreed.

'Ever since she started doing all that stuff. I said to them all, I was the one born with a caul, but you don't see me flaunting myself to the bereaved.'

'I don't—' my mother began.

I looked around the room. It wasn't a big room but it was bigger than her bedroom – I hated it when we had to go and see her in there. The garibaldi biscuits and Imperial Leather talcum powder – *Imperial Leather*: in another universe it was a fetish mag for colonialists – all got me asking how I could ever enjoy an evening again. How could anyone?

'As for those cards,' Granma continued, 'they used to do it when they were little and I never paid much attention. Eleanor brought some home from a boyfriend one day and a whole troupe of them went up to the loft to use them.'

'That was a Ouija board,' my mother said, fluffing a cushion for no one.

'I heard screaming and went up there and there was a girl with a broken leg lying wailing in the corner.'

'Something broke her leg?' I said.

'No,' my mother said quickly.

'She already had the broken leg when she went up there,' said Granma. 'But her crutches had come alive and started hitting her. So they all said, anyway.'

My mother looked down.

'What?' I said. I had never heard this story.

'Still, she made an okay living out of it in the end. Not that I ever saw much of it.' Granma turned to me. 'You were supposed to get rich and look after me,' she said. 'When are you going to marry a rich man?'

'*I am a rich man*,' I said, quoting Cher.

'I was in *Coronation Street*,' my mother said.

'For one episode,' my Granma said. 'No good at putting yourself forward, that's why. Expects it all handed to her on a plate. Expects *them* to come chasing *her*.'

'I need you to sign something, Mum,' said my mother, and reached into her bag. She pulled out a small stack of stapled papers.

I looked at a woman sitting in a chair opposite. She was holding a baby doll and trying to feed it from a small plastic bottle. The doll didn't want to drink from the bottle, so the woman started rocking it instead.

I heard Granma say, 'Forget what you need. There's something I need to say to you, Carmen. Something I need to ask you.'

I turned around and looked at her, and for a second it was like she was the old Granma there – lucid as you like. Eyes that could split light.

My mother put the papers on the tray table and looked at Granma expectantly. 'What?'

There was the sudden, unmistakable stench of hot piss. My mother sat back. None of us looked at each other. I put my hand on Granma's back. Her spine felt like the end of an escalator, vertebrae rippling under rubber. She gripped her stick. 'I forgot.'

After a minute or so had passed, my mother placed the papers gently on the side table. 'You need to sign this so that we can sort the money to pay for this place.'

Granma looked at the form. 'I'll have the lamb.'

'No,' my mother said, 'it's not a menu. It's something for you to sign, about money.'

'Lamb,' Granma said, 'just put lamb. You're getting on my nerves, now.'

My mother handed her the pen. 'You need to sign it, Mum. Here.' She pointed with her finger.

Granma took the pen and diligently wrote the word 'Lamb' in the signature box.

'Oh no, that's not right!' My mother snatched up the form. 'Your name's not Lamb, is it? I'll have to get another form.'

Lamb's eyes were big and frightened behind her glasses.

'It's okay,' said my mother. 'We'll sort it.'

There was a tone in my mother's voice that made me feel sick with hope.

ALL MY CIRCUS, ALL MY MONKEYS

I meet Nicolette at eight in the cheap pub near Goodge Street with the stained-glass windows and stained upholstery to match. I'm wearing a 'Nostromo' T-shirt and an amber necklace. It's an outfit that I think suggests a rich internal life. My hair is done but not too done, and my black denim skirt is short enough to suggest tasteful but empowering nudity.

Nicolette arrives in a bad mood.

'What news from town, sister?' I cry.

'I've cracked my screen again,' she rages.

'Oh. Here, have some awful wine.'

'Thanks. Oh, it's even more awful than usual. I almost want to congratulate them behind the bar.'

'It's just so cheap, you can't argue.'

'You really can't. I also think something about it pleases me when the rest of my life is relatively tasteful.'

Nicolette puts her phone on the table. It is indeed very cracked.

'What happened?'

'Mood malfunction.'

'Ah.'

'So that's sixty quid even with insurance.'

I sigh. 'I have my own courtesy-phone debacle to deal with right now. Look. The fact we have to pay for all these devices is in itself outrageous. It's like a modern version of the window tax.'

'Oh my god, that's EXACTLY what it is. Charging me for my windows on the fucking world!'

This is how we have these times together. We drink and we riff in our own little echo chamber. We've even started calling it 'The Prosecco Chamber'. Gross, right? But here we are. I know that Nicolette has had as sheltered a life as me, devoid of any real hardship, which is depressing, although it does make the whole thing easier to work with.

I drink more wine and gag.

'So, how are you?' Nicolette says. 'I keep seeing his stupid photos everywhere.'

'You don't have to say that.'

'No, I mean it. They're everywhere.'

'I meant the stupid bit.'

'Oh.'

'You're a pal.'

'So, how are you?'

'Pretty awful. I got fired, had a fight with my oldest friend because she objected to me leaving her grown-up child in the street, and, worst of all, Art's seeing a woman I'm obsessed with online.'

Nicolette makes a sound like a human balloon withering and I am just so elated and relieved that someone finally gets the enormity of this. I put my hand on her arm. 'Thank you, Nicolette, for making that awful sound.' She makes it again. I thank her again. 'So in answer to your question, all I can say with any surety is that I am . . . *continuing*.'

'Well, that's something,' says Nicolette. 'I'm going round in circles. Or maybe it's a vortex, spiralling slowly inwards to its inevitable own obliteration. On my way here I walked past a place called Highcroft Mews and I had a flash of my future: gated suburban blocks of identical houses, clipped bushes, jet-washed brick. I thought to myself, *Someday I'm going to have an affair with someone who lives in a place like this. We'll share average bottles of wine and only fuck drunk. And the worst thing is, it'll feel like a break from the old routine.'*

'You're not even married.'

'It doesn't matter. I've always known that a dire, depressing affair is my ultimate fate. Much more than the marriage part.'

She goes to the bar. When she gets back I start telling a story about someone who says *I'm back in town!* at the point of orgasm. As I'm telling the story it dawns on me that it's actually *her story I'm telling back to her.* Fuck. This has happened to me before. Sometimes it's harder to back-pedal than others. I wonder whether I've got the sympathetic bias right. I'm telling it from the point of view of taking the piss out of the person who says *I'm back in town.* It's so hard to be spontaneous and thoughtful at the same time. This is why you're generally better off staying in and watching TV or interacting safely on the internet behind a semi-affected persona. The outside world demands too much reality. And I find reality stressful in the extreme. Reality doesn't give a person enough thinking time. It renders one ill prepared. For a moment, I'm fucked. I pull things round by telling her an embarrassing thing I once said after an orgasm: *Mmm, that's welcome!* If in doubt, self-denigrate.

'I know a story like that,' Nicolette says. She looks confused. 'What am I going to do about my phone? It's the fourth one this year. Did you know 15 per cent of phone users in the UK are operating with a cracked screen?'

'I believe it.'

'It's like they DESIGNED it to be painful, difficult and expensive. A glass phone! Fucking larks.'

We drink through the pain.

Hours later, we are in a private members' bar. Everyone loves a private members' bar until they're in one. I've been to the toilet twice to take cocaine and I think everyone in here is highly aware of this fact, particularly the pianist. I also possibly have a nosebleed, or a runny nose, one of the two. I feel genuinely fantastic. We have had a bottle of expensive wine because this is the kind of place that sells nothing else – a rash proposition when I am literally sinking into debt. Fuck it! We have thus far put three pictures each on Instagram, and one video of us flossing with a doorman.

'Let's promise not to regret these and delete them tomorrow,' Nicolette says. 'It's always such a giveaway when people do that. Let's OWN the social media fall-out.'

'Agreed.'

The wine slides down my throat. It is cocaine's throat now. It is cocaine's world.

'What did you fight about with your old friend?' says Nicolette. 'Kelly?'

'I haven't met Kelly, have I?'

'No. I don't think so.'

'I know who she is, though. I saw a picture of her online – she left a funny comment on a picture of yours so I clicked through.'

'Hm, yes, she does that.'

'She looks quite moody in her pictures. I'm generally scared of women with big fringes. They always seem more noble or judgmental, or both. She seems to wear a lot of dungarees and Breton tops.'

'She does love a Breton top.'

'What did you fall out about?'

'It's too involved to go into at this stage. But I think she might be leaving me.'

'Leaving you?'

'And London. The whole shebang.'

'God, I can't imagine leaving London. I am going to live in the city *forever*. I feel as though the capital is the perfect place to continue my studies of love and life. So many hearts, lost and hunting.'

'What's going on in your dating life?'

'Oh, it's a ride, for sure. You'll have to get on this! I'm thinking of changing my Tinder profile to men and women.'

'Why?'

'I'm sick of the men. I am increasingly sick of men.'

'Such an extreme response though, for a heterosexual.'

'I might not be a heterosexual.'

'Not even a sex tourist; a *sexuality tourist*.'

'What's wrong with tourism? Tourism is how you find out whether you want to emigrate.'

The next time I take stock of my whereabouts, I am in the smoking area of the same bar – a tiny New York-style black iron fire escape with a few ferns waving from the landings. Six or seven of Nicolette's media friends are with us. I cannot remember a single one of their names, but I am enjoying telling them what I think about everything very much and in that way they are my most treasured audience to date. I also find I have acquired new and abundant knowledge on matters such as globalism, juvenile correctional facilities, and the output of Radio 4. Someone asks me whether I am familiar with the work of Rembrandt. I say: 'Was he the one who wrote the theme tune to *Friends*?' No one laughs. I fear this is because few of them are familiar with the work of *Friends*.

Two hours later. Where am I now? A flat. There is music on – 'Blister in the Sun' by the Violent Femmes – and most people are dancing, apart from me and one man, who is bald and talking to me by a small marble side table covered in drug detritus. I suppose I am trying my best to look very, very infertile. I feel like Frankenstein – nose stuck to my head; leg in my armpit. It is dark but – oh god is that daylight outside the window? No, it's just reflected light, thank Christ – there is a piece of neon on the wall opposite that says CRYWANK in Tracey Emin font, bright pink. The bald man is called Konrad, I think, I *think*, but it doesn't matter because his current raison d'être is telling me why this is his favourite song ever and why he has chosen to put it on. It seems there is no end to his reason but really I can't wait for him to shut the fuck up so I can start telling him about MY favourite song, which is actually from this century. I nod, encouraging him – to finish and shut the fuck up. He goes on, and then it slips out at one point that he works as a hospital porter.

'I don't judge you for that,' I say. Mainly to just infiltrate the monologue.

'No,' he says, 'why would you?'

I say: 'Some of the most intelligent people I've known have worked as porters.' Is this true? Who cares!

'I'm from Poland originally,' he says.

'What's that brilliant fucking phrase,' I say, grasping for it, holding the conch – he looks annoyed as he tosses his head and says with me: '*Not my circus not my monkeys.*'

'Yeah,' he says. 'I really fucking hate that phrase.'

'Oh.'

'Yeah. Why do we not want to look after each other any more? My grandmother, who was a woman who taught me everything I know, said *it's all my circus and all my monkeys*. And I think we've really got to band together and sort out these monkeys because man, these monkeys are everywhere. When did loving other people more than yourself start to become such a bad thing? All this "self-care" bullshit is just about buying things. It's because society has let you down and you're burnt out, so you're going to throw money at the problem and reinforce the very thing destroying you.'

I have decided I like Konrad a lot. I also feel like I am struggling to compete, and I despise him for that. Imagine meeting someone at a party who is more intelligent than you. Surefire way to ruin your whole fucking night. 'How old are you?' I say. 'You're not in your twenties, I can tell.'

'How can you tell?'

'You're not dancing.'

'Neither are you.'

'I can dance. Look. Watch. You see? I've got moves. I've got shapes. I'm a motion wizard.'

'You can stop now because you have proved your point.'

'Thank you. I think you are younger than me.'

'How old are you?'

'Thirty-five.'

'Wait, what? Thirty-five? I was thinking more like thirty-one or two.'

I don't know whether the music actually stops or just feels like it stops and suddenly there are two other people in the conversation. *She's thirty-five? Fucking hell!*

'Oh no,' Konrad says. 'Really? No way. I never would have said that.'

'What? Why?'

'Oh no no no no no.'

'What?'

'You have to go home.'

'Why?'

'Do you have a husband? Partner? Kids?'

'No.'

'Do you want them?'

'Maybe.'

'You have to go home. You can't be doing this.'

'You can't send me home!'

Konrad looks at me like he is truly sorry for me. I say: 'Look, buster, you are the one who is almost completely bald. So. Who needs to go home? Not me. I think the bald person. Who votes for the bald person going home before me? Let's have a referendum on this.'

Everyone is looking at me, a little sadly.

Konrad is almost my age. Is this why he gravitated to me? I don't know whether he is bald by nature or design. It's not the kind of thing you can ask on a first meeting. It bothers me every time I look at Prince William, the recession of his hair to almost nothing, because I do view him as a contemporary for some reason. When Prince William is fully bald I will know that I have to stop going out, for good. But then – where is my own body and hair going? We've lost touch. It's doing its own thing, that's for sure. It has plans.

Nicolette comes over. 'What's going on? Are you okay?' She bats everyone away. 'She's had a tough day.'

I suddenly feel very weary – very weary indeed.

'Let me get you another drink,' Nicolette says.

'You know what, I don't think I can.'

'Don't let them send you home!'

'No, it's not that – it's just . . . I am all asunder, Nicolette.' I think of the sofa, and the faces of the people in the TV drama I'm watching, those friends waiting for me on Netflix. I think of a sandwich. I am shamefully, helplessly allured. 'Is it terrible that I would rather go home right now, Nicolette?'

'No. I mean, that's okay, if it's what you really want.'

'I have to confess: whenever we have a night out planned, I'm relieved when you cancel. I love seeing you, but I'm so . . . tired at the moment. There, I said it. When you're going out the night before we're due to go out a little part of me always hopes you'll get fucked up and feel dreadful so you have to cancel our night out. Or you'll get sick. Sorry. Or you'll realise you're too skint. Anything really. It's nothing personal, it's just I can't really do this. It doesn't make me happy. I can do a bar or a party for like half an hour, then I'm done. Do you hate me?'

'No, of course not.'

But she's making a face over my shoulder – is she? Oh god, is that daylight, now? When it gets light that's the really grim bit. And my mother will wonder why I'm so late, but at least she will be there in the morning and maybe she'll boil me an egg. No, not a boiled egg, I do not like the thought of that at all. Maybe pour me a cold sparkling drink that will refresh me and exfoliate my mouth. Yes, that would be nice. I swallow. I see that I have possibly been working very hard. I have been simultaneously trying to figure out the codes and rituals of a realm, an institution, whilst also trying to present myself as appealing. I feel very, very stretched and thin, like I might almost snap. I have been connecting, and connecting, and connecting. I'm like an algorithm system with feelings.

'Nicolette, I'm going to go now.'

And I go. The failed pseudo- (antisocial) party girl.

On the way home I eat a pizza so hard I feel each point stab the back of my throat. It is my throat again. Boy, is it. I find myself having to spit on the ground shortly after – a big cokey, tomatoey gob. A woman walking her dog stops and stares at me, disgusted.

'I have cancer,' I say.

'Oh,' she says, understanding.

It's not an outright lie. To be fair, I probably do, on some level. Most people do, after a certain age.

On the bus, pizza crumbs embedded in my skirt, I see a man who looks like Art would, old. He looks like a chamois leather thrown over a marrow. He moves his bags for me as I make to get off. He has learned how to be kind – I can tell by the pride he takes in it, this acquired skill. He is a social craftsman. I think: Time will take you too, Art, eventually. It will dampen your spirits. It will mock your desires. And you will be a better man for it. And I will be a better woman.

Emma Jane Unsworth

JUNK EMAILS

Hi! Just really wanted to reiterate how pleased I am about you and Suzy XXXX

I mean Suzanne

Floozanne

hahaha

Like. realy pleased so pleased

I do hope I can meet her son

Soon! Autocorrect makes drunks of us all!

Imagien if she had a son with you lol

I would be fine with tho

With it

I woud givei t my blessing

The blessed child

Speak soon! Xxxx

JUNK TEXTS

Hey Kel, how are you? X

Kelly?

Kellyyyyyyy

Keeeeeellllllllllyyyyyyyyyyyyyyyyyyyyyyy

BURNOUT

I go to look at Suzy's page but instead somehow find myself looking at Kelly's. I go through all of Kelly's recent posts, seeing where she's been. It strikes me, surely, somewhere deep around my solar plexus, that I have missed some major events in her life. Not just Sonny's birthday, but her birthday. Her mum's seventieth. A trip up north for her great-aunt's funeral. I look at who else she has been spending time with, who she is currently seeing as a more valid and mature person than I am. I look at who has been commenting on her posts. I see a comment I left on there ages ago, months ago – the last comment I left her, I think. On a picture of her doing a jewellery class with her mum, I have written:

HI HO SILVER!!!! WORK IT, YOU ABSOLUTE GEMS!!!! XXXXX

It is a comment I have obviously thought about a lot. The sight of my own rabid communication, the ECG spikes of exclamation marks, of my leaping emotions, is wearying.

Why am I looking at this now? Wearying my weary self with my own wearyingness?

I say it out loud. I say it right out of me. *This is ill behaviour. I am ill.*

214

THERAPY SESSION #2

The second therapist I saw, when Art's pictures had hit the big time – possibly *because* Art's pictures had hit the big time – listened straight-faced, even when I cracked jokes, and that put me off (*Is it protocol, to be dour?* I wanted to say), so I gabbled to fill the silence. I told her how I was scared and jealous of Art's success, about how I was sure he'd leave me now for someone famous and cooler. I told her how I saw women flinging themselves at him, sometimes otherwise respectable women, desperate to touch the hem, and that made me feel even sadder and more scared and I wasn't sure whether that was for him, or them, or me. After forty-five minutes had passed, I ran out of steam and material. She nodded sagely and said, 'I think that was very good work for today, Jenny. Same time next week?'

'I'm not sure – am I . . . meant to feel different?'

'Not yet. Give it time.'

Time was something I knew I didn't have much of. Time was already a fucking worry.

'Okay.'

I pulled on my coat. Picked up my handbag. As I stood, we shook hands, and she said, 'What's his name, by the way?'

If she'd have asked tentatively, I might have understood. But she showed such a lack of self-awareness that my trust in her evaporated in that instant.

'Whose?'

'Your partner's. The famous photographer!'

'Art Wilson,' I said, instinctively.

'I'll Google him!' she said.

I looked at her face, trying to ascertain whether she was joking, whether she was making an ironic reference to the exact cause of the problem. It became apparent that she wasn't. She was . . . well, there's no other word. The simplest of reductions. She was *excited*.

I blinked and bade her farewell.

I cancelled my appointment the following week, before the required forty-eight-hour notice period.

By text.

IN

THE

BIN

(ONE WHOLE DAY)

APP IDEA

Gin is not my friend, I realise for the hundredth time. But more than that, I need to stop using my phone drunk. When oh when will they create a breathalyser app that disables your phone when you're over the limit? A phone in the hands of a drunk person can do more damage than a car. I swear I'm first in the fucking queue to be liberated from this risk. There should be some kind of SAS service you can subscribe to that detects when you're about to use your phone fucked and sends out special forces who crash through the nearest window and wrestle you to the ground and prise your phone out of your stupid drunk hand and incinerate it in a portable incinerator. Then they force-feed you a pint of water and two ibuprofen and two paracetamol and a burger and put you to bed. I would pay for this service, why does it not exist? It's unthinkable it doesn't. Yet another example of technology being ahead of humanity.

Sometimes I feel like it would be safer to stay in and never go out or see anyone or communicate at all, just to be sure there's nothing to regret.

The day after Bin Day, I get up in the afternoon and cycle to the park. I steer my bike around a root-crinkled patch of tarmac. A teenage couple pass me. They're holding hands and having a stilted conversation. Their hoods are up. I hear myself go *Ah*.

Evening is coming. The path is banded with the shadows of trees.

Sometimes I could weep, quite tenderly, for the London childhood I never had. Then I remember the pollution problem. I sit on a bench and get out my phone, which I've had on silent, because that will show it.

Kelly has replied! (FINALLY.)

> Hey love thanks for your message. Bit tied up but I'll get back to you asap x

> Don't thanks for your message me – wtf????

Big wait. Two minutes. Then:

> I just need a little time away. Take care x

> Kelly?????

I look around in the park. There is nothing soothing. Everything is dead and dying and dirty. I look at Suzy Brambles' feed. And, horrors (seek and ye shall find), there's a new picture of Art and Suzy at a café. They are messily eating ice creams, is there anything better in life! This warrants several ice cream emojis and some starbursts. They're really going for it now, no holds barred. Jenny knows, so let's let rip. Fuck off. Fuck off both of you. And mostly fuck off ice cream. It's November. Has no one any self-respect? I've always believed that emoji use is a pretty good gauge of mania, and right now, from where I'm standing, Suzy is on the edge.

I leave a careful comment: *Looks delish!* With one emoji. A sane, simple yellow heart. Not as demanding as a red heart. Sort of more carefree.

Suzy does not like my comment.

I imagine them discussing my comment. Naked, post-coital, with espresso martinis. *So delightfully capricious wurhahhah . . .*

219

I wait ten minutes, and then I delete it.

I instantly regret deleting it.

I wonder whether I can retype it quickly and put it back or whether they will have noticed and see that I typed it twice. I don't want to look unconfident or weird.

But maybe I do want them to talk about me. I want to be in between them as they're walking along. I wonder whether he's giving her a hard time for using her phone.

I could always blame it on a bad connection. I've posted things twice by accident several times before. Well, once. It's feasible. But when – *when* would I get my chance to explain myself? Unless I put it in an email to Art, or would that seem excessive?

With every second that passes I feel more panicked. My mind incessantly shrieks: *It's now or never!* There's a good chance she didn't see it before I deleted it. Not everyone checks their comments every ten seconds. And if they do then that makes *them* the ones with the problem, does it not? Yes! This justifies it. If Suzy notices that I posted the same comment twice with two minutes in between, then SHE is the loser. Perfect.

I type it again.

I post it.

I look at it.

Oh god, I hate it.

I hate myself. I writhe inside. I feel uninhabitable. I need to bite something. Anything. Maybe my fist.

I notice that someone is looking at me from the next bench. They look away quickly into their burrito.

DRAFTS

BURRITOFACE,
DID YOUR MOTHER NEVER TELL YOU THAT IT IS RUDE
TO STARE?
REGARDS,
JENNY MCLAINE BA HONS.

LOOK NO HANDS

Hi Jenny I just happened to notice online that Art is with that Suzy person again, I think perhaps you do have cause for concern. Mummeeeeeeeee xxx

I'mon my bike please don't text me a out thia

So she's got her feet under the table

WHY DO YOU THINK IT IS IMPORTANT FOR ME TO HAVE THIS INFORMATION

She looks like a praying mantis crossed with Wednesday Addams

Stop

SOMEONE JUST ALMOST KNOCKED ME OFF MY BIKE

I'm just saying she got her claws in quick. We should probably go to the exhibition

I ALMOOST DIED HOPE YOU ARE HAPPY

Stop being dramatic

STOP TEXTING ME JESUS CRHIST I AM COMMANDEERING A VEHICLE

Can you pick up some lemons if you pass a shop?

WHAT DO YOU NOT UNDERSTAND ABOUT THIS
SITUATION

DRAFTS

Subject: To the woman in the Fiat 500 who cut me up on the corner just now

Dear Madam,

Huge thanks for almost knocking me off my bike, but even more for alerting me to your precious cargo with the prominent 'Baby on Board' sign. This piece of information is invaluable to me as another road user. I tend to smash willy-nilly into cars containing fully grown people. However, I make sure to drive exceptionally carefully behind vehicles such as yours, knowing that you are transporting The Future rather than just another worthless adult human.

BR,

Jenny McLaine BA Hons.

HI HI HI

In the corner shop I say *Hi* to the man behind the counter and then I examine the two fridges. I buy three lemons – all he has left – even though one is mottled with something unfortunate. I take a can of diet cola and a can of diet cherry cola because one thing – lemons – feels like too little to purchase. I don't want him thinking I'm using his shop in a trivial manner, because that sort of treatment can be demoralising, I know. I look at the cheeses. I pick up a packet of feta. I make an approving noise so that he knows that I like his feta. It's a small sound, somewhere between the word 'Nice' and just a 'Huh' – something like a high-pitched 'Nah'. I put the feta back – carefully, respectfully – because even though I am not going to buy it, I am not being dismissive of this feta. I want him to feel that. I look at a few other things, handle them, and make similar sounds of approval. Eeaorw. Aoooirw. Mmmmooooer. I want him to know that I like everything he has in here. He has pleased me with his choices at the warehouse, or the wholesaler, or wherever he selects his goods. He has done A Good Job. He is A Good Shopkeeper. As I pay I say, 'You have a wonderful shop.' I take my change and it jangles, just like me. Why do I want to look more nervous than I am, too? So he'll like me? Feel less threatened? I have got myself into a mindset where it's almost as though a display of nerves is a social compliment; not to show them is an insult. To be confident shows a lack of respect, somehow.

This whole thing is getting quite difficult to live with.

BACK AT HOME

my mother greets me in the hall.

'Jenny, are you all right?'

'I'm fine. Here are your lemons that almost killed me.' I hand her the bag. 'I hope they taste as good as near-death. One of them is rather shop-soiled.'

'Aren't we all, darling?'

She takes them. 'Are you really all right?'

'Yes! Godssake.'

'What are you doing tonight?'

'I have some freelance work to do and I'll probably just watch TV. Something soothing like a nature documentary.'

'Soothing? They send you berserk.'

'Maybe going berserk is how I relax.'

She takes a lemon out of the bag and inspects it. 'How are you feeling about Art's exhibition? Do you want to go?'

'No. Yes. Maybe. I mean, of course I do.'

Curiosity will get the better of me otherwise, I know it. How can I not meet her? In the flesh. The least fleshly of all beings. The wraith who has stolen my life.

My mother takes the lemons to the kitchen. I walk into the lounge. Her phone lights up on the table. Instinctively, I walk up to it and look. I defend myself thus: we are conditioned to look at a lit screen these days, are we not?

226

It's a message from Art.

I peer at it, confused.

Is it my phone? Have our phones somehow got mixed up and she has brought my phone? My brain scrambles for an explanation.

No. It is her phone. Her obscene designer case with the magnetic clasp.

The message says:

> I am heartbroken too Carmen but this really is the way it
> has to be x x

I stare at the words. I grab the phone and unlock it. Her passcode is my birthday.

I open the messages and scroll through. She has been texting him since I told her. I scroll and scroll.

> I just need
> to understand xxx
>
> Maybe you need to talk to Jenny x
>
> She hasn't talked to me for 20 years xxx
> NO ONE EVER THINKS ABOUT THE IN-LAW XXX
> She loved you when you were a nobody how can you
> abandon her now xxx
> Please take her back Art PLEASE XXX
> I know she's hard work but it's not her fault. She's always
> been difficult but I still love her xxx
> I see a bright future for you two, I always did.
> The true mark of a man comes out in the end doesn't it.
> They all warned me about you xxx
> Just miss you so much xxx

There are reams of them. Reams. Swinging from needy to abusive and back again.

My insides churn. Now, I see it all so clearly. Is it any wonder I am alone and anxious when this – this duplicitous *fiend* – has raised me?

SENT ITEMS

Subject: Column idea

Hi Mia,
I wonder whether you might consider this idea for a column?
My mother has moved in with me and it's a complete nightmare.
How about I do a weekly expose of how hideous it is? The
primal female relationship, skewered.
Best,
Jenny

INBOX

Subject: Re: Column idea

Jenny,
If you can crank up that skewered to crucified, you have your-
self a gig.
M.

Subject: Re: Re: Column idea

Mia,
Of course! You've got to fight pain with pain.
Jenny.

EXHIBITS A AND B

I get ready in my room. I think, what would Suzy Brambles like out of my clothes? A long black skirt and good boots and a ruffly blouse. I cover my body, layer by layer, not looking until it is dressed. My own nakedness is a historical fact to me.

When I am ready I wander along the hall towards the sad back room with the draughty window. The house creaks around me. The complaining crackles of the pipes and the floors. Familiar and unfamiliar sounds. For the first time, I feel the house's loneliness. A wintry sort of longing. My mother is in Sid's old room. Also the room of something that was not to be.

My mother is doing her vocal exercises. I peer in. What was once a big, bare space is now a messy, pleasant room. There is a tapestry throw over the bed. On the bookshelves are various objets d'art, French-sounding perfumes, powder puffs. There's a Cow & Gate formula tin, one of my old ones, that she keeps samples of beauty products in. She is half naked, on the bed, her back to me, sitting on a towel. She is wearing the 'quick-drying' pink towel turban she always wears when her hair is wet. She stops noodling when she sees me. She puts on a hotel bathrobe from *The Shelbourne, Dublin*. As she changes, I ogle her body the way I have always ogled it – with wonder, gratitude, fear, and a profound self-reflexive humiliation. Her lower back and thighs are clawed with fading red stretch marks that, if I'm not careful, I might start to romanticise.

'You kept that old tin! Why?'

'It's as good a receptacle as any. Just because all of your shit is in a cloud, darling.'

'It's not. A lot of it is in your garage.'

My childhood and teen years are chronicled in six or seven boxes in her double garage. Polaroids and airline tickets, soft toys and plastic tat, paperclips and hairgrips shoaling like krill. Tax receipts, key rings, snapped candles in whisky bottles. The fall-out of every ending. The episodes of my life set in amber. I have moved from mammal to mammal, like a flea.

'Not any more,' she says, starting to apply her primer. 'I had a clear-out.'

'What?'

'I skipped it. Sorry, darling, I applied the six-year rule. If you haven't needed it in six years, it can probably go.'

'Those were my old school books! My A-level files!'

'You did all right on them, didn't you?'

'In spite of you! You never respected my work!'

'Ditto.'

She moves and I catch a scent of her coconut body butter – the same brand for thirty years now. She starts on her foundation, smoothing it over her cheekbones and eye sockets. She overplucked her eyebrows in the seventies and has been drawing them in ever since in a thin Garbo arch. There are two gin and tonics on the dresser.

I sniff. 'One of your eyebrows is higher than the other today.'

'Eyebrows are sisters, not twins, darling.'

I stare hard at her face some more. And some more.

'Look, if you're that bothered about those files and books, you should have said one time when you were home.'

Home. The word still presents itself, ludicrously. I am thirty-five years away. 'Away' rather than 'old', that's how it feels sometimes.

I shake my head. 'Don't worry about it.'

'Let's have a gin.'

'It's very early. We should watch it.'

'I have a very good relationship with all intoxicants,' she says. 'Much healthier than any human relationship I've ever had. I've never had a comedown I couldn't handle. Never had a hangover I couldn't talk myself through.'

'Good for you. They finish me off for days, now. I obviously didn't inherit that resilience from you.'

She daubs bronzer up her cheeks. I pass her a gin and sip delicately from the other glass.

'Are you almost ready?' I say. 'I don't want to be late.'

'What – don't tell me you're ready? Are you just going like that?'

'As you see.'

'You seem . . . agitated, darling. Are you agitated?'

'Maybe a little. It's understandable, don't you think?'

'Well, drink up. Good girl. Now, why don't you let me lend you something to wear.'

'Because I am two sizes bigger than you. Why do you think we have the same bodies? We haven't been the same size for a long time now. Why are you labouring under this delusion? God, this is strong.'

'It's medicinal. We should have two. You could wear a belt.'

'I like what I'm wearing!'

'Want me to do your make-up?'

'No, thank you.'

'You should look good.'

'I do look good.'

'You could look better.'

'The last time you did my make-up I looked like the Babadook.'

'It was a smoky eye!'

'I didn't ask for a smoky eye! Who wants a goddamn smoky eye? It's not 1996.'

'It's a classic look '

'I am not classic, I am modern.' I say: 'I am so modern it hurts.'

She says, 'Even though you don't want to be with Art, it is important you look better than you have ever looked in your life before.'

'That is just a disgusting terrible cliché, and you should know it.'

'That may be true, but I'm sure Suzy is going to be making an effort.'

Once, when I was comparing myself to a dark-eyed friend, my mother said: *There are some people who can wake up in the morning and look good and you are not one of those people, Jenny, but when you do yourself up you're as good-looking as anyone.*

I sit down at the dresser. 'Okay,' I say, 'but if you over-smoke me I'm not going at all.'

'Fine. Now, don't smile.'

As we stand waiting at the Tube station, I look online to see if Suzy and Art are preparing, but they are giving nothing away. I look at people I know they know and might be there, but nothing. No clues. I should be a lot better at waiting, since I spend so much of my time doing it.

I take the crook of my mother's arm as we get on the Tube. Walking with her is like steering a full shopping trolley. We sit down. She says: 'The last time I took the Tube these PHENOMENAL ACROBATS got on.'

'Shh,' I say. 'You're being too loud. No one talks loudly on here.'

'Oh, no one gives a monkey's what I'm saying, least of all you.'

'Shhh!'

A man next to us laughs. Seeing this as active encouragement, my mother gets louder.

'Not everyone is interested in our conversation and lives!'

'He is!' I hiss. 'He just laughed.'

The man straightens his face and gets out his phone.

Another man gets on at the next stop and walks past us and down the carriage. He has no top on. His chest hair gleams. His nipples look like baked beans. I look away. The man next to us looks away. 'Well,' my mother says, 'the things you see when you've not got your gun.'

The man next to us guffaws.

My mother leans towards me. 'I'm trying to make you laugh,' she says.

'Why?'

'Because I can hear your nerves jangling.'

'That's just my bracelets.'

'My proud girl. I'm proud of you.'

'Don't say things like that now, for god's sake!'

'Sorry, darling.'

We sit in silence the rest of the way.

At Embankment we get out and walk towards the bridge. Two women dressed as hot nuns walk past. It strikes me that I haven't seen a nun in ages. It's like even God's been avoiding me.

DRAFTS

Subject: A request

Dear God, or whoever picks these up,
Please let my death be comical. Please let it be the sideways
spring off the trampoline into the unsuspecting mouth of the
yawning hippopotamus. Please let people be applauding before
they realise there's been a terrible accident.
Thanks,
Jenny McLaine (CHRISTENED)

GOOD FAMOUS PEOPLE

Art and I once went for dinner with an American pop star who Art had shot album artwork for. He was passing through London, as American pop stars do. Ray Brazier. We had dinner at a swish place off the Strand. I dressed up, course I did. I even wore Spanx under my satin dress – god knows what possessed me, I never usually subjected myself to such things, but I must have felt the occasion called for it. I was misguided. They cut into my thighs viciously, and the hems kept poking out when I sat down. I was conscious of them, especially when Ray Brazier decanted himself into the restaurant (late) wearing nothing but a sly smile and a loose purple kaftan. He stank of weed. The really famous didn't have to try – I knew that from doing celebrity profiles; from Art's slow but sure slide into huffy, comprehensive self-acceptance. Makes sense, really. They've done their trying, haven't they? And there's nothing – *nothing* – a famous person loves more than another famous person (ideally, another famous person who is *slightly more famous* than them). I stood out like a sore thigh.

'Oh, hal-*lew*,' Ray drawled – soooo satisfyingly Californian. He sat down and raised an eyebrow. 'Look at you tew.'

Art was wearing a suit. Nevertheless, he didn't flinch. He gracefully straddled worlds – the high and the low, the smart and the casual – talking about his latest shoot with a band in the mountains, and another he was doing for an Icelandic film director. Ray chuckled and marvelled and proffered his own latest stories, amongst the olives and breads and butters (*Would you like some water, for the table?* the waiter asked. I almost said, *Yes — and some accolades. Bring some more over, would you? We don't have nearly enough over here . . .*). Instead, I sat there, quiet — too scared to speak in case I sounded stupid, or worse, mundane — discreetly (not discreetly) yanking my Spanx periodically back under my dress. They asked the waiter's name and visibly committed it to memory and then used it at every opportunity like Good Famous People, who acknowledged the little men. I caught them, both of them, having a moment as they perused the menus (Ray had the duck, since you ask) and they sighed in time, laughed and shrugged at each other. They were both in the *New York Times* and here they were, together, in the flesh. It was so . . . *pleasing*. They could hardly believe it themselves.

NO photos, Art had said before we left the house. He was quite strict about it.

I was so alone, in my big body, with all that breath. I looked at my phone under the table for most of the meal and smiled benignly whenever I looked up. At the end of the meal, as we said our good-byes, Ray had clearly forgotten my name. 'Je-*mima*?' he said eventually. Well, I wasn't going to relieve him. 'Jezebel,' I said. And I let my Spanx slide down as I waddled to the door.

Back at ours, we drank tea in the lounge. Art said: 'You were quiet tonight.'

'I was just listening.'

'You were looking at your phone. I bet Ray thought you had narcolepsy. Your head kept dropping.'

'I didn't feel I had much to add to the conversation.'

'You just sound jealous, now. Who are you, Jenny, between these parameters you batter?'

I think he was right. My ambivalence about life. About people.

About everything. Art saw straight through it to the nothingness beyond: the nothingness that was me. The many flying fragments.

He sighed. I sighed. The elephant in the room trumpeted.

'Listen, is it really really okay?' he said.

I looked out of the window, across the street, into the window of the ground-floor flat opposite. A man was often there in his kitchen, pottering around. He was there now, making a hot drink. We had never looked at each other directly but I felt connected to him in that way we often do in cities: by proximity, by similar living spaces and activities. I had fantasised about going over there, pressing his buzzer, walking into his flat and fucking him against his cooker, looking back out through his kitchen window and across to my lounge, straight into the eyes of Art.

I said: 'Define okay.'

'I guess I might just feel like you're starting to resent me.'

'Resent you about what?' I mean. Bless me.

He looked at me. 'The baby thing.'

I wondered whether to say it. I thought of my options in the quickfire way I always do – down every avenue like a rocket, to each conclusion and back again and down the next, testing each hypothesis, a series of blistering speculations. For some reason I decided to be brave. I said, 'I just know that we have both refused to budge but in that, it's my desire that has been pushed down. How is that?'

'Because yours is the thing rather than the not-thing, and the thing is too much of a risk.'

It was a prepared answer, I could tell. Our conversations had been going round and round.

Why should I back down?

Why should I?

Why should I?

But how?

How do you know you want one?

How can you be sure?

We could have gone round in circles a lot longer, I suppose. If we were younger, easier, less proud. All I was left with was: 'I DON'T FUCKING KNOW. I'm sorry if that isn't good enough. I'm afraid it just has to not be good enough. You know how sometimes you just have to start walking to see which way the blob is going on the map? That.'

'Why are all your analogies about phones?'

'Oh for god's sake.'

'You need to be a lot clearer on this if you want me to understand, Jenny.'

'Well, I don't know 100 per cent whether I want one, but I want to keep the possibility open.' *I feel rushed and limited and very mortal.* I said: 'Do YOU feel that you've interrogated things fully?'

He looked frantic, then. 'Don't pin me down on this!'

'You're the one pinning me down, asking impossible questions about resentment! I'm not a fortune-teller!' *I'm a fortune-teller's daughter.*

He nodded and looked out over the street at the man in his kitchen. He was still making a cup of tea. For all I knew, Art had been having similar fantasies about him. And then Art said: 'I just don't want us to get to our fifties and you be resenting me. That's all.'

'I promise you I won't let it get to that.'

'But how do you know, if you're not a fortune-teller?'

'Maybe I have a little of it in my DNA.'

Art looked at me and said, with a horrible gentleness: 'I don't want this to become a point of self-torture, because neither of us have time for that.'

'Oh, I always make time for self-torture.'

MY MOTHER

and I walk towards the gallery. She takes my hand and I let her.

'You're not off the hook, by the way, about binning my school files.'

'You really should have said if they were so important.'

And then I see the milling crowd through the glass windows. I tell myself to be strong. To walk tall. That's it. Hold yourself together. Walk like a man. I am Ripley in the lift with the flame-thrower. I can do this.

We step into the spacious gallery. I always hated galleries and could never tell Art, but they give me an instant migraine, like shopping malls and churches. It's the pressure of a building with intent. My mother takes two glasses of wine off a tray and hands me one. I drink half of it. I can feel the gin inside me, looking for a friend. It finds the wine. They hit it off. My head is a party. I look around at all the people and for a second I am happily lost – and then I feel the darkness of their clothes and the situation. It is inevitable I will see Art – the one my soul dreads and seeks (there's always one at any given time) – any second, even if I try to talk to my mother, even if I pretend to smile at a stranger, even if I look for the bar or the toilet when I do not want the bar or the toilet or maybe I do want the toilet, even if—

Now. Look. There.

STILL

LIFE

I take him in – hunched and shaven-headed, the warlock he always was. And, next to him: her. Perched on a stool, pinching the stem of a glass of red, she is like a buzzard in a distant tree – elegant, solid, rare, doubted-at-first, and then: THERE.

She is smaller than she looks on my phone.

I take a moment, on my own, bent over with my hands on the top of my knees. I breathe deeply. A few yogic lion breaths.

My mother says, 'There's Art!'

I stand up. Straighten myself.

'Where? Oh, yes. There he is.'

'Let's go over.'

Art jumps up as we approach. 'Hello! Gosh, I didn't think you'd come! It's so great that you've come!'

We should not have come. I look down at the floor. Then I realise I do not want Suzy seeing me looking at the floor in case she reads too much into it, so I look at her. Except I cannot look at her. Especially not when she is looking at me so . . . vibrantly. I look down again.

'Your hair!' says Art. 'It looks *great*.'

'It does not.'

'It doesn't,' says my mother. 'Well, look at this!'

Art says: 'Jenny, Carmen, Suzanne. Suzanne, Carmen, Jenny.'

My mother is straight in there with the double kisses. I look at Suzy.

Art says: 'Suzanne has been dying to meet you.'

Suzy says: 'He talks about you all the time.'

She says this, to me, to my face, in real life. I realise I have never heard her speak. Her voice is soft and sonorous and all the things my voice is not. Reality is so discourteous, don't you think? I have a sudden wild fantasy where Suzy takes me by the hand and we run towards the river, laughing, everyone watching – *who are they, these mystical nymphs?* – and we strip and jump and swim naked together in the cold but refreshing water. We start to swim away to a far, foreign land.

Art says: 'Carmen! So glad you could make it too. It has been too long.' He looks at my mother meaningfully but then I don't know whether I am just trapped in a maze of meaning right now. Everything is so maxed out with meaning.

Suzy says: 'Art tells me you're a journalist. How exciting.'

I am not prepared for this interview. I say: 'More of a columnist, really.' She nods. The air around us bristles. 'So,' I say, 'what is it you do?' The question catches in my throat.

She smiles, looks down, modest. 'Bits and bobs. Art said you follow one of my accounts on Instagram. That's kind of you.'

'What's your name again?'

'On there? Suzy Brambles.'

I look as though I am trying to place it. *Suzy . . . Brambles, you say? B-R-A . . .* 'Oh, yes, I think I do know you on there!'

'Yes,' she grins. I grin.

It is all so superlatively congenial. The tension is at critical mass.

I say, 'I think you might have followed me, too. Until recently.'

'Did I?' Her brow buckles, almost convincingly. She is choosing to play this game, and I must play along. I decide that maybe I can turn this whole situation around – from extreme discomfort to blissful solace – when I convince her to start following me again. In fact, I will not leave this place until it is so. I relax a little. In a way, it's what I've wanted for so long: An Audience with Suzy Brambles.

I say: 'What kind of bits and bobs do you do?'

'Arty things, mostly. Also I teach French to underprivileged children.'

French. My only B at A-level. Now I do know, categorically, that France has always had it in for me. I wonder if she speaks Frenchly to Art when they're—

'You've travelled a lot, then?' my mother says.

'Not as much as I'd like.'

'Are you from London?' I ask.

'Suzanne could not be more London,' says Art. 'We just spent the weekend at one of her mother's places, in Belgravia.'

Places. I want to whistle. My mother does.

'And I understand you're from Lancashire?' Suzy says.

'A long time ago.'

'I'm still there!' my mother says. 'I'm just down visiting and helpin' out.'

Helpin' out! Dear Christ. Like she is some hokey Texan mom.

I look at Art's arm. His tattoos.

His skin.

WE'D GONE

out for drinks, to talk. It pained me, but I also felt sort of exhilarated by my own proximity to emotional danger. Like I was prodding my own parameters. I was wearing a different perfume to seem altered and unfamiliar. I'd replaced most of my clothes and perfumes anyway, after.

As the night wore on, we moved outside to smoke more thoroughly. We graduated from small to large wines. Whisky chasers. I was shitfaced, spectacularly. Adrenaline held me together, kept me upright, kept me talking. We discussed another exhibition he had been offered. His ideas. His travel plans. Then it came to peeling-off time and neither of us wanted to go. So, one look led to another, we fumbled through the apportioning of suggestion, of potential blame and power, and, subliminally, via an off-licence and a taxi, he ended up back at our old house. He went straight in. I took a deep breath and followed.

I saw him looking around the lounge. There was our plant, 'Robert'. The record player. The TV. Everything, still existing, without him, so blasé. There was the sofa with the waxy patch on the back where his head sweated when he played video games. I looked at it and felt like I could be forever fond of it, which felt somehow magnanimous. Everything seemed to hum in his direction. *Hi hi hi, hi hi.* I thought of Nick Cave's 'objects and their fields' – everything with its own shape and potential. Everything with its magnetic history. There were – literal – gaps where he'd been:

spaces on the walls that had once held his photos. I saw Art looking at those spaces, and I felt like I understood. This was his dream, and my dream, somehow; our narcissistic ideal: to be adored with zero pressure. To leave a gaping hole in which we could be loved.

Art said, 'You've hardly looked at your phone all night. Impressive.'

I'd wanted to. I'd been dying to get a surreptitious shot of us both together and post it, to prove we were still friends. But it felt too jarring. Too slapdash. I had a point to prove that was bigger than my reputation, even. The point was: my body can still kill you. He'd walked away, I pulled him back. Through fucking him, I could use his body to leave my body. The chastity I had been preserving had been waiting for this moment. I surveyed the size and shape of him and I thought, *Why do you get to walk around like a free agent? We'll see about that.* The stage was set.

Rekindling an old romance, even for a few hours, is a byzantine affair. I'd almost kissed him in the cab, but was enjoying the tension too much: that small window of time when you know that it is *on*, that it is indubitable, but there's also a slim chance the world or the vehicle could blow up in the meantime. It's the Christmas Eve of hooking up.

In the lounge, Art sat down. And very nearly put me off.

'I know this must be very strange for you, me being back here.'

'Strange for me?'

'I know it must be harder for you, out there. You're such a catch, though, Jenny.'

Reader, I fucked him anyway.

I straddled him on the sofa – clumsy at first and then all-encompassing. He hadn't shaved in days and the stubble was invigorating. I knew exactly how to put my lips on his lips, precisely how to put my tongue into his mouth. He stiffened.

He had lost weight. There were nubs where no nubs had been previously. There were juts and corners. I kissed them all. I reacquainted myself with his penis. I took my time. I didn't want him to go down on me because it made him feel too far away.

He fell asleep in my arms, in our old bed, that too-big bed that had been too big before he moved out. I felt him take his penultimate pre-slumber breath, a big hard deep one, and then relax on the outbreath – a huge sigh, like a child does after they've been sobbing.

I lay awake, listening to him breathing.

We woke up the same way. 'Babes in the wood,' I said, and he laughed, and his breath was foul, and I didn't care. It was his old foul breath and it would be coming out of him until the wrinkles on his face sank into trenches and I would breathe it in and out and it would take me closer to the inevitable rushing personal death of myself in a world of unwelcome. Sunlight spilled through the blinds. His toe ticked against my heel. I wondered whether we would have sex again. I wondered whether I should allow myself to want to. I wondered whether I just wanted him to want to. He got up to make coffee.

As I was sitting on the toilet, I felt around inside the pockets of his jeans, which were on the floor, and found a black kirby grip. I looked at it for a while, thinking about time and how no one is ever anyone's.

I got fully dressed because that felt the least presumptuous thing to do. We sat down together at the too-big wooden table in the kitchen. I picked up a teaspoon and stirred my coffee but I didn't put milk in. I was still harbouring a wild desire to seem different; to seem new. Black coffee was a start.

He said: 'So I have a date tonight.' Then he laughed. 'It's sort of depressing, isn't it? The futility of romance.'

The clock on the wall ticked. A bird outside chirped. I realised how tightly I was holding my teaspoon. My index finger was white and bloodless.

'Yes!' I laughed.

He left in a breeze of fineness.

DRAFTS

Subject: [No subject]

Dear Art,
You cunt.
Jenny

'FUNNY'

Suzy says, 'how Art and I are both photographers.'

'I take photographs, too,' I say. 'Recreationally. I am a recreational photographer.'

'We all are, these days,' says Suzy. 'I'm lucky I can make 220k a year out of my humble little snaps. With the right promotional attachment.'

My mother's head rolls round on her neck and back again. 'Excuse me?' One of us says it.

'That's right,' says Suzy. 'It's nuts, really.'

My heart is crashing. My brain is crashing. Someone turn me off and on again. And then I see the opportunity. What a beautiful fiction I could cannibalise from this terrible pain . . . I pull my phone out. 'Do you mind,' I say, 'if I get a photo of us all? I always do this when I meet interesting people. To prove I still have an interesting life. Being over thirty, I mean! Haha!'

Art looks at me unusually. I almost can't believe my own behaviour but I have nothing to lose now, literally nothing. I hold my phone up for the selfie. I don't even care that I'm at the front, in potato position. This is pure gold. They are all mine now, captured in my little memory box. I move to take the shot, to seal the box.

'No,' Suzy says, ducking out of the way, 'no, sorry. I'm quite careful about privacy. And besides, tonight's all about the work!'

'You can see it,' I say. 'You can authorise it.'

'No, I don't think so,' says Art. 'Let's just get to know each other, shall we? Let's be friends first, facilitators later.'

'Hahaha!' says Suzy, relaxing.

I put my phone back in my pocket, chastised.

'I have to be extra careful because of Clemency,' says Suzy. 'And please don't repeat her name elsewhere as we are keen to protect her privacy. We have an Instagram account just for her with just a picture of praying hands as the avatar. That's all the world gets of her.'

'Is Clemency a dachshund?' I say. 'No, don't tell me, Italian greyhound. Did you get the dog to look like the dog? I have a theory about this.'

Suzy is looking at me oddly. So is Art. Do I sound like a stalker? I don't want to sound like a stalker.

My mother says, 'Oh.' My mother says, 'Ah.' My mother says, 'Jenny, I remember something I needed to talk to you about regarding something urgent, come with me now . . .'

I brush her off. I am enjoying my wine and dog chat with Suzy B.

'How's work, Jenny?' Art says.

'Great.'

Suzy says, 'Art showed me a few of your articles. I particularly loved the one about being big spoon for a change.'

'Thanks, yeah, they're usually a lot more political than that.'

'I love your nineties smoky make-up, by the way. I've been meaning to try that, but I never really wear make-up.'

'Don't you?' says my mother. She looks at Suzy closely.

'No. All au naturel! I suppose I might have to change my tune when I hit thirty-three or thirty-four. But I'm only twenty-eight, so, you know, I have time.'

I want to say to Suzy, *Let's not do this, you and I. Let's not be part of the deforming sexual competition.*

'I did Jenny's make-up,' my mother says. I want to throttle her. 'We're all in the creative industries. It's a lot of maintenance.'

Suzy says: 'We are all about natural beauty here at the show.'

'Nature is not beautiful,' says my mother. 'Nature is the ugliest thing of all. Mother Nature is a misogynistic bitch. You just have to look at childbirth to know that.'

'I'm very interested in this,' Art says. 'Tell me more, Carmen.'

Suzy laughs again, more of a titter. I do what I think is a silent impression of her but it actually comes out as a squeak. I cover my mouth and pretend it was the beginning of a strange cough. My mother tries to catch my eye but I expertly avoid her. I down the rest of my wine and take another from a passing tray.

'Art tells me you're a psychic-medium,' says Suzy, to my mother.

'I used to be an actress,' my mother says. 'I have trodden the boards.'

Suzy smiles politely.

'Now she just goes for the board of producers,' I say.

Suzy roars. Like the lion of Great Britain. Like one of those big ones, by the Thames. 'You're so funny!' says Suzy. 'Just like Art said! So delightfully capricious and contradictory.'

I make a laugh-shape with my mouth, but I am stricken. Is this what I have become: an anecdote he recounts in bed – something that they can both titter about? I am not that small or tragic. Am I? This is the version of me that Art wants me to be – and she does too, on some level. They both want me to fade into a safe, defined dot, receding into nothing on the road behind them. So they can look back and go – *Is that . . . ? Ah. No. It's just a speck of dust on the lens.*

I look at Suzy – at her bird-like face and scrupulous restraint. The water in Suzy's inner bowl is a millpond.

I have almost finished my second glass of wine. At the bottom of the glass is freedom.

'Oh, I almost forgot,' Art says. 'We must make a plan to give you back your cups and saucers.'

I frown.

'So adorbs!' says Suzy.

They both look at me, like I am an enchanting dog. 'Jenny used to throw these wonderful parties.'

'You said,' says Suzy, still smiling.

I shrug. 'It was just some mulled wine and hot punch. Look, I really don't want them back. Just give them back to charity.'

Art opens his mouth to speak but then a little girl runs up to us. I look at her, this lost child. She stares at Suzy. 'Mummy, I need the toilet.'

Suzy reaches for her bag. I look back to the little girl, and see she has the same haircut, the same face.

'You can go,' says Suzy. 'Just check in with me straight after, okay?'

I stare, perplexed. The little girl runs off.

'Kids,' says Suzy.

I stare. 'Yes,' I say, 'they are.'

My mother says, 'Well, how nice this has been! See you soon!'

I do not move. I keep staring at Suzy.

'I know,' Suzy says, 'people are always surprised at my . . . situation. I do try and hide it mostly. Motherhood doesn't define me. I mean, I'm glad I've done the procreation thing, but it's not really how I want to be *seen*.'

'Mm.'

'And Art is so great with her. It was her birthday last week and he bought her a stack of presents. He dotes on her. He's a natural. He makes everyone feel seen and valued. Are you okay, Jenny?'

'Yeah I just have to nip out.'

I run fast through the gallery – and outside, I puke, heartily. It's mostly bile. Slick fluoro-yellow. Nice clean edges. Rope-like, almost. *Rapunzel, Rapunzel* . . . Ten seconds or so of silken unspooling, culminating in a single dry retch, unproductive.

As I turn around, wiping my mouth, I see my mother and Art waiting by the gallery door. I point at him. It is not dignified to have a row outside an art gallery at 7 p.m., but here we are and believe me I am going to go for it.

I shout: 'You know, Art, when you said, "Fuck the establishment" I never thought you meant *literally*.'

He blinks at me. His fuck-you blink. Some people have a power stare but Art has a *power blink*.

I cross the street. Suzy appears. With child. I move towards them. 'I know you want me to give this my blessing, so that is what I am going to do,' I say. 'I'm going to be the bigger person here. You have my blessing.'

'We don't need your blessing,' she says. She looks at Art. *Yep. Just like you said. Crazy.*

'Maybe women everywhere need to make a deal to not hear their predecessors bad-mouthed,' I say to Suzy. 'When my next boyfriend – should such a thing happen again – tries to tell me that his ex was crazy, I'm going to say, *Was she really crazy, or did she just get sick of pandering to your fads?* Because I think the answer will be interesting.'

'Hey,' says Art. '*Hey*.'

Suzy says, 'I know it must all still be pretty raw for you and that's why you sound like a conspiracy theorist. But I want you to know, I'm not mad about it. You just strike me as a person who is quite loose and lost.'

I swallow. 'Well,' I say, 'that's the opposite of how I am. Neither of you know me at all.' I turn to Suzy. 'Listen. He'll just be telling the next one *you're* crazy in a few years, because this is what men do. They make women pass the baton of crazy.'

Suzy shakes her head. 'Art is a feminist.'

I look at Art. 'Thank you.' My mouth is saying it on behalf of all of womankind. My eyes are saying it on behalf of My Disbelieving

A-hole. 'You've started laughing with just the bottom half of your jaw,' I say to him. 'Like a ventriloquist's dummy.'

'You're just being vindictive now,' Art says. I look in his eyes. There is nothing of him in there as he says this. He is Art imitating Life.

'And please stop leaving comments on my posts,' says Suzy. 'It's inappropriate.'

I punch the air and scream: 'I KNEW YOU FUCKING KNEW ME!' I look at Art. 'VOILÀ!' Then I regret speaking a French word because of Suzy's perfect French.

'I think I wouldn't mind so much if you weren't so . . . sales-y.'

'Sales-y?'

'You are quite sales-y, yes.'

'This from the woman who has her name on a black scented candle from Bergamot Brothers, the UK's foremost scented-candle-makers. "The Suzy". I even fucking bought one. It's going in the bin now. Why didn't you just mute me? Or did you want me to know?'

'It felt inappropriate to continue following you.'

I stare at her and try to split her with my compound eyes. The water in my inner bowl has evaporated into a desert whirring with locusts.

My mother says, 'My daughter and I are leaving now.'

She leads me by the arm down the street. I still have things to say but I can't formulate them properly so I allow myself to be led.

'You always get the chance to say everything you want to someone,' my mother says. 'It's okay. There's no hurry. Let's get home.'

'Okay,' I say quietly.

Art follows us. My mother hails a cab.

'It was always your show, Art,' I say, gesturing to the building. 'I thought it was mine for a while, but now I see I was just opening for you.'

A cab stops. My mother opens the door.

Art puts his hand in his pocket and grimly hands the cab driver a twenty-pound note through the open window. He is a Decent Man doing the Decent Thing.

'Thank you, Art,' my mother says, pushing me into the cab.

'No, no, thank you.' I throw his money out of the window. 'Stop trying to be Charlie Fucking Big Potatoes.'

'I am not trying to be Charlie Fucking Big Potatoes!'

'Drive on!' I say to the driver. 'Drive on, driver, please!'

Art pats the side of the taxi.

'Go pat something else, you patronising bastard!'

The cab drives off.

'No more wine for you,' my mother says. 'Ever.'

'You can fuck off, as well.'

'It's sixty quid if she soils the vehicle,' says the driver.

'I am not going to soil the vehicle! I love the vehicle.'

I put my hand on the deliciously cool window. It is so nice and cold and glaaarrrgggggggymmmmmmm. We drive over the Thames, where the river is swirling and churning. The city passes in bursts of grey and yellow.

'I don't believe them,' my mother says. 'This is a rushed, desperate affair. It's all wrong. All very wrong.'

I raise my head up, which is hard. 'How can he be playing happy families with her? Layers of duplicity!'

My mother sighs. 'Well, darling, maybe he just hadn't met the rich girl.' I look at her, hurt. She continues: 'I mean *right* girl.'

She laughs – and I laugh. Despite myself, and everything.

Back at the house I go up and wash my face and then I change into my pyjamas and get into bed.

My mother follows me up silently, still with her coat on. 'What are you doing?' she says.

'This is an act of hibernation.'

'It's barely November.'

'It's going to be a long, cold winter.'

'You're just drunk, darling. I'll make you a melba toast.'

She goes downstairs to the kitchen. I put on a nature documentary and watch it until I fall asleep.

OUTGROWN

Art was antsy in the waiting room at Whipps Cross. He kept pacing and scratching and going outside. After half an hour or so, he asked me if he could leave and get back to his studio because he had a big job on for an advertising agency, which I already knew. There was no point the two of us staying, was there? I could see the logic in that. The proud part of me hustled forward inside and I heard myself say *Okay*. Because – also – (and I know I'm letting myself off the hook here, as well as being philosophical) how can you allow yourself to need someone who refuses to be needed? Don't you just know that they are not right for you, that they don't love you enough? The answer is in the question, is it not? They do not love you *enough*. If you make them stay, under duress, it changes the nature of any possible fulfilment. Best to turn off the need. Best to let the need do what it will, inside.

So, he left and I watched him go – through the revolving door, out into the sunshine. I think my heart broke in that moment. It snapped clean in two, like a biscuit; a brittle, little, domestic thing.

The room where I had the blood test was windowless, with grey walls. There was a single small bed with grey sheets and a plastic bucket in the corner. The heavy door swung shut with a clank. They took the blood out of my arm, which was funny because so much of it was falling out of me anyway. They took me for a scan.

'There's nothing there,' the sonographer said. 'There's nothing there.'

Back out in the waiting room, I sat far apart from anyone else. There were pregnant people in there. It didn't seem right, to put my particular curse amongst them.

Do you want to know the punchline?

As I was sitting there, bleeding, failed, confused, sad, mad as fuck, I glanced up and saw a man I'd got off with once on a drunken night out in Camden. He was sitting opposite with his very pregnant girlfriend. He was holding her hand. He recognised me and I couldn't bear it, so do you know what I did? I pretended not to be me when he said hi. (This is a woman in her mid-thirties, remember. Pretending not to be herself. In that moment, I really think I wasn't.) He probably thought I was crazy. And, in that moment, I suppose I was. I pulled out my phone and I started scrolling. I didn't know what else to do, where else to go. I composed an email so as to compose myself.

When I got back from the hospital, I went down to Art's studio in the basement. I put down my carrier bag. It was full of all the banned cheeses: Brie, blue. I'd bought pâté. Salami. All the fuck-yous to the Unborn.

'Hey,' he said softly, turning round from his computer and coming over to me. He hugged me like I was made of glass. 'Are you okay? What did they say?'

'Bizarrely they said there was so little of the hormone in me it was as though I'd never been pregnant. So I don't know whether it hadn't grown much or what.'

His computer switched to sleep mode. Photos of me in different locations appeared in a slow montage. Me feeding a horse. Me eating an ice cream. Me pretending to like the sea. Smiling, always smiling. Smiling on demand. Being fine and nice about it all.

'Can I get you anything? Come on, come upstairs.'

He put me on the sofa, under a blanket.

'I'm still bleeding quite a lot.'

'Let me make you some tea and toast.'

While he was in the kitchen I pulled off a big hunk of Brie and rammed it down my throat.

He came back in and put the tea and toast down.

I said, 'Thank you.'

He said, 'Listen, babes, I've been thinking.'

I looked at him.

He said: 'I'm not ready to do this. Start a family. I'm not sure it's for me.'

I thought of the condoms in his leather toiletry bag, batched in bright foil squares, like confectionery. The way I'd obsessed over them in the early days. Resisted counting them each time he visited. We were heading there again. Beating a retreat. To distances. To speculation. To protection.

'Okay,' I said. 'So why did you do this with me for so long? Were you just playing along?'

'No,' he said – and then, seeing that was unsatisfactory, added, 'My therapist understands. It's a psychological thing. I also need a lot of artistic headspace.'

Art's therapist was a piece of work. They bought each other gifts. He had Tony Soprano aspirations. She loved treating a famous photographer. It was all very bad practice. I imagined her like Sharon Stone, sitting waiting for him in a desk chair, legs open, the dark recess of her skirt holding crotchless panties. Early on, he told me that she had advised him to see an older woman, that I was too young for him (I was two years older than him). She, on the other hand, was conveniently a whole ten years older. 'Your therapist has an agenda.'

He didn't say anything. He walked across the room and punched the door. He punched it so hard he made a hole (a frayed, clumsy hole that stayed there for weeks while we both skirted the issue of discussing its repair – and, by proxy, *it*). We both looked at the hole. It was good to have something real to look at.

'Oh god,' he said. 'Jesus!'

He put his head in his hands and stood there for at least five minutes. I stared at him, and as the time passed I started to think, incongruously, how he looked like a child playing hide-and-seek.

Subject: Notes From Purgatory

Dear Man I Once Snogged,
I am sorry I am ignoring you while you sit opposite me here in this waiting room between worlds – for you, Heaven; for me, Hell. It has nothing to do with the fact that you were a dreadful kisser. It is just that I am in a bad place right now and can't handle social interaction of that sort. I hope you have been a good, honest, consistent person since we last facially connected. I hope you have not subjected your nearest and dearest to sea changes of heart. I marvel at men, I really do. The liberty! ENJOY. It'll hit you like a ton of bricks at sixty-five and then won't we all hear about it. I hope you have a happy life with your partner and child – who I hope will be a boy-child, so as to have a better chance in this whole fucking shitshow.
Kind regards,
Jenny McLaine BA Hons.

ART SAID

'Are you sure? Like, sure it was actually a man that you knew in there?'

'Yes. Don't say it like that.'

'You do tend to be a bit paranoid about these things.'

'What things?'

'Knowing people you don't. Not knowing people you do.'

He was right, too. Sometimes I walk down the street and feel like I know everyone; love everyone. Other days, bad days, I can walk right past someone I know.

BODIES OF WORK

The next morning there is an uneaten melba toast on the floor next to the bed, along with the unpuked-in washing-up bowl. It is very much a tableau of self-possession and restraint. I decide I am not going to get up today, or maybe even ever again. I put my nose into my armpit and inhale the sweat-scent feedback loop. I text Nicolette.

I can no longer deny the malaise

Don't talk to me about malaise – this morning after my shower I couldn't even be bothered to moisturise my second leg

I knew you'd understand

I almost reported a man for having a wank in the park and then I got closer and realised he was sanding a chair leg

Clapton, man

Clapton. What's up?

My soul has been pureed in an unspeakable act of betrayal

Did someone regram you without a credit?

264

No, Art's new girlfriend has a secret child

Like Mick Jagger???

Sort of

Dude. That burns

I am in bed and I am staying here until further notice. It is the only respectable thing to do

I am coming round

You don't have to

I have ordered a cab

Will you bring alcohol and Camel Lights

Yes. Will bring a nice bottle of white I've got in

What country is it from?

Dunno. France mebs

I can't drink it

Why?

Nothing French

Is this a Brexit thing?

No

You drank French wine the other night

I AM NOT DRINKING FRENCH SHIT GODDAMNIT

Okay I'll get some fucking Chilean then!

I am going to smoke in bed I am that unmaternal

I am going to swing by the Scottish restaurant, would you like any supplies?

Filet o fish

Do they still do those

Yes

How many?

Three. One for each eye

My mother comes in. 'The Kraken wakes!' She sits down on the bed. 'Are you getting up today?'

'Negative. I am exploring my fertile void.'

'Sounds messy. Will I need to change the sheets?'

'A therapist once told me about it. It's about the useful nothingness you have to go through occasionally in order to prepare for the next thing. It's about stopping to reassess.'

'It might be more useful if you took a break from your phone.'

'Don't turn off my life support! I know you would, given half the chance!'

'Ach. Do you want a cup of hot chocolate?'

'Maybe later. Nicolette is coming over. She's swinging by the Scottish restaurant if you want anything.'

'What is the Scottish restaurant?'

I look at her.

'Do you mean McDonald's?'

'DO NOT SAY ITS NAME!'

'I've had my smoothie and some melba toast. It's 11 a.m.'

'If you wanted something to do,' I say, 'you could have a whip-round on the cleaning front downstairs. That would be so helpful.'

She goes downstairs. I hear her sing a line of Madonna and I think maybe this time it isn't to dispel the spirits but more to dispel her own anxiety. Imagine that. I hear the hoover start up. Then the hoover stops and I hear her walking to the front door and opening it.

'Hello!' says Nicolette's voice. 'I'm Jenny's friend, Nicolette. It's Carmen, isn't it? We've never met but I've heard a world about you. I've come to get in bed.'

'Let me guess,' says my mother. 'Leo.'

'Yes! Oh my god!'

'Are you spiritual?'

'I am VERY spiritual. I love a ghost. I am always ghost-hunting.'

'GET UP HERE, NICOLETTE.'

KELLY SAID

'So he's been lying all this time? You've been trying, like actually trying. You could have got actually pregnant!'

'Yeah . . .'

I couldn't. I just . . . couldn't.

I said: 'He says he's talked it all through with his therapist and he's sure.'

'No way is he. For starters, having kids is the ultimate vanity project. And Art is *very* vain. He will have kids, for sure.'

'Well, he says he won't have them with me. He has decided not to sire my young.'

'Then you've got to leave him,' Kelly said, deadly serious. 'He'll string you along until you're fifty and then he'll leave you for a thirty-year-old and have twins. You have to trust me on this.'

She poured two glasses of wine and I topped them up to the brim.

'Woah,' she said. 'Someone's on a mission.'

I think probably part of me wanted to beat my body up – because that's how it has to be, sometimes, for us to truly own ourselves, doesn't it? I didn't have time to go through the *maybe-if-you-loved-yourself-more-you-could-forgive-your-body* rationale. I was on the fucking minutes. By 9 p.m. we'd got to the second bottle of wine, the second pack of fags, and the eighth circle of Truthtalk.

'Do you think I'm maternal?' I said to Kelly.

Her brow buckled. 'Huh?'

'Don't feel pressured to answer.'

'Not really,' she added, 'when I think about it.'

'Why not?'

'You like to do your own thing.'

Now I frowned. 'It's strange, isn't it. The either/or.'

'I thought you judged me when you found out I became a mum so young.'

'What? How?'

'If you knew me without Sonny – not that that would be possible, but try and imagine it. If we'd just met in a bar, say, would you think I was maternal?'

'Yes. I think so. You're very authoritative.'

She laughed. 'What?'

'And organised.'

'Oh, stop. I feel too sexy.'

'And you are very caring. You care about me. I feel that.'

We were silent for a moment. I thought about the first time she'd left me alone with Sonny and I worried about child abuse, the way I always do when I'm left alone with strange children. Not because I have any desire to do it, but because people might think I do, or I might do something inadvertently.

Kelly said: 'I thought you thought I was a dumbo.'

'I didn't think that, Kelly. At all.'

We sank another glass.

'Well,' she said. 'I thought so.'

'What made you think that?'

'You referred to me as your "mum-friend" in a column one time, maybe even a few times.'

I opened my mouth to speak. From the corner of the room, Siri said:

'*Sorry, I couldn't find any matching restaurants.*'

I cracked up. So did Kelly. We both looked at her phone. 'I think what this tells us,' she said, 'is that there's just no way to win.'

FAKE NEWS

I'd done it once with Art. Towards the end-end. Sent him a shopping list and put 'chicken breaths' instead of 'breasts' and considered changing it but then left it there because I thought we could both use the laugh.

GOOGLE ME

Nicolette stamps up the stairs and into my room. She's wearing a sweatshirt that says KILL ALL PODCASTS on it in arching capitals, like the logo of a university.

'Nice room,' she says. 'This is a different one though, right?'

'Yes, I moved rooms since last time.'

She takes off her shoes and gets into bed beside me. She unpacks the burgers from the paper bag and throws me a few. I unwrap one and shove it into my mouth. 'Obviously, this is just a brief hiatus from my veganism.' I recall the time I caught a vegan friend tucking into a dish of sweet and sour pork in Chinatown. *Oh!* I said. *A meat tourist!* Genial, you know. She never returned my texts after that.

'Just happen,' says Nicolette, chowing down. 'Just allow yourself to be happening. Stop pre-defining yourself.'

I polish off all three burgers then light up a cigarette. We are side by side in bed, the ashtray between us.

'Do you think I'm unmaternal, Nicolette?'

'I think that question is unmaternal, that's what I think.'

'You're so right.'

'Thank you. I accept the compliment.'

'You have ketchup on your chin.'

'See?! You are so maternal right now.'

'Let me wipe it off for you.'

'More than my own mother ever did.'

My mother shouts up from downstairs. 'Do you girls need anything?'

'No thank you!' we shout back.

'She's just trying to get in on it,' I say. 'She'll be up in a minute with an extravagant drink.'

Nicolette sucks her fingertips and bats a crumb off her phone screen. 'So what's she like, his new girlfriend?'

'She's my ideal woman.'

'Fuck.'

I show her some photos of Suzy Brambles.

'Oh,' she says, 'I see your predicament. They look like a cool couple.'

'What? Why? Because they're both wearing black?'

'I like her hair. I'm only being honest.'

I puff on my cigarette. Nicolette pulls out her vape.

'My love life's just as disastrous, if that's any consolation.'

'It is.'

She sucks hard on her vape and releases a sweet guff of applemint. 'Last week I went on a date with a man who started off by showing me the floor plans of a flat he was buying. *Started off.* Most boring date ever. I was like, how do we climax? With your ISA statements? When I said I was leaving early, he said, *What makes you so great?* I said, *Google me.*'

'You actually said "Google me"?'

'I did.'

My mother comes in with a jug of lemonade on a tray.

'What's this?'

'Homemade. I found a recipe online. It's very good.'

She pours two glasses.

'It is good,' says Nicolette, taking a sip. 'My mother only ever microwaved me pizza. One time a boy came round and she tried to cook a pizza in the oven and he told me afterwards part of the reason he dumped me was because it was burnt on the outside and frozen in the middle. Which I think is a pretty perfect analogy of my romantic experiences to date. I gave away my sexual prime to Facebook. I'm a tundra on two legs.'

'Have to say I sympathise more with your mother than the boy there,' says my mother.

Nicolette drinks all her lemonade. 'More?' says my mother, gratified.

'Yes please,' says Nicolette, holding out her glass. My mother fills it from the jug.

'Hey,' says Nicolette, 'so you do tarot?'

'No!' I say. 'Not in my room!'

'Oh, let her stay! I want my cards doing.'

'You don't believe in this shit too, do you?'

My mother pulls a pack of tarot cards out of her pocket and hands them to Nicolette. Nicolette squeaks with delight and shuffles them. 'Like this?'

'Like that.'

'Soooo exciting.'

I roll my eyes and drink my lemonade.

SOCIAL CATERPILLAR

I started going online, drunk, at night, alone. Setting up semi-knavish profiles on dating sites. Stalking old spars. One time, in a stunningly productive vodka fug, I ordered fifty cardboard boxes to pack up my books. I skipped supper. I forgot the alarm code. Warning shots across my bow from the good ship *Self Sabotage*.

I sent away for a pack of those caterpillars that you incubate and watch grow into butterflies. Painted Ladies. I kept them patiently in a tank in the corner of the dining room, watching them slow down and slowly form their chrysalises and hang like seed pods. They made it look so easy. When they hatched, the butterflies clung to the side of the tank, drying out. If you kept them too long in there they died, but I released them too soon. Or maybe it was too late in the year. I found them dead and dangling from hedges and bushes. I came in carrying one, once. Art was in the kitchen, holding a pack of five beer cans by the empty loop where the sixth had been.

'Where've you been?' he said.

'Work, then round at Kelly's.'

'What's that?'

'A butterfly.'

'Looks dead.'

'It is dead.'

He slept down in his studio. I slept in the bed – or rather I lay there, staring at the ceiling, stalked by my own thoughts.

He came in first thing. He hadn't slept either. His breath was beer. He said: 'Are we breaking up?'

I nodded. He started to cry. I got up and went to the toilet. The smell in there. In the end, it was like cutting open a shark's stomach. Tin cans and toddlers' limbs. Everywhere we'd been.

REALLY THO

I'm terrible with endings in general. Sometimes I turn a song off halfway through because I can't bear the demise. When the battery on my phone or laptop gets below 50 per cent I can feel the anxiety start to build in my stomach. By 30 per cent it's in my throat.

DEALS WITH STRANGERS

'Hand them back when you feel ready,' my mother says to Nicolette.

Nicolette instantly stops shuffling and is about to hand over the cards when she stops and looks uncertain. 'No wait,' she says. 'Maybe I'm not ready. How will I know when I'm ready?'

'You're ready when you're ready,' says my mother. 'Don't overthink it.'

Nicolette's face splits into a grin and she nods. 'Thank you,' she says. 'So is this just about the future, yes? Not about the past. I would like to just know what's going to happen. I don't want to . . . dwell on anything that's been and gone.'

'Of course, in simple terms,' says my mother. 'Although really they are one and the same.'

'I love how you talk.'

'I see a man with glasses and a kind face in your near future. Can you accept that?'

'Accept it?' says Nicolette, 'I'm counting on it! When is this happening? Can you give me a ballpark figure. Weeks? Months? Can I request he has a job and no fungal foot issues?'

'Now,' says my mother, 'I'm going to lay the cards out in what we call a classic horseshoe.'

I pretend not to look. I am giving my lemonade all of my attention. Would you look at this lemonade, would you just, oh wow I mean this is a thoroughly engrossing lemonade.

'Can you do it so it's mostly about love,' says Nicolette. 'That's all I'm really here for. I'm just being honest. You can cut the health and money stuff.'

'That'll change.' My mother deals the first card. 'Death.'

Nicolette gasps.

'It doesn't mean "Death", it means "Regeneration",' my mother says. 'Christ, Nicolette, have you never watched a horror film?'

'It's got a freakin' skeleton on it, Carmen.'

My mother turns the next card. 'The Three of Cups.'

A new arrival. Also, the 'party card'.

'That looks better,' says Nicolette.

She deals the next.

The Sun.

'There's some travel on the horizon,' my mother says.

'I'm so ready for that,' says Nicolette. 'Just don't let me get delayed at the airport for god's sake or it's not worth it, not for a short break. Unless you think it'll be something longer? Do I need to start looking into visas?'

My mother and I look at one another. Next.

The Empress.

My mother peeks under the next card and then puts it down flat. She sighs and sits back. 'Darling,' she says to Nicolette, 'I'm not sure these are for you. They just don't feel right. I'm sorry, something is going wrong. Sometimes the energy interferes with surrounding forces. It could be someone in the next house. These walls are thin.'

'They're not that thin,' I say. 'This is a well-built, structurally sound property.'

'It all feels right to me,' says Nicolette. 'Keep going!'

My mother turns over the Ace of Wands, then the Page of Cups. She looks perturbed. 'Do you think . . .' says my mother. 'No, I shouldn't say.'

'What?' says Nicolette. 'Do I think what?'

'Well, is there any way you could be pregnant?'

Nicolette laughs. 'Fucking hell, I hope not! I only sleep with dicks!'

'Must be for someone else. Sorry, it's not always clear.'

I feel suddenly sick. 'Thanks, but we'd appreciate some time alone now to talk.'

My mother smiles at Nicolette and pats her knee. Then her face changes. She and Nicolette hold each other in a gaze that lasts a few seconds but looks like a wondrous sad love. Nicolette jolts out of it. My mother puts the pack of cards in her pocket. She picks up the tray of lemonade and walks to the door.

'Don't you think it's a bit pathetic to stay in bed much longer?' my mother says.

'Oh quite the opposite, Mother. This is a vital and bold protest. We're like John and Yoko.'

'I'm Yoko,' says Nicolette.

'What are you protesting about?' says my mother.

'Life! And our experience of it!' I reply. 'I have emotional whiplash.'

'Lifelash,' says Nicolette.

'Yes, that's it. We have lifelash.'

'Right,' says my mother. 'Do you want a gin?'

'Yes please,' says Nicolette.

My mother runs off.

'Don't let her make you a gin,' I say. 'You'll never get out of bed again. She does all-inclusive-package-holiday measures.'

'It might help me forget about last night. I had the worst date. I thought it was going well and then he left after half an hour, because he could "just tell it wasn't going anywhere". Half an hour! You spend longer than that viewing a house!'

'How rude.'

'So rude. And I wasn't about to let him get away with it. I pressed him for a reason and he said: *Okay, Nicolette, I don't normally do this, but I'm going to tell you the truth because you're a nice woman and I think you deserve the truth. So here it is: I simply don't have time to pursue things that aren't 100 per cent worthwhile — and I can tell this situation is only potentially 50 per cent worthwhile, tops, so it's nothing personal, but I'm not feeling the fire, so I'm going to save us both some time and leave.* And he left.'

'Jesus.'

'Half an hour!'

'You don't lack anything. He is lacking, to write you off so quickly. Is there not some kind of captcha thing you have to do when you sign up to these sites, to prove you're not an automaton? How did this guy get through? He sounds in every way soulless.'

'It's all binaries. 1 or 0. Yes or no. That's what they send you, these men on these dating apps. Questionnaires with yes or no answers. *Indian or Chinese. Chocolate or sex. Black or white.* No nuance. Just polarity.'

'Oh god,' I say, the light bulb in my brain exploding, 'we are thinking like computers! That's what's happening! *That's* what all this is doing! Define yourself as one thing or the other! Do not be wrong! Do not contradict yourself! YES versus NO, thumbs up thumbs down, all of us junksick robo-emperors in a little blue arena.'

My mother brings three G&Ts in on a tray.

I look at Nicolette. 'Do you think what is happening here is some kind of evolution?'

Nicolette looks at me, terror in her eyes. '*Into robots?*'

My mother turns around with the tray. 'You two don't need any gin.'

'What if,' Nicolette says, 'we thought it was taking us backwards, giving us less thinking time, and actually it's all going in the right direction for us to be fused with the machines psychologically into a super-race. Like love-children of Cylons and humans.'

'Good grief,' says my mother. 'I thought you were talking about dating. Can we get back to dating?'

She hands us our gins. We all cheers and take a large slug.

'Anyway, I'm going to delete all my dating apps,' says Nicolette. 'I don't want any more vacuous property imperialists or bankers taking me out to schmancy restaurants in Kensington. Oh no, I am just going to walk into a scruffy bar, walk up to someone, smell them, and if that smell is right, I'm going to ask if they want to fuck.'

'I'm not sure that's the best approach.'

'We need to get back to the sensorium. I get PLENTY of abuse on these supposedly "clean" dating sites. Men rating me on my boobs, my hair, my teeth. They say way more suggestive things than that. I'd like to do this to you. I'd like to do that to you. Let me buy you dominatrix shoes for your ugly feet. Send me your oldest shoe and I'll Paypal you a hundred dollars. Would they say those things to my face? Some of them would, for sure, but not as many of them.'

'Tell me more about these dating apps,' says my mother.

'I'm on about six,' says Nicolette. 'I can send you the details if you give me your number.'

'Mum, I really don't think you should go on dating sites. Someone your age will get eaten alive.'

'I'm not going to sign up for anything!'

Nicolette hands her phone to my mother and my mother taps her number in with a long blue nail. She hands it back. Seconds later, my mother's phone pings with messages.

'Just be careful though with those, Mum,' I say. 'Don't agree to meet anyone without running them by me first.'

'I'm just looking for friendship,' my mother says.

'Ah yes but that's what they lure you in with,' says Nicolette. 'Watch the friendship thing. They sneak up on you. They're like, *My closest friends are women! You're in your comfort zone, you're in your comfort zone, you're in your comfort zone . . . TAKE YOUR TOP OFF.* Be vigilant, Carmen.'

'You're forgetting who you're talking to.'

I locate my phone under the covers.

'Are you signing up?' says Nicolette. 'If you do I might not delete them just yet.'

'No,' I say, 'I just want to leave a comment on Art's exhibition posts to say I had a good time and am proud of him. Hoorah for you. All that shit.'

'NO!' say my mother and Nicolette. Nicolette sprays gin on my arm.

'I also want to say NEVER CONTACT ME AGAIN.'

'NO!' they shout again. Another boozy hosing from Nicolette.

'You'll regret it!' adds Nicolette.

'It won't achieve anything!' says my mother.

'It will make me feel something, which is an achievement. And I regret EVERYTHING, so what makes this worth avoiding, unless I'm going to start avoiding everything?'

'NO.'

'At least let me unfollow Suzy Brambles.'

'No! Stop being so aggressive. This is a peaceful protest.'

'It will symbolise my detachment from the situation.'

'UNFOLLOW HER IN YOUR HEART, JENNY,' says Nicolette. 'That should be enough.'

'It's all too raw,' says my mother. 'You need to trust yourself.'

'I don't know who to trust because I don't know who I am. At thirty-five years old, at halfway, I am still waiting for my life to start.'

'Do you think you're halfway? Are the mid-thirties halfway? Do you think you're only going to live to seventy? My dad is seventy!'

My mother says, 'Thirty-five is just the beginning. You're not even remotely menopausal.'

Nicolette and I share a look.

NEWS ITEM

It has recently been discovered that killer whales, one of three types of mammal, including humans, to have a menopause, have this menopause due to a complicated relationship between mothers and daughters. Beyond their fertile years, older females play a crucial role in the life of the group. Grandmothers help improve survival in larger matriarchal groups because they often find and share food resources communally. A pod of killer whales is made up of multiple family units, known as matrilines, which travel together. During the prolonged post-reproductive life of humans and toothed whales, a wish to avoid conflict has pushed them to abandon fertility.

NICOLETTE SAYS

'Apparently, social media is worse for women.'

'Is that right?' my mother says.

'Yep.' Nicolette taps her head. 'The amygdala in your brain processes emotional learning, fear and memory. They tested a bunch of men and women and found that the women became depressed when they were presented with the same negative stimuli over and over. Men could blank the familiar stuff out and only responded to the new stuff – terrorist attacks, stuff like that. But the women reacted to the familiar stuff. It chipped away. They got anxious and depressed. And yet here we are, partaking. Perpetuating.'

'Why?' I say. 'Let's stop and ask that.'

'I keep telling you to!' says my mother.

'Well it's part of my process, I think. Going round and round. I can allow myself a few more months. My therapist told me,' Nicolette says.

'What process?'

'Our process. You know. Our thing. I told my therapist all about you.'

'Right.' Sometimes I think about how many therapists in the world know about me and I feel sick with fame. 'What did you tell her?'

'That we are similar. That we are . . . playmates.'

I wait for more, but Nicolette just looks at me blankly.

'Playmates?'

'We know how to distract ourselves while we process what we're processing.'

'You mean like the world and meaning and . . . stuff like that?'

Nicolette looks at me. Her lip curls in a way that doesn't look particularly controlled. 'Yeah, but the underlying thing too. We're comforting ourselves, aren't we, you and I. We're living in repeats and circles because they're reassuring. That there'll be no surprises. No more hurt.'

My mother has her head at an uncomfortable-looking angle and is hanging on Nicolette's every word. She looks at me when Nicolette stops talking.

'Mother,' I say, shaking my empty glass, 'I think we need a refill, if you don't mind.'

She reluctantly takes our glasses and leaves the room.

I look at Nicolette. She turns her body towards me and tilts her head to one side.

'That's why we started talking to each other, wasn't it?' she says. 'We were both grieving.'

'What?' I shake my head.

'I didn't need the details; I just got that vibe from you. Our sad bits attracted and joined up. You seemed so agitated. Like you were on high alert.'

All this time I suppose I felt superior somehow, when in fact she was the one who knew my true heart.

'Really? You didn't just think I was . . . fun? I was in a Garfield suit.'

'You seemed to me like a person in a lot of pain. Did I not seem like that to you?'

'No, you just seemed . . . wry.'

'Oh. I thought that was how we bonded. Over our horribly unspoken heartbreak.'

I pause. Swallow.

'And . . . what *is* your heartbreak, Nicolette?'

I am dreading the answer, and also I know that this layer has always existed between us: the vast salt flats of the post-corporeal mind. Grey, cold and dissolving in fine mizzle. Nicolette ánd I meet there nightly, and we dance a slow dance.

Nicolette hunches over. There is musty silence. She raises her eyes to meet mine, and then cringes like she is about to receive a blow. 'My sister killed herself,' she says. 'Last January. She drank three bottles of wine and hanged herself. I can't stop wondering whether it was the wine or whether she'd have done it anyway.'

'Oh god, Nicolette.'

'It's okay. I don't believe in closure so I'm just . . . assimilating. And I do believe she's still out there in the universe somewhere, doing something. I do.'

She weeps, effortlessly. I put my hand on her hand and I squeeze. Her hand is warmer than mine, I can feel it. 'I had no idea,' I say. 'I'm so sorry, Nicolette.'

'So funny, I thought you could see right through me. I thought I didn't even have to say it, because you just always knew. It was implied in a thousand unspoken things, I was sure. I think maybe you did have an idea.'

My mother comes in with our gins. She doesn't ask what has happened and I think she has probably listened or guessed or tuned in or who knows and who cares. For the next ten or twenty minutes, we are just three women sitting together, looking out from our faces, doing our best. Life goes on. That's the great insult of it, I suppose.

When Nicolette has gone, my mother goes down to make dinner. I lie in bed, staring at my phone and into the bowl of flies that has taken the place of my heart. With my other hand, I tweak my nipple hard. Nothing. I press the button of myself. Nope. I miss my body. I do. I miss it. Deeply and hard. The exchange between neuron and sensor. The inner interaction. I want to think with my body again. I miss that innocence. I am so sick of thinking with my brain. I tweak my nipple harder. Nothing.

I draft an email. And then I do a strange thing.

I send it.

SENT ITEMS

Dear Art,

Good to see you at the exhibition. I just wanted to say that I know my mother has been texting you and I'm terribly sorry that you have been subjected to that kind of onslaught. I had no idea that she had a problem, and I do think it is a problem that she has (one of many) and I hope it won't affect our friendship or your opinion of me. I trust that we can move forward and you will not judge me on this. I don't even know why I feel the need to apologise on her behalf because we are such drastically separate and different people, but I suppose I just wanted to acknowledge it like the adult I am. Lots of love to you and Suzy and her very real child.

Bests,

Jenny

I wait for him to reply. I flick through my apps and channels. Flick flick flick flick. I become increasingly irritated when junk emails come through. I didn't sign up for any of this shit. Tooth-whitening. Budget-airline flight sales. Then one from a pizza company I ordered from once a few weeks ago in a fit of nocturnal starvation. Their winter offers.

I reply, incandescent.

SENT ITEMS

Dear Pizza the Action,
IT WAS ONE NIGHT. ONE NIGHT!!! THIS IS HARASSMENT.
NEVER EMAIL ME AGAIN.
Regards,
Jenny McLaine BA Hons.

HALF AN HOUR LATER

Art replies.

> Jenny – please don't worry. I took it for what it was, an upset
> and lonely old lady not knowing where else to vent her frustra-
> tions. I also took your outburst at the exhibition for what it was
> – an upset and unstable person venting her frustrations the
> only place she could. Hope you are well and that you are getting
> the help you need x x

I stare at the message for a few minutes and try and work out all
the ways in which it enrages me. When I think I have them all in
my mind, I reply.

> Hi Art,
> Firstly, she's not that old. And she has plenty to occupy her;
> she's working hard and making a success of herself. Also, what
> do you mean by frustrations? Because if you're thinking she's
> somehow unfulfilled either in herself or in her opinion of me and
> my life, then you're wrong. Secondly, I was upset and unstable
> but at least I'm trying to be better. I might not be a premium
> kind of person just yet but I am slowly coming in to land.
> Jenny

ASS FIZZ

I get into the *Foof* office and there is a balloon tied to my chair. The balloon is in the shape of a huge fist.

'This is to celebrate the number of hits you're getting!' says Mia. 'Your column is the top read on the site, you little fuckwit!'

'I chose the fist,' says Vivienne.

Mia merrily whacks me about the head a few times with the balloon.

'Ow.'

'Excuse me but I am JUST SO GRATEFUL AND PLEASED FOR YOU.'

'I appreciate it but please could you stop that now.'

'Here,' says Mia, pulling up her phone on the cord around her neck. 'A photo. For the *Foof* feed. This is a celebration.'

There is a collective gasp. No one ever gets put on the *Foof* feed unless they are an extremely attractive intern or a celebrity.

'Come on,' hustles Mia. Vivienne and a few others shuffle into the shot.

'I'm not going at the front,' says Vivienne.

'I'm not going at the front,' I say, 'especially if you're going to tag me.'

'Fucking hell,' says Mia. 'Rita-Kathleen, get the clutch drone!'

Mia's assistant runs off to her office and seconds later, the clutch drone buzzes in. it circles us, taking pictures as we all pose.

Vivienne is a sharp poser. I get elbowed and kneed out of position by her several times. For the last shot, she has her leg up on the desk.

'Amazing,' says Mia, looking at the pictures on her phone. 'Well done, Jenny.'

'Thank you. This is . . . very unexpected.'

'In fact, your success is so epic,' Mia says, 'you have inspired me to take a sabbatical and write a memoir.'

'Spare us,' says Vivienne.

'So I might need you to deputise under Vivienne for a while. Which will mean a pay rise.'

'Don't count on it,' says Vivienne. 'Bitch needs diamonds.'

'A memoir about what?' I ask Mia.

'Well, about . . . me.'

'Is that . . . enough?'

Mia comes close and puts a hand on my shoulder. She stares deeply into my eyes. '*You are enough*, ginge, and the sooner you start believing that, the better. Your friend Kelly obviously thinks you're worth something. She came to see me and Vivienne and read us the riot act. Said we're not looking after you and should give you compassionate leave.'

'Compassionate leave? For what?'

'That's exactly what I said. I mean, you've got your mother living with you. You couldn't be more spoilt. But Kelly said your mother and her were in cahoots about it. That they were working together to get you offline.'

'What?'

'And then she said,' Mia looks at Vivienne, whose mouth is a volcano, 'and we are still reeling from this – she said: *Female stories are not a genre. Feminism is not a lifestyle choice. And that is not "a story"; it's a fucking jumpsuit.*'

I burst out laughing.

'The arrogance,' says Vivienne. 'The ignorance.' She adjusts the top of her jumpsuit. 'If I was bi I would definitely ask her out.'

I go back to my desk, sit and try and imagine Kelly coming in and sitting opposite Mia and Vivienne, giving them pure hell. I wonder if she wore her white suit (her only suit)? I don't like being discussed. Even more unlikely: Kelly and my mother sitting in my lounge, planning an intervention. But there's something about it all that makes me feel fizzy down low, like the first plunge of a rollercoaster. I'm feeling a subterranean buzz.

I text my mother:

What are you and Kelly plotting?

Did she tell you?

No my boss did. So that was a hoot

We are worried about you. Kelly came round to see me while you were out. She thinks you need us to step in as no one else will stand up to you.

What else did she say?

That Art never truly challenged you and that was why he wasn't right for you. But as a friend the greatest act of love is to challenge you. You are not okay. She said that.

I put down my phone. I have never felt so happy putting the phone down after an interaction with my mother.

After work I go to Kelly's flat with the portable speakers from my desk and a microphone from Gemma's product cupboard. I set up on the pavement, next to a sapling ringed with metal. I hop about keeping warm while I dock my phone. I press play. The backing track to 'Wind Beneath My Wings' starts up. I crank the volume to max. When the verse kicks in I start to sing. I see the blind go up in Sonny's room. His head appears, silhouetted – I'd know his ears anywhere. I continue singing. By the chorus, Kelly is there – her smooth hair giving her the outline of a Russian doll.

'Shut the fuck up!' someone shouts from across the street. I ignore them and carry on. A few people have stopped. Someone takes a picture. Kelly disappears from the window and then appears at the front door.

Sonny stays at his window, holding his phone up and occasionally shaking his head.

When I've finished, I give Kelly a perfunctory nod and dismantle my equipment.

Kelly shouts: 'I reckon a lot of scornful reviews of you just went viral.'

I give her a thumbs up.

I walk off. She shouts after me: 'Makes it all worthwhile, you know, freezing my tits off in your shadow.'

On the way home, I email her, and I send it:

Dear Kelly,

I appreciate you going to speak to Mia – I know how much you hate her and the *Foof* office, so that must have been a genuine endeavour. I see that I have been in an oubliette of self-regard. I thought boundaries were a bad thing, but now I see that knowing where I begin and end tells me what I can forgive of people, and what I can ask for forgiveness for. Because you're mine I walk the line and all that. I have also Googled friendship therapy to see if it exists and it actually does so if you think we need to go for that to fully repair the damage, then I am game.

Love,

Jenny x

THAT NIGHT

I sleep the whole night through for the first time in a year.

The next morning, Kelly has replied.

INBOX

> Dear Jenny,
> Thank you for the special gift of your music last night and for
> your thoughtful email. Do you have time today to meet for a
> coffee – this morning maybe? I can get out at 11ish for 55
> minutes or so.
> Let me know,
> Kelly x

Fifty-five minutes.

Whatever, Kelly.

Still, I do find the 'let me know' sort of thrilling. I am clearly
so needy that even someone *demanding* a response from me is joyous.

I feel like she's chasing me a bit, and I like that.

It feels like a beginning.

IT HAPPENED TO HAPPEN

I go in the café and quickly buy two coffees and two croissants and sit down at a table by the window to make our meeting as light and optimistic as possible. Kelly arrives on time. She comes to the table and I show her the coffee and croissants. 'I got you a cappuccino – that's right, isn't it?'

'It is. Thank you.'

I point to the croissants. 'And some pastry-based fuel.'

'Perfect.'

She takes off her coat and sits. I sip my coffee and watch her tear into a croissant. I pick up the other croissant and take a bite. It could have sat under a heat-lamp for a week and I wouldn't give a shit. I think of the microbes in my gut, receiving the white fluff and debating what to do with it. Billions of little voices, desires and commands and orders and opinions. Shut it, I tell them. Shut the fuck up, you and the rest of the world. I'm concentrating.

Kelly looks at me and smiles. 'Only *you* could send an email that contained the phrase "oubliette of self-regard",' she says. 'Dickhead.'

I smile, uncertainly. 'You still love me, though.'

'I do. And this is a problem. Because you're *such* a dick.'

I eat more croissant, encouraged. 'How's Sonny?'

'He's okay.'

'What's happening with the flat? Is Esther definitely selling?'

I am aware of being careful, considerate, gentle, selfless. Like an

297

addict who has been burned, I am reapproaching this with the caution of a novice. And maybe that's what I am where Kelly is concerned. A new friend. And this is our year dot.

'Yes, afraid so. Her kids are really pressuring her. Fucking kids.'

'What are you going to do?'

'Dunno. Still figuring it out.'

I nod and sip my coffee.

'How are you?' says Kelly, and it isn't a normal version of the question. It's a proper How Are You.

'There's something I want to tell you.'

She nods.

'I didn't want to tell you when I was asking you to forgive me because I didn't want it to be like . . . the dog ate my homework.' Kelly nods again. She eyes me with the deep, patient curiosity of a friend. 'I had a miscarriage. With Art.'

'You were pregnant?'

'I was. And then I wasn't.'

'You didn't tell me? *ME?*'

'Art and I agreed to do the twelve-week silence thing. And then I was so ashamed.'

'How many weeks were you?'

'Nine.'

'Ah shit, Jenny, I'm so sorry.'

'It's fine. It was just like an abortable bunch of cells.'

'Well, it was *your* abortable bunch of cells.'

'If it's abortable you can't care about it, can you?'

Kelly frowns.

'I don't know how to feel about anything any more, Kelly.' I start to cry. 'It would have been the size of a strawberry.' She puts her arms around me. 'I didn't see it come out. Just pieces of what looked like raw liver. I don't know why I'm crying.'

'You're grieving,' she says quietly.

'But what am I grieving for? Because I didn't love it. I didn't love being pregnant. I felt like a success and a failure all at once. I felt simultaneously progressive and devolved. I was ambivalent about it.'

'Maybe you loved the possibility of a future life? Or a better love, with Art?'

'Maybe.'

'How was Art about it?'

'Oh, I don't really know. He walked out of the hospital like a free agent.'

'He left you in there?'

'I let him leave me.'

'Fucking bell-end.'

I sigh deeply. 'I guess he was going through something, too. And it's like Dorothy Parker said: *Serves me right for putting all my eggs in one bastard.*'

Kelly laughs. After a moment she says, 'What died that day was your relationship with him.'

I smile. 'If only it was that neat. But it was much more than that. Until that moment, I didn't know what I was.'

'And what are you?'

'This, and only this.'

She points up and down me. 'This isn't so bad.'

'It fucked up. My body fucked up.'

'How do you know that? It could have been his faulty sperm. It just happened to happen inside your body.'

'I wish I could get out of it.'

'You know what I read the other day? The egg is an aggressive cell. The sperm isn't the only one with a mission. Women's bodies have a plan. They just get called crazy for it.'

'I think I probably have quite aggressive eggs.'

'I definitely have aggressive eggs.'

'But I have no integrity, so it's no surprise it didn't stick.'

'You're being too hard on yourself.' She swallows. 'I take it back,' she says after a moment, 'you're not a child. You grew up while the man you were with didn't have to.'

'Maybe. To be honest, I still feel like a child pretending to be an adult.'

'And your best friend didn't know what you were going through because you were doing your "I'm fine" dance all over town.'

I sense Kelly searching for the next question. I think this is how it will be between us now, for a while and maybe forever. Careful, not careless.

'How's it going with your mum?' she asks.

'Okay. Thanks for getting together with her, for me.' She blushes a bit. I sit up in my seat. 'I'm writing about her, actually.'

'I saw. Does she know?'

'No, I don't think so. She owes me, anyway.'

Kelly looks unconvinced. 'The eternal debt.'

'She's been texting Art. It's too dire to go into.'

'She does care about you, you know.'

I glance at my watch. Our fifty-five minutes is almost up.

'We should do this every week, at least once,' I say. 'Let's make a regular arrangement and honour that. Have a think about when would suit you best and we'll try and coordinate our diaries.'

Kelly laughs. 'Sounds very formal.'

'Maybe it needs to be. Maybe if it isn't it won't survive these next years of our lives.'

Kelly says: 'Why don't you and Carmen come over for a roast on Sunday. Sonny would like to see you. He says to tell you he's created a gif of your song and it's doing really well.'

'Tell him that is very comforting. That knowledge bathes me in comfort.'

Kelly puts on her coat. She sighs. 'I was very hard on you.' She sighs again and blows the air out through pursed lips. 'On reflection, I don't know where quite all of it came from. I suppose I am a bit jealous sometimes about your freedom to give a shit about the meaningless things. I have to plan *everything* I give a shit about. Very little of it is accidental.'

I hug her. She hugs me back.

'Oh, before I forget, Sonny says can you bring his present.'

'Tell him no.'

'Okayyy,' she says, confused. She leaves. I watch her go.

#FROTHEH

The next evening I'm in bed after my column has gone up. I'm watching the comments and the likes. I've really sent her up in this one. I've even got a codename for her now. 'Frotheh'. Or should I say, #Frotheh. After the way she pronounces 'frotheh coffeh'. I felt mean coming up with that but then I thought about how embarrassed she makes me feel, and those texts, and I thought, she deserves it, and more. Anyway, it's entertainment. I've written about how she was in *Corrie* and had one line and repeats it regularly after a few drinks – as well as all the impromptu singing she does in public, on the street, especially now in the run-up to Christmas.

Someone has commented:

She's fucking insane

And I have liked it.

There's a knock on my bedroom door. She comes in with a G&T. 'Here you go, darling. Evening shade.'

I angle my phone away as I take the drink. 'Thanks.'

She looks curiously at the phone and I can see the screen lighting up with more comments. I sip my drink and wait for her to leave the room. She gets the hint.

I look at the space she has been standing in and feel like I want to call her back. Her expectant face . . .

How dare she be expectant with me? It's not fair.

She turns at the door. 'These columns,' she says. My stomach

302

plummets. 'Someone told me that the last one was . . . um, was about me?'

Like she hasn't read it.

'Possibly,' I say. 'Inspired by.'

'I think we need to have a chat about what constitutes reality and what is fair and what is not fair.'

I feel positively cruel, then. Also incensed. 'It's the way it works. It can't just be real because real isn't enough to keep people reading. I only exaggerate for dramatic effect. You know about that. We aren't so different, you and I.'

'Mmmmmmmm.'

'You have no idea how hard I work.'

She looks on the verge of tears. I can't bear it.

'Look.' I get out my laptop. I show her. 'They're a hit. There's a comment here from a man who says you sound hilarious.'

She looks for a while. She scrolls. 'Okay,' she concludes. Her face brightens.

'And,' I say. She looks at me. 'I know you were texting Art.'

She looks ashamed. 'Truce?' She sticks her hand out.

'Truce,' I say, shaking her hand.

'I'll never text Art again about you,' she says. 'I can promise you that wholeheartedly.'

'Good.'

She sits down next to me on the bed and leans around my laptop.

'Now if these highly successful things about me are going to continue, I want to have some say in my character development . . .'

MY MOTHER SAYS

'I think if I was going to live anywhere in London, it would be Crystal Palace, just for the name. Just so I could say it, every day, several times.'

'Can you turn down the New Age for just an hour? The air is purple and sparkly.'

We get out of the cab. Kelly answers the door in a pinny that says LICENCE TO GRILL on it. I instantly want to photograph it, but I resist.

We go in. Kelly's flat is laid out in almost a square of corridors, with French windows opening to a large sunny (was it always sunny here? It felt like it) garden at the back.

I go to use the loo. I love Kelly's bathroom. It has a teen feel: bath salts, Body Shop products, cotton-wool-ball dispensers. The sink is too small, one of those sideways ones you usually get in nail salons, but it's just big enough for washing your hands and it makes you really concentrate when you're brushing your teeth. On the back of the toilet door, for ten years, there has been a child's drawing of a Dalek with a speech bubble saying: *Are you my daddy?* I used to look at it and think: *Same.*

When I get back to the kitchen, Kelly is tending to something in the oven. My mother has found a gin balloon from somewhere and filled it with gin and tonic. They are laughing, like old pals. I wonder whether Kelly is doing that thing where you're nice to someone's family as a way of bashfully showing you care, like when Mr Darcy helps Lydia but really it's just so Elizabeth knows he's a powerful man hot for her pants. I'll take it.

'Breastfeeding, though!'

'Oh, it's INHUMANE.'

'Until they get those artificial wombs developed there's no hope of equality for the human race. I'm coming back as a male seahorse.'

'Good choice.'

'It's a bit sexual, too, right?' says Kelly. 'Breastfeeding.'

'WHAT?' I say. 'Desist, before I become unwell.'

'Well, it is. Of course it's massively fucking taboo to talk about any of this. Any combo of sex and children is like such a no-no. But it's complex. It's human. Oh god, you're both looking at me funny. I can't talk about this.'

'No, I know what you mean,' my mother says. 'Jenny used to be sexual. Before she became this clinical little insect.'

'SHUT UP.'

They both laugh.

'Please, stop. I didn't bring you here to mortify me. Get your cards out. Anything.'

'Jenny would only feed from my left breast.'

'I'm going outside,' I said, 'to play football with Sonny.'

'Good luck with that. He's not played football for about three years,' says Kelly.

'What does he do now?'

'Watches porn on his phone.'

'WHAT?'

'I don't know. Sorry, I think that was just my worst fear that came out of my mouth.'

My mother pours herself another gin.

'I'll join you,' says Kelly.

'Single or double?'

'Single. And then I can have one more, and that's it. I've realised that I've spent my whole life chasing the two-drink high.'

'Two drinks?' my mother says. 'Dear god. That's when I just start feeling good.'

'What have you been up to in London, Carmen?' Kelly asks.

'Oh, I did a bit of a course. A few other little things. I'd love to get back into acting while I've still got my looks. And I've started online dating.'

'What?' I say. 'We agreed to discuss this.'

'No we didn't,' says my mother. 'I am a grown woman. I've been chatting to a few nice men on there.'

'They're all at least ten years older than they say. Just so you know.'

'One of them was helping his mother lay a patio, so he can't be that old.'

'Is that his dating chat? Laying a patio? Jesus.'

'Come on, then,' Kelly says. 'Show us some of these fellas.'

My mother gets her profile up. We crowd around her phone. She clicks open her matches.

Dino, 66 — I try to be the change I want to see in the world. I am my own future. I know who I am and what I like. I support equality and became aware of my genital privilege decades ago.

Wimpywilly, 51 — Looking for someone who would enjoy making fun of a guy with a small one. Someone who would enjoy making me feel even less of a man than I do already. More than happy to try n make up for my size with my tongue x

'Saints alive!' I say.

Kelly is on the floor, laughing.

'You're crazed!' I say. 'You have to promise me you'll never meet any of them. These men are clearly psychopaths of the most dangerous order.'

'There's someone else,' my mother says. 'But he's not on a dating app. He's on Twitter. We just got chatting on there because I signed up to his mailshots.'

I do not like the idea of my mother signing up for someone's 'mailshots'.

'He's a lifestyle guru,' my mother continues. 'I'm interested in what he's doing. I think he has some good advice. I respect his output and his utils.'

'His what and his *what?*'

She gets him up.

Dan Mosel

Life guru. CEO of Becoming Who You Are. Daily #LifeTips

'What do you think?'

'I think he looks like a man unmolested by the rumblings of a soul,' I say.

'You're harsh, Jenny.'

'He has two hundred thousand followers on Twitter. That should impress even you.'

'But how many people is he *following*? Probably two hundred and ninety-nine thousand. You can't trust the follower count. It's all about the ratio.'

'Well, no look, see, he's only following two thousand and thirty-eight.'

'Ah, then he's probably one of those awful types who follows and unfollows. He'll follow tons of people and then sneakily unfollow them once they've started following him back.'

'I need a manual for this.'

'How much are you communicating with him? Direct messages, is that it?'

'We message each other daily and we've shared a few pictures.'

I look at Kelly. 'Oh my god. Pictures of what?'

'Relax. I am a pretty good judge of character, remember. I have inside info.'

I look at Dan Mosel's picture. He has sparkly eyes and is grinning with all his teeth. He is also possibly wearing eyeliner.

'He looks like a naughty king from the Bible.'

'I like naughty kings.'

'Ugh.' Does my mother fancy him? If she has a 'type', does he – could he – look anything like my . . . you know?

'I can't see myself getting back into dating any time soon,' says Kelly. 'I don't see the point, really.'

Because you've done the procreation thing? I think, helplessly. This brain!

'Do you think you'll have any more?' asks my mother.

I laugh in shock. 'Mum, you can't ask that question. It's off-limits. You can never ask a woman about her plans to have or not have children, or more children. You just don't know where she might be at with it all.'

'I'd like another,' Kelly says.

'What?' I sit down. 'I can't cope with today.'

'Well, you've got to have two, haven't you?' Kelly continues. 'In case one dies.'

My mother cackles.

'This is news,' I say. 'How would you do it?'

'Artificial insemination. I've got the names sorted and everything. Helvetica for a girl and Kale for a boy.'

'Gorgeous,' I say. 'And so modern.'

'I don't know whether you're being serious or not now,' says my mother.

'I am about the baby part,' says Kelly. 'But I'd have a C-section and I'd want savings in place for more childcare.'

'I just wouldn't do it at all,' my mother says. 'I wouldn't have gone through with it, if I'd known how hard it would be. It's nothing personal, darling.'

'No,' says Kelly, 'you can't say that in front of Jenny. You have to wait until she's in the garden. That's the rule.'

'I'm really going!' I walk towards the French windows, out to the garden. 'There, now you can let loose.'

As I walk outside, I hear Kelly get her guitar and strike up the first few bars of 'Love Is Like a Butterfly'. My mother will do the harmonies, no doubt.

I want to see Sonny anyway.

THE HEART CROSSES IT

When I reached Kelly with two-year-old Sonny in my arms, he scrambled to get to her and I got that shameful feeling I always got – immaturely, stupidly – when babies and children preferred other people, even their mothers, to me. Kelly hugged him hard. Her chin wobbled.

'I just nipped to the loo,' she said. Her Northern accent hit me like a warm breeze. I wanted to say: *Do they understand you when you ask for nuts in a pub? Because they don't understand me.* 'I was away for thirty seconds. I normally take him with me, but he was watching telly and – I had no idea he could do handles.'

'It happens,' I said, as though I knew what I was talking about.

'Thank you,' she said. 'Thank you from the very bottom of my heart. I'll never be able to thank you enough. Do you want to come in for a drink?'

On the way to the house, she showed me the back gate. 'I don't know who left that open. Fucking numbskulls round here. Where are you from?'

'Manchester. Originally. Near there, anyway. How about you?'

'Huddersfield.'

'Do you miss it?'

'I miss my mum.'

'Were you never tempted to move back?'

'Nah. I don't miss her that much. I see her often enough. And Sonny's dad's up there and he's pulled a few stunts. And I like my job. I'm just a receptionist but it's easy and they're really flexible.'

We drank wine in her living room. There were posters from festivals up – Green Man, End of the Road – alongside shamanic art. My wine glass was chunky and dark green. Kelly's was different. Pink, maybe. Sonny banged his toys together on the rug. After an hour or so, she put Sonny to bed. I heard the sound of a lullaby tinkling from his bedroom as she shushed him.

When Kelly came back in, it was with another bottle of wine.

Out of nowhere I said: 'My mum was a single mum.'

What was I aiming for? Bonding? Some intimation that I understood her life? I get an anxiety shard when I think of myself saying that, now. The LOVE ME LOVE ME factory setting of my lost little heart.

Kelly didn't prolong the moment for me. 'Where does she live?' she said.

'Still up near Manchester.'

'Where's your dad?'

'I never knew him. My mother barely did, by all accounts.'

Kelly smiled. 'What's your mum like? I bet she's a glamour puss.'

'She's like a baby bird,' I said. 'All mouth.' Kelly laughed. I went on. 'She puts the "other" in "mother".'

Kelly laughed again. 'Don't we all.'

It was too soon to offend her. I backtracked. 'I guess we all get Stockholm syndrome where our mothers are concerned.'

'Right. No wonder he broke for the border.'

'No, I didn't mean—'

'Shut up.' She poured more wine.

We chatted for hours, I completely lost track, and then she got out her guitar and sang 'Love Is Like a Butterfly' by Dolly Parton. She had a good voice, raspy in the right places, and she played well – she'd taught herself. Only when she'd finished did I remember my taxi driver and rush out the back to find that he – like my loneliness – had long gone.

MANCHILD

I walk down the garden and find Sonny sitting on the bench outside the shed. He is looking at his phone. When he sees me he stops and puts it in his pocket. He looks so grown up I almost stop in my tracks.

'Heya.'

'Hey.'

'What you doing?'

'Revising.'

'What for?'

'GCSEs.'

I sit down next to him and look at both of our sets of trainers, lined up on the ground. 'Sonny, don't watch any freaky shit online, will you?'

'Don't you start.'

'I mean it. I know you're smart but that will teach you all the wrong stuff about sex.'

'Okay, you need to just stop being so extra.'

I nod slowly in agreement.

'Did you bring my present?'

'No. I brought you twenty quid instead.'

He looks at me. I look for Kelly in his face, like always. 'Bet you've smoked them, haven't you?'

'*Do as I say, not as I do.* God, my Granma used to say that and I hated it.'

'Not surprised. I hate it, too.'

'I don't know how to talk to you, Sonny.' I look back up towards the house. 'I am stuck between a rock and a hard place.'

'Which one am I?'

'Oh, you're the rock. You're all rock.' I make rock horns with my hands.

He laughs and looks mortified for me.

'Take over the world and be quick about it,' I say.

'Maybe that's why I don't feel like a kid,' Sonny replies. 'Because the planet is dying and someone needs to take responsibility.'

'You have baths,' I say, uselessly.

WHO YA GONNA CALL

In the cab on the way home, she says: 'I remember the moment I fell in love with you. Like, *you* you. The person, not just the tiny human who'd come from nowhere. You don't have a moment like that, do you? A falling-in-love moment. Children don't. I didn't with my mother, god knows I didn't. It's just part of you, your love for a parent, until it isn't. But parents *actively* fall in love with their children. It happens. There is a moment. You were in your highchair in the kitchen and I was making a coffee. Coffee and sugar kept me going at that point. The radio was on. The *Ghostbusters* theme tune came on and I started dancing, and you started laughing. I exaggerated the moves, made it all ridiculous and over the top. They way you laughed at that I knew we'd get along. And I knew I loved you. As you. The little individual you were, with your duckling hair and your dirty laugh.'

I look at her hands in her lap. I think of all the times I watched her from the wings. The real times and the remembered times and the imagined times. I say: 'I think children do have that moment. I think they do.'

If we were more evolved, more mature, more comfortable people, we would embrace or something at this point.

NAKED AMBITION

I'm leaving the *Foof* office, high on my latest column glory. I walk out of WerkHaus with a spring in my step. I decide to get some-thing nice for dinner, something to take home, a gastropub bistro dish for two. As I walk past Oxford Circus, I see the homeless man I ranted at that time. I stop. He looks at me, expectantly.

'I'm sorry for ranting at you drunkenly,' I say.

He looks at me as though he doesn't know what I'm talking about.

'I'm sorry,' I say, 'of course you don't remember me. You must have hundreds of people giving you shit every day. Why would you just remember one?'

He narrows his eyes. 'Wait a minute,' he says. 'Were you the one going on about Facebook?'

'That's me! That was me!'

It is so good to be remembered, even negatively.

'Yeah,' he says.

'Well, I'm very sorry anyway. I'm a bit better now.'

He says, 'That's okay.' He says, 'I thought you looked like a person in great pain.'

I nod. 'You weren't too far off the mark.'

I can see now how unwell I was. This culture of constant checking, of feeling as though everything can be instantly sorted, and accounted for, and validated, and gratified – that has to rub off on us psych-ically, doesn't it? I'll check, I'll check, I'll check. The weather, my thighs, my politics, my lunch. Erasing all mystery. But does it? Does it, really?

As I turn the corner at the end of the street I see her. I blink. It's definitely her. My mother. For sure. She looks different, but it's her. She's wearing a little green hat and lots of make-up and a natty little black suit jacket and jeans. She looks all dressed up for a . . . well, for a date.

Uh-oh.

A fever strikes me – I must save her from whatever she has got herself into. With that dreadful life guru or any other opportunist on a heartless dating site.

I think about shouting to her, but then I think, no, don't. I follow her.

I have to make sure she doesn't end up catfished or dogfished or kidnapped or shown floor plans of someone's prospective flat.

I follow her, down street after street, until we end up at a tiny theatre in the West End. Funny time for a matinee. She goes inside. But something's not right. The theatre looks dead. No one is around. What kind of pervert attacks a middle-aged woman in an empty theatre? I guess that's the problem with the internet. The fetishes are infinite. There's a fetish for everything. Even middle-aged women in empty theatres.

I hear muffled voices, and then my mother's voice – easier to pick out the words of that one, attuned as I am to it. I pick up my pace – quietly, quietly as I can – down the corridor.

She says, 'I'll just get straight on with it then, shall I?'

And then I hear Art's voice.

Art's.

I reach the main auditorium and peek inside. My mother is standing on the stage looking forward, her clothes off and thrown in a lump on the floor. I make myself flat as I can against the wall and look through the sides of my eyes.

Art is moving around, stalking and shooting, with his camera. People are moving beside him – hair, make-up, people holding lights and reflectors. Everyone is looking at my mother as she poses there, naked – oh god, naked – on this stage in the middle of London. My mother: the Greatest Show on Earth.

'That's really great, Carmen,' Art says. 'Just a little more of the leg, of the stretch marks. This piece is all about those beautiful lines.'

'These things!'

And then I see her – Suzy – next to Art. Standing there like it's just normal to be someone I am obsessed with standing next to my ex. The world is turning in on itself, and also exploding. I flatten myself more against the wall.

Suzy says: 'You grew too quick!'

And my mother – MY MOTHER – replies: 'I shrank too quick.'

'Because you grew too quick,' Suzy says.

My mother is contorting herself into various unrecognisable poses – not of humans but of writhing insects or swarming reptiles. I can't bear to watch. But I do.

Suzy says: 'Can I post one of these? Please? They are so raw and perfect. So immediate.'

Art says: 'Sure, but credit me.'

My mother says: 'Credit *me.*'

Suzy raises her phone and lines up the shot of the scene.

I've got to either puke or move. Puke or move, Jenny, puke or move. I move. I might also puke, but I am moving. I stride right in and I say: 'WHAT DO YOU THINK YOU ARE DOING?'

I want to say YOUNG LADY.

Or OLD LADY.

But mostly ARRGGGGGGGGGGGGGGGGGGGH.

Everyone and everything stops. The people who don't know me clearly think I am some prudish theatre worker or zany wandering type. The people who do know me know that I am all of those things, and also – righteously angry. I stand looking at them, one by one – my mother, Art, Suzy. All of their mouths are open.

I say: 'WHAT KIND OF DEPRAVED ARRANGEMENT IS THIS?'

My mother reaches for her clothes to cover herself up. I am aware on some level of the innate ridiculousness of myself. This is me: I am half panic, half pantomime. And this is about me, all of this, is it not? Has to be.

Art says: 'Carmen, I thought you said you cleared this?'

My mother bats her hand and mutters, 'My daughter's not my keeper.'

This prompts a kerfuffle of sudden understanding amongst the attendees who don't know me. *Oh, it's her daughter* . . .

Suzy says: 'She is free to be the woman she wants to be.' She says it with the barest edge of civility.

I point at her. 'Don't you even THINK about making this a feminist thing, Brambles.'

My mother says: 'How did you find me here?'

Art says: 'I can explain. This is a full story. Your mother is part of my next exhibition: *Scars and Girls*. It's about motherhood.'

My mother says: 'It's going to be a beautiful and important exhibition.'

I look at the three of them, from face to face to face. Suzy looks irritated, as though me turning up here is ruining her day. My mother is looking at me in a panicked sort of way, like she's only just realised what a monumental fuck-up this might be. Art is watching me with a look in his eye that is deliciously fearful.

I am Ripley with the flame-thrower. The elevator reaches the bottom floor. Ding.

I take a deep breath. 'You win, Art. You win.'

He coughs and looks unsure, shuffles from foot to foot, looks at the buttons on his camera. 'I don't want to win.'

'Doesn't matter. It's not your fault but it's what you were primed for. You bided your time because on some unconscious level you were playing a long game. A long game I could never play.'

'I'm not playing any games.'

'Your whole life is a game! You're like Peter Pan or Picasso. The *puer aeternus*. But I'm glad to know what I know. To be what I am, in this painful age of personal enlightenment.'

With that, I turn and walk out, out from the dark theatre into the daylight

She'll follow me, I know she will. And when she finds me I will be ready.

Outside, it is not sunny, it is overcast, but it might as well be the height of summer. It feels as though a big light has gone on after so many months in darkness. I'm like a critter that has shed its skin and come out sturdier.

SOHO SQUARE

I look at my phone. Suzy has posted the picture of the shoot already, with the caption:

Such an honour to be here at my paramour @ArtWilson 's shoot for his next exhibition exploring motherhood with remarkable women like Carmen #scarsandgirls #motherhood #stretchmarks #ageing #bodyinspo

It looks pretty good in black and white. Iconic.

I type:

Must be plenty you can relate to, yuppie mum of the year — is he going to do your C-section? #OWNYOURTRUTH

I stare at the comment. Like it is a little draft missile, lined up, ready to fire. Boom, Suzy Brambles, down you go.

And then I delete it.

And then I mute her. Not angrily, but because I know there will never be any good feeling for me now in looking, and there probably never was. This is a private act of sanity. There's a sign pointing towards her in my mind, a big old sign carved out of an oak tree, and it says: *Only Trouble This Way Be* >>>

I hold my phone close to my temple and imagine tumours blooming inside.

When she appears at the far gate, it is like a reckoning. Like my own death has caught up with me. I stare at her and she stares back. The air between us crackles. She starts to walk over.

I fantasise about saying it, standing up and screaming it: *I HAD A MISCARRIAGE.* I watch her fling herself to the ground and beat the earth with her fists. NOOOO NOOOOO NOOOOOOOOOOO! I watch her weep for the grandchild that will never be. For her daughter's shame and agony. *Why didn't you tell me? Because you're a grief leech! A misery vampire!* I watch her tear her own hair out and hurl it towards me in bloody clods—

She sits down next to me. I look at her but she doesn't look at me now – she looks dead ahead. She is everyone who ever loved me, everyone who ever left me, everyone who ever admired me, everyone who ever ignored me. She is a Bloody Mother Fucking Arsehole, as the song almost goes.

'I know what you must think of me.'

I see her wringing her duchess hands. The blue polish is chipped on her thumbnail.

I look to the sky. 'That's your job.'

She makes a firm mouth and bows her head low, like a scolded dog. She used to do this. Martyrdom, I believe they call it.

'I have my reasons,' she says. 'I have a right to still want things for myself, Jenny. I wasn't thinking of you.'

'Evidently. All of it is you. I cannot shed you. My work patterns. My love patterns. Good god.' I look at her, into her big blue blood-shot eyes. 'You're scared.'

She doesn't argue.

'Did you approach him, or did he approach you?'

'He said he was looking for models for a new project. I put myself forward and he said yes instantly. He was worried about what you'd think, but I said I'd tell you.'

'So why didn't you?'

'I told you a million times in my head, but I kept putting it off.

I even wrote you an email that I didn't send. Texts I didn't send. Ridiculous, really! I just got so anxious about it and then it was the day of the shoot and you were off to work and – well, here we are.'

'Why did you come? To London?'

'Same reason you always came. To take the taste away.'

I light up another cigarette.

'Can I have one?'

I light one for her, too. She smokes it with her fingers curled, like an amateur.

The day is fading. The last bands of sun sneak across the square.

She says: 'I suppose part of me was, on some deep unknown level, hanging on to the idea that you might come home.'

'What? You turned my room into an en-suite! You threw away all my schoolwork!'

'I suppose I was trying to look like I'd moved on, you know, to not seem bothered. I think it still hurts that living with me isn't an appealing prospect for you.'

'There is no one I want to live with right now, Mum. And I don't know what I'm going to do.'

She sighs. 'That's always been my problem. I knew the kind of man I wanted to die with, but I could never find the one I wanted to live with.'

CHIEF EMOTIONS

So I have a confession to make

You posed naked for Art, too

No, worse: I'm following your mum's new crush

OH ARE YOU INDEED

Yes

(I am too)

Hhaaha

He's SUCH A NAUSE

SUCH a nause

He calls himself the CEO, that's 'Chief Emotions Officer',
of motivational site Becoming Who You Are

CHIEF EMOTIONS OFFICER

Did you see what he posted this morning? He posted a
picture of a zebra in sunglasses with the caption 'Are you
a baller or a bailer?'

He tweets fifty times a day

My intelligence wants to take out a restraining order on him. When I read his dross I feel physically assaulted

Is this actually his job???

I'm so glad we're bonding over this, Kelly

SHE SAYS

'One day I'll travel light, but not in this lifetime. He thinks I'm the best person in forever.'

She brings the last of her bags into the hall. The van is waiting in the street.

'Watch your step with him, Mum.'

'I think he really likes me! Like, *me*-me, I mean.'

'I'm pleased for *you*-you. Really.'

'He's invited me to do some travelling with him later this month. LA, San Fran. A few conferences and a bit of a jolly. I think it'll be good for me, and I'd like to get to know him better. Would . . . that be okay? Would you mind?'

'Why would I mind?'

'It's over Christmas.'

I look at her. 'S'fine.'

She says, meaningfully: 'Thank you. He's a bit younger than me, but it's not like that,' she says.

'How much younger?'

'Ten years. But I don't feel sixty. Truth is, I feel twenty-five. I've felt twenty-five since I was twenty-five – it's like my personality was set then when I had my calling and I've never changed. And it's not like anyone's pulling the wool over anyone's eyes. We've got all that out of the way. He has his children. I have you. There are no secrets.'

'Does he have an ex-partner?'

'His wife died four years ago. I'm going to try and put them in touch.'

'Like hell you are.'

'I'll do my best.'

'*Love does not advance by weddings; love advances by funerals.*'

She shakes her head.

'He organises these big spiritual sessions. Gatherings, really. Five people doing reiki on you at once.'

'What, *gang reiki?*'

'Jennifer. Apparently, people hook up to do group meditations online and when there's enough people in a city the vibes are so strong that the crime rate falls.'

'So he's a superhero.'

'He's a man who knows what he wants.'

'You mean he's rich.'

'He's found his niche.'

'You mean he's rich.'

'It's better to be with a . . . companion. Retirement terrifies me. Old age terrifies me. Not death, never death, but being old and poor . . . It's an optimistic sort of pragmatism I'm employing here. I'm looking for companionship first and foremost. And if it means subverting from the inside, so be it.'

She comes close and I think she's about to hug me when she says: 'How do you feel about the photos?'

'The ones Art took? I'm sort of detached from it all. How do you feel about them?'

'They're black and white. Very tasteful.'

'Yes, that would be the main word I'd use to describe the whole thing. Tasteful.'

She laughs and then her face is serious. 'I've been thinking, you could freeze your eggs. We could raise a child together.'

'You're getting ridiculous now.'

She reaches to hold my hand. 'I do love you, darling.'

'I love you, too, Mum. I do. Even though we'll never be friends in the normal way.'

'Inmates,' she says. 'That's what we are.'

I nod. 'And Kelly's moving in so you can't just come back here as and when you please. I won't be your candle in the window.'

'Understood.'

She moves to hug me, and I let her. Our clavicles clash like antlers. I pull her in tight and try not to think about every single contact point between our bodies and how long this embrace might last. I do pull back first and that feels empowering but also potentially insulting and oh god I just need to stop analysing every single fucking thing all the time brain PLEASE.

'Oh, my darling,' she says, into my hair. 'At least I only had to try and look like Twiggy. You've got to sing and dance and fuck and work and mother and sparkle and equalise and not complain and be beautiful and love your imperfections and stay strong and show your vulnerability and bake and box and pull fucking pork. It's much too much.'

I say, 'Alexa, play "Age Ain't Nothing but a Number".'

'You don't even have an Alexa.'

'Hahahahahah.'

INT. JENNY'S ROOM. NIGHT

A lamp on. Jenny in a double bed, reading a book. Her phone is face down on the bedside table, next to a pint of orange squash.

The phone beeps and lights up. Jenny looks at it, hesitates, looks back to her book, and then puts her book down and picks up the phone. She reads the name on the phone, hesitates again, makes a decision, nods and answers.

ART: Jenny! How ARE you?

JENNY: I'm okay, Art. Yes, I think I am.

ART: Thanks for picking up. I wasn't sure you would. You've always been such a textual being.

JENNY: How are you, Art? It's been months.

ART: Oh, okay. You know. Suzanne is doing my head in slightly. She's pretty crazy.

JENNY: Wait – either I've heard this before or there's been a glitch in the Matrix. You don't need to slag Suzanne off to me, Art, you know? You don't have to be the big man protecting my puny feelings.

ART: And Clem got sick last week and it's taking over EVERYTHING. I'm behind on my shoots. I feel like saying, hey – I am a person too! I am a human, with needs! Suzanne seems to forget this when her kid is around, and as for the kid – well, the kid has no concept of it at all. She does not give a shit about my work, this kid!

JENNY: Extraordinary.

ART: Isn't it. You know, Jenny, you sound different. You sound good. Like . . . I dunno, the old you.

JENNY: Nah. This is the new me. But don't you think the new is probably the oldest thing of all, Art? As in, it has to contain all the old, in order to exist in the here and now?

ART: Yeah. You sound a lot more like the girl I fell in love with.

JENNY: You sound drunk. Where's Suzanne?

ART: Away.

JENNY: You're drunk and your girlfriend's away, and you're on the phone to your ex. Dearie me.

ART: I'm not slagging her off. I'm . . . concerned more than anything. I thought she was more in control of her shit, you know, but . . . You thought that too, didn't you? You used to idolise her.

JENNY: I suppose I did. But it was never really about her. It was more like I was pouring my need into a Suzy-shaped hole. Blame mirror neurons.

ART: You genuinely sound good. It's good to get my Jenny fix.

JENNY: Happy to help!

ART: No wait. I'm . . . sorry, Jenny. For leaving you. In the hospital. I think about that, you know – it's come out ashamed when I'm drunk to other people, but never you, until now.

JENNY: It wasn't all you, it was some me. I think I've always been waiting to go to pieces.

ART: No it was definitely all me.

JENNY: You can't have it all, I'm afraid. I think for me it was a largely narcissistic injury. I didn't know what my body was.

ART: I don't have it all.

JENNY: You know, you and Suzy should probably have a child together now.

ART: That's very big-hearted of you, Jenny.

JENNY: I mean, think of the important work you'd be doing for the gene pool.

ART: Aha. Okay. *Okay.* Listen, Jenny, my career isn't certain, you know? There are no guarantees. I don't come from money. My parents lost most of their pensions, remember? And she's nice, really nice. Really very kind.

JENNY: I understand. I appreciate that, as a woman.

ART: It's not all one way, anyway. I hooked her up with some contacts. I think I've helped all the women I've been with, and that's a source of great pride for me, to be able to help with your careers. It means a lot to me, to be able to do that, for my girlfriends. It makes me proud, being able to help women. I know it was a big help to you to come to all my exhibitions, move in those circles, with those kinds of people. It's helping Suzanne now, too.

JENNY: You're beautiful.

ART: Don't be like that.

JENNY: I will always love you, Art, after a fashion. The fashion being velour leisure suits. I'll always love them more.

ART: Hahaha. Oh, you.

JENNY: Yes, me. Delightful, capricious me.

ART: She's forced me to live with her, at least, and I'm so glad.

JENNY: Forced you?

ART: Yes, like you did. I never would have done it otherwise.

JENNY: I certainly did not.

ART: You did!

JENNY: No, Art, I really didn't. Maybe it just suits you to feel like the adventuring wanderer, dragged in from the forest and civilised by a woman ennobled by her missionary status. But you're not. I'm a lot less civilised than you, I can assure you. You don't get to be the wild one tamed. You have absolutely no concept of what it is to be in a cage. You don't get to be the adventurer who comes in from the storm to a woman's cosy hearth. I never had a cosy hearth for you.

ART: I know it.

JENNY: So. Don't get off on that one. And give Suzanne some credit.

ART: God.

JENNY: There, you see. It's just like the beginning all over again. Me telling you off and you being impressed rather than insulted. A perfect circle.

ART: So you don't despise me?

JENNY: No. [sighing] You sort of wasted my precious time, but you will always mean something to me, Art. I mean that. This is the heartfelt bit.

ART: Oh good, I've been waiting for this.

JENNY: We helped form each other. I will think about you every day in some way and I will hate you for that but with a deep, impossible, death-conquering love. And I'll never be able to hear Mariah Carey's 'All I Want For Christmas Is You' without thinking fleetingly of you and what went wrong, and wondering whether you still want me in some way during festive times of year, even though we'll never act on it. Again. And that is a modern classic, ruined. This is what you have done to me, Art. All that said, I would like us to try and be friends. I've never managed that with anyone else, but I've never really had an ex like you, and I think I do need you in my life, as a friend. I think I might be ready. I certainly feel like I can say anything to you now. Like, I don't want us to talk like this.

ART: Like what?

JENNY: Like we're reading off a script. Some kind of 'how to talk to your ex' script.

ART: Okay, so what do we do?

JENNY: I don't know. Try and relax?

ART: Your speciality.

'Hahah.'

I hear him breathe a couple of times and then he says, 'Hey, I've got my new exhibition opening in spring. *Scars and Girls*. Will you come?'

I take my time preparing to reply, and then I go for it. The words pour out of me, like a sudden rush of dammed water through a crack. 'Listen, Art, I probably won't. I fucking hate art galleries. I always did. It's a relief to be able to tell you this, finally, as a friend.'

There's a rush up my back. I hear his lips make a wet sound and then he says, 'Okay. Thanks. That's okay.'

'Now go to bed. Good night.'

'Okay.'

He stays there, breathing. I stay there breathing, too.

'What is it, Art?'

'You know, you scare the shit out of me.'

KELLY SAYS

'Is this it? Are we doing it? Did we retire?'

'It's not about retiring. It's about not waiting.'

We can just about make it work with my pay rise and there's a spare room for the mothers to stay in – if and when they visit.

'If we are going to be truly modern about this,' she says, 'then we have to see it through. If you want kids, I mean. You could get a sperm donor. We raise the kids together. We have a life and home and future together here, as certain as any anywhere. Think about it.'

'Have you and my mother discussed this?'

'No!'

'Good. Because there are more pressing things at hand. We need to get a chores rota going,' I say, 'and a list of house rules. Or a family agreement. If this is a project, then it is a PROJECT.'

Kelly laughed. 'What the fuck. Okay, whatever, we'll try this.'

I look at the picture on the wall, of my mother on stage a few years ago, in her element. I have put it in a frame, next to a framed print of a letter Anne Sexton sent her daughter. *Be your own woman. Belong to those you love.*

'I'll keep you there, Mother,' I think. 'Now be a good girl and smile.'

Kelly gets her phone out. 'Check this out,' she says, pointing the screen towards me. 'They're at Chateau Marmont.'

'I love how obsessed you are with my mother online now. I thought you were immune.'

'Watch.'

The video plays. My mother and Dan Mosel are at the piano in the hotel lobby. My mother is on top of the piano, holding a thunderball glass. She is singing 'My Baby Just Cares For Me' and Dan Mosel is playing the piano, and not badly. There are people around of various ages, whooping and cheering her on. My mother is, categorically, having A Ball.

'I think your mum is having a better retirement than us so far,' says Kelly.

I look at my mother's face as she sings, and I look at the way she looks over at Dan, and the way he looks back. She looks different – like a little girl but also like a person I have not seen before. I think, *Okay, okay, now I get it.*

My mother has found her people.

GENUINE QUESTION

Does the five-second rule apply for penises?

What?

You know like when you drop some food on the floor well what if a penis only goes in for five seconds

I'm not sure it reliably applies to food on the floor, Nicolette

You know I'm all for condoms but I think in your late thirties they are offensive – they're either saying you're diseased or a bad mother amirite

The dating's going well then

Literally every man who contacts me online asks me whether I want kids within five minutes, and the other day someone asked me if I could send a straight-on photo as all the photos on my profile were 'slightly angled'. I was like DO YOU NEED A PASSPORT PHOTO, ARE YOU SPAIN

I don't think I'll ever date again. I can't even hold down a hobby rn

You should try a non-verbal activity

Not a bad idea

Although you do yoga

I try

You must be really good at yoga by now. I bet you can do handstands on your clit

I'm going to get you a non-verbal Christmas present – something arty

Intrigued

I know just the thing. I interviewed a painter the other day and she said she had come to accept self-loathing as part of her process. Isn't that liberating?

Maybe. Right gotta go – time to give Kelly back my phone

What?

She's rationing me. Two hours a day. She's my Social Media Carer

Wise

She's enjoying it because she is part sadist. If the receptionist thing doesn't work out she could easily become a prison warden

Hi I just wanted to let you know Suzanne and I have agreed to tell each other everything about everyone we've ever had sex with and what it was like x x

Oh

It feels really healthy and open x x

Fascinating that you should want to inform me of this. At 1 a.m.

As a friend x x

I'm starting to think friends are worse than mothers.

LIFE DRAWING

Before the class I stand naked, post-shower, in front of the full-length mirror in my room. I look at my body, and I think, I can beat you again. I can love you again. You are mine to kill.

Twelve of us sit waiting in a sunny upstairs room of a pub that doubles as a vegan restaurant. The tutor explains the principles of life drawing for those who haven't done it before, like me. We sit, poised with our pencils and papers. I suppose I feel like we should all be naked. Is this person being paid to be naked? Is it worse if they are? A naked person comes out from behind the bar. Their body is supple and softly lit. It is the afternoon and I have had a wine in the pub downstairs – a pale rosé that kissed me on the lips and slid down my throat like a promise. The sky outside is pink and grey. The person sits and gets comfortable. They look so comfortable they make me comfortable. They are not posing and nor am I, nor is anyone. We all start to sketch. I let the silence gather around me once more. The shapes I make with the nib of the pencil are fat and light and easy, then grow into human parts and then I stop thinking altogether and—

RELAX

Almost. I suppose you could call it something like that.

Four hours later. Now I am naked too, but I stand smoking by the open window and the no-smoking sign, regarding this person with whom something is about to happen. I put out my cigarette still looking at them.

Our clothes lie like stepping stones to the door.

WE LIE

still in the full quiet of the room. Our bodies are like sucked sweets. We don't even know each other's names and this makes us both smile as we say goodbye. I order room service and eat it sitting in my own divine stink.

When my meal is done I creep into the bathroom and take a milky piss, slack and sensual. The porcelain gleams meanly. My hair is wild in sweat-dried curls around my head.

I go back to the bedroom and lie on the bed, ass aloft. I look at my nakedness in the full-length mirror. I make a square with my fingers and put myself inside. Click.

I leave the hotel at 5 p.m. I weave between people and cars, through the rush hour, but now the rush hour is outside. I am aware of my body as a shape that is cutting the same shape through the world, over and over as it moves forward, leaving behind it a concertina paper chain of women holding hands. We hold each other together.

I hold myself together.

When I get home, Kelly looks at me and says, 'Have you done something different?'

'You could say that.'

DRAFTS

Dear Jenny,
It seems to me you have two options:

1. Embrace the terror
2. Die

As a high-functioning introvert you are terrified of everything, but you get through. You were never going to settle for a bearable life. But you've come a long way and I have high hopes for you. I reckon by the time you're sixty you're going to be halfway on the way to being a semi-sorted-out person. Maybe not the goddess Durga, but someone who can confidently wear a beret. You will have stopped waiting for your life to start because you'll understand that this is based on the idea of waiting for a perfect moment to arrive so you can stop and have a rest. Spoiler alert: that perfect moment will never arrive, because it is based on a fairytale you were told in a bid to keep you lacking. It is a pretty lie on a paper horizon. Your life is happening without you, so best be in it.

You'll be happy enough living with Kelly. She snores like a fighter jet with a fifty-a-day habit, but that snore-cancelling app is really helping. Who knew she sounded exactly like a crackling fire? The app. THE APP KNEW. The friendship therapy is also helping, even if the therapist is technically a marriage counsellor. It's not your fault you're ahead of the curve again, culturally. Friendships go through cycles, orbits, and you are coming back round to Kelly again, very close, you can feel it.

You still haven't forgiven Mother Nature but when things get really bad you can put Christian the lion on YouTube until your faith is restored. Truly the darkest mood will dissipate at the sight of that grown lion running towards the men who saved it from the toyshop and putting its paws on their shoulders. Dear god! There is goodness out there. Amongst lions.

Finally, a small note about housekeeping. It's about time you started eating more brassicas and wearing better brassieres. In fact, that's your mantra for next year: More Brassicas, Better Brassieres. Catchy, and sexual.

Let's make this happen.

Forever yours,

Jenny x

My dearest darling Jenny,

I thought I'd send you a postcard to cheer you up in that dank little house, so here you go! It is so hot here you can feel it strengthening your bones and the sushi is To Die For. I am having a sensational time with Dan, whose friends have welcomed me warmly and are very respectful of my work. We are getting along so well and I'm thinking about living with him more than dying with him, so that's a real plus. The best thing is it looks like there is a lot of work out here for someone like me and as you know I've always wanted to travel so Dan and I are looking into longer-term possibilities but of course I will keep you posted. The other day we went to see the Hollywood sign and do you know it looks ever so flimsy up close. Anyway, let it be shouted from the rooftops (and the hillsides): CARMEN MCLAINE HAS MADE IT TO HOLLYWOOD!!!!

Love and light,

Mum xxx

SILENT-ISH NIGHT

I get back from the *Foof* Christmas party to find Kelly lying on the sofa, wearing a Santa hat. She's halfway down a bottle of port.

'You are scrumptious.'

'This is as far as I go.'

I sit down and help myself to a small glass of port. She shuffles around, making room for me, and puts her legs either side of me. There is one of those loathsome nostalgia programmes on TV. *Weren't the 90s Great?* No, I think. Let the nineties die with dignity.

She grunts and shifts on the sofa, pulls my phone out from underneath her and hands it to me. 'There you go. Half an hour.'

'You're a cruel mistress.'

'You know it.'

I take my phone and turn it on.

'I feel really sorted, you know,' I say. The phone starts to come alive.

'Did you have any tea?'

'A few festive snacks,' I say, mindlessly going through my apps.

'Hmph.'

'Yeah,' I say. My phone awakens with alerts and new messages.

'Jenny?'

'. . .'

'You're getting that glazed look. I think you'd better give that back.'

But I can't.

'JENNY.'

Kelly puts her port glass down and starts getting up. I run into the kitchen with my phone.

'Jenny!'

She is chasing me. I will wrestle her if I have to. Hahahahaharrgggggggggggh.

She loves me.

INBOX

Suzy Brambles started following you on Instagram.

FIN

THANKS

To my friends, for loving me and letting me steal their gold, particularly: Sally Cook, Katie Popperwell, Natalie O'Hara, Nicola Mostyn, Maria Roberts, Sarah Tierney, Alison Taylor, Emily Morris, Jesca Hoop, Holly Smale, Alex and Simon Glew, Eden Keane and Romana Majid.

To my agent and friend Clare Conville, who always steers me to shore and has picked me up off too many decks to mention. To all at Conville & Walsh. To Camilla Young and all at Curtis Brown.

To Sophie Wilson, for terrific and much-needed early guidance.

To my editor Charlotte Cray for faith, kinship, and pushing this book to be the boldest thing it could be. To Ore, Suzie, Ann and everyone at The Borough Press.

To Anna Burtt for being a solid cheerleader and the best Suzy Brambles.

To Sarah Brocklehurst, dear friend and workwife.

To Jenn Ashworth, for the gimp whippings and naked photos.

To the Society of Authors for the grant when I was trying to combine new motherhood and writing. Do apply if you're a skint author.

To my family: Mum, Dad, Grandma, Lucie, Dave, Charlie and Matilda. And to Ian and LF, for sharing me so graciously with my work.

Finally, to every reader who got in touch in the abyss between *Animals* and this. Thank you. You kept me going. X